WHOLENESS

WISING UP ANTHOLOGIES

ILLNESS & GRACE, TERROR & TRANSFORMATION

FAMILIES: *The Frontline of Pluralism*

LOVE AFTER 70

DOUBLE LIVES, REINVENTION & THOSE
WE LEAVE BEHIND

VIEW FROM THE BED: VIEW FROM THE BEDSIDE

SHIFTING BALANCE SHEETS:
Women's Stories of Naturalized Citizenship & Cultural Attachment

COMPLEX ALLEGIANCES:
Constellations of Immigration, Citizenship, & Belonging

DARING TO REPAIR: *What Is It, Who Does It & Why?*

CONNECTED: *What Remains As We All Change*

CREATIVITY & CONSTRAINT

SIBLINGS: *Our First Macrocosm*

THE KINDNESS OF STRANGERS

SURPRISED BY JOY

CROSSING CLASS: *The Invisible Wall*

RE-CREATING OUR COMMON CHORD

GOODNESS

FLIP SIDES

ADULT CHILDREN: *Being One, Having One &
What Goes In-Between*

THE POWER OF THE PAUSE

WHOLENESS

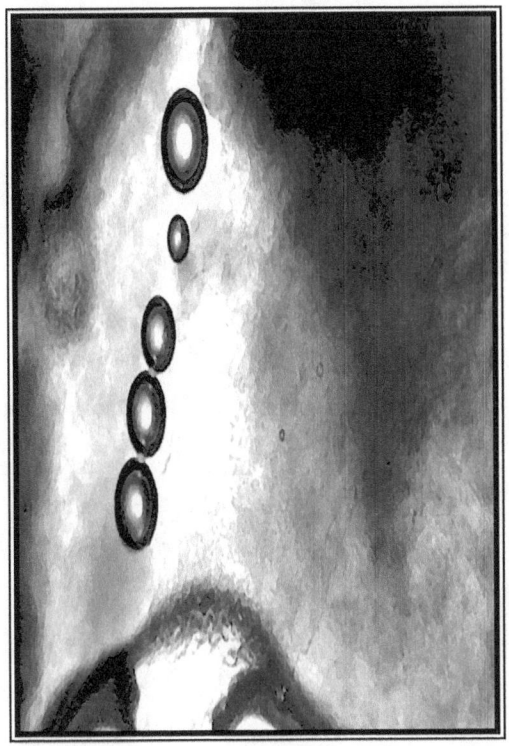

Heather Tosteson & Charles D. Brockett
Editors

Wising Up Press

Wising Up Press
P.O. Box 2122
Decatur, GA 30031-2122
www.universaltable.org

Catalogue-in-Publication data is on file with the Library of Congress.
LCCN: 2023942237

Wising Up ISBN: 978-1-7376940-7-6

To the Wising Up Writers Collective—
Kerry, Michele, Kathleen, Bill, Murali, and Felicia—
who have given so much to us and to the press,
including a wonderful sense of wholeness and depth to our vision
"Finding the We in Them, the Us in You"

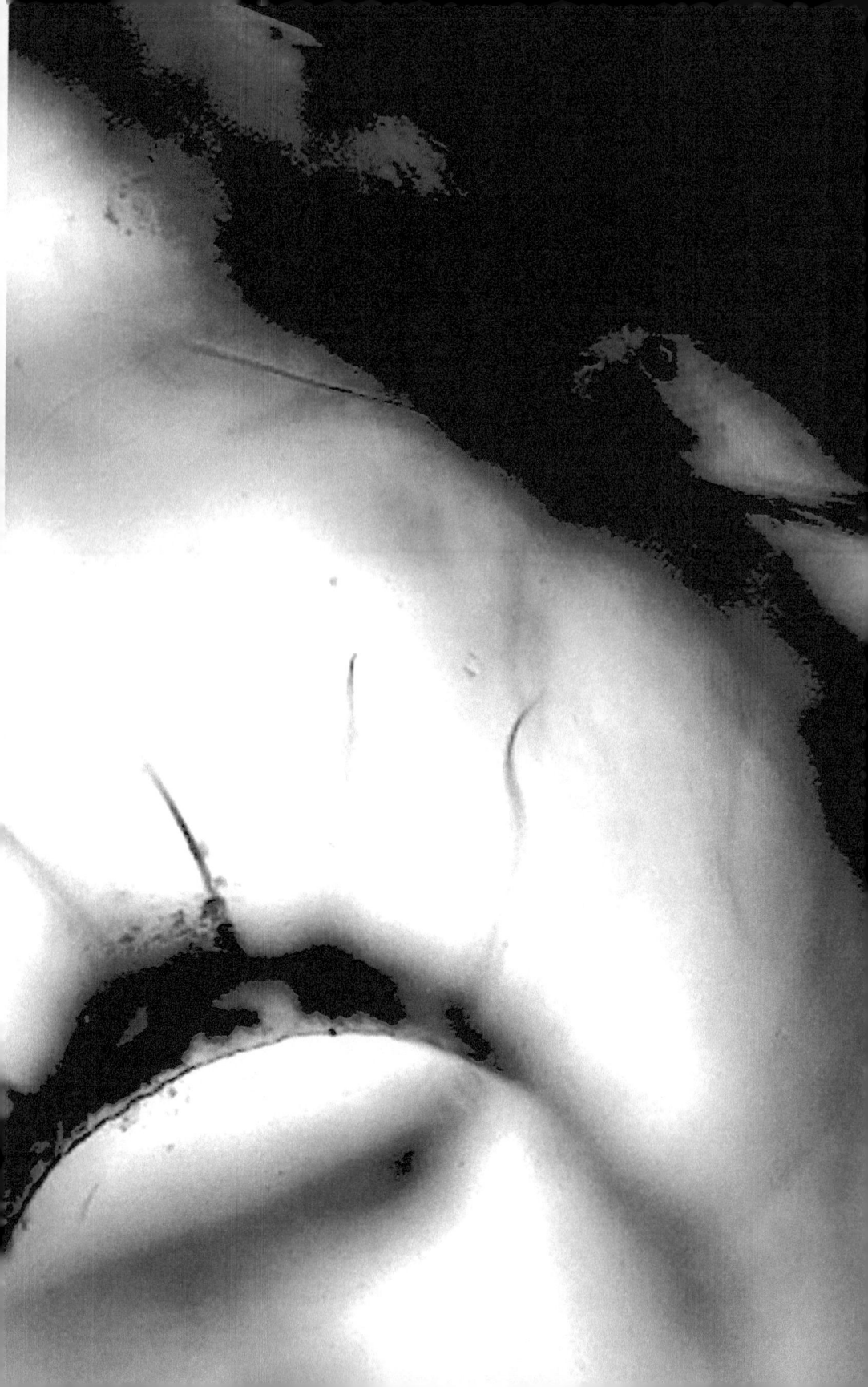

CONTENTS

HEATHER TOSTESON
Introduction: Wholeness   *1*

I. ARC OF LIFE

LAURA APOL
Hanna on the Monkey Bars   *12*
The Gift of Yes   *13*
Light, Water, Bones   *14*

THEA HEARD
A Girl No One Can Trust   *15*

WILSON R. M. TAYLOR
Crossing the Lagoon   *17*

DEIDRA SUWANEE DEES
Fragment: Negotiating Identity in the South   *25*

ISABELLA OJEDA-AHMED
All the Pieces   *27*

BETH CHRISTENSEN
Part, Part, Whole   *32*

CYNDY KREY
Promises   *39*
Finding Your Way   *41*

PATRICIA CANNON
Wild Heart   *43*
Inspiration   *46*

JASON A. NEY
The Life of the Blood   *48*

YESSENIA GUTIERREZ
The Kidney Queen   *50*

MAISIE MCADOO
At Water's Edge   *53*

MARIAN MATHEWS CLARK
Journey of Aloha   *61*

JAMES WYSHYNSKI
Womb — 74
At the Carwash — 75
Catastrophic Molting — 76
Interior Dialogue — 77

JEN WEBB
World Wildlife Fund — 78
The Last of the Futurists Arrives in the Suburbs — 79
On Beauty — 80
On Love and Lovers — 81
That "Formal Feeling," Emily — 82

RANJANI RAO
The Opposite of Perfection — 84

GABRIELLE LEMAY
Night Peepers — 91
Night train — 92
Prom Night — 94

LISA HOCKSTEIN
A Love Story in Eight Short Acts — 96

ELLEN BIRKETT MORRIS
Where I'm From — 100
Reel to Real — 102

KESHAWNA MOONEY
A Predictable Crisis — 104

GEETHA NAIR G.
Testing Time — 116

JEANETTE MILLER
My Mother, My Child — 121

SHERRY SHAHAN
Joining My Mother for Breakfast at a Downtown Motel — 129

RICKS CARSON
Just To Let You Know — 132
And After Dinner, a Book — 133
My Father, in Heaven, Is Sorting — 134

SHARON LASK MUNSON
Glimpse into a Marriage   136
Grace   138

NORITA DITTBERNER-JAX
Park Point, Duluth   140
High Up: Sunrise   143

RANDY MINNICH
Late Winter Soliloquy   144
Something Lies Beyond Dementia   145
Then You Walked In   146
The Colors of the World   147

II. SOCIAL CONTEXTS

LAURENCE SNYDAL
Thrift Store   150
The Whale Line   151

C.P. SURENDRAN
Invitation   152
Surprise   153
Self Portrait with Bandaged Ear   154

SARA BROWN WEITZMAN
Rodin's "The Hand of God"   156
Adam   157
What's Missing   158
Van Gogh's Room   159
Ecosphere   160

DANIEL M. JAFFE
Enchanted   161

LARRY LEFKOWITZ
The Perfect Woman   168

BRIAN MICHAEL BARBEITO
Breath   174

MEERA JACOB ELAMATHA
Honor Among Women   180

GAYE D. HOLMAN
The Elusiveness of Wholeness   184

CHARLES BROCKETT & HEATHER TOSTESON
Anthony 187

NANCY WERKING POLING
Intrusion 205

EISHA A. MASON
Vigil for Charleena Lyles 211
How to Walk on Hot Coals 214

LINDA QUINLAN
Babysitting Danny 216
Father Tom 218

JOHNNY TOWNSEND
Reparations, One Family at a Time 220

III. MYSTERY OF THE MOMENT

TED MILLAR
GPS Never Works (in My Dreams) 224
One Kind Favor I Ask of You 226
Five Million Years 228

MARY KAY RUMMEL
Welcoming Night 229
Eighty Autumn Moons 230

SUZANNA C. DE BACA
Everything Is a Shadow 232
Everything Is a Grave 234
Mortuary Bee 236

HEATHER TOSTESON
Mary Salaam 240

SARAH ROSENBLATT
Ephemeral Matters 249
Resilience 250
To Have Loved 251
Against All Odds 252

DEIDRA GREENLEAF ALLAN

    Nomad   254

    Farmhouse, Mountain Lake Park   255

    After a Lecture on the Numinous, Montpelier, Vermont   256

    What She Heard the Room Say   257

    Woken   258

RICHARD SCHIFFMAN

    Melting Time   260

    Eden in the A.M.   261

LOUIS FABER

    Carrying   262

    Not Speaking   263

    Quantum Romance   264

CHRIS ELLERY

    Every Beautiful Name   265

ACKNOWLEDGMENTS   270

CONTRIBUTORS   272

EDITORS/PUBLISHERS   280

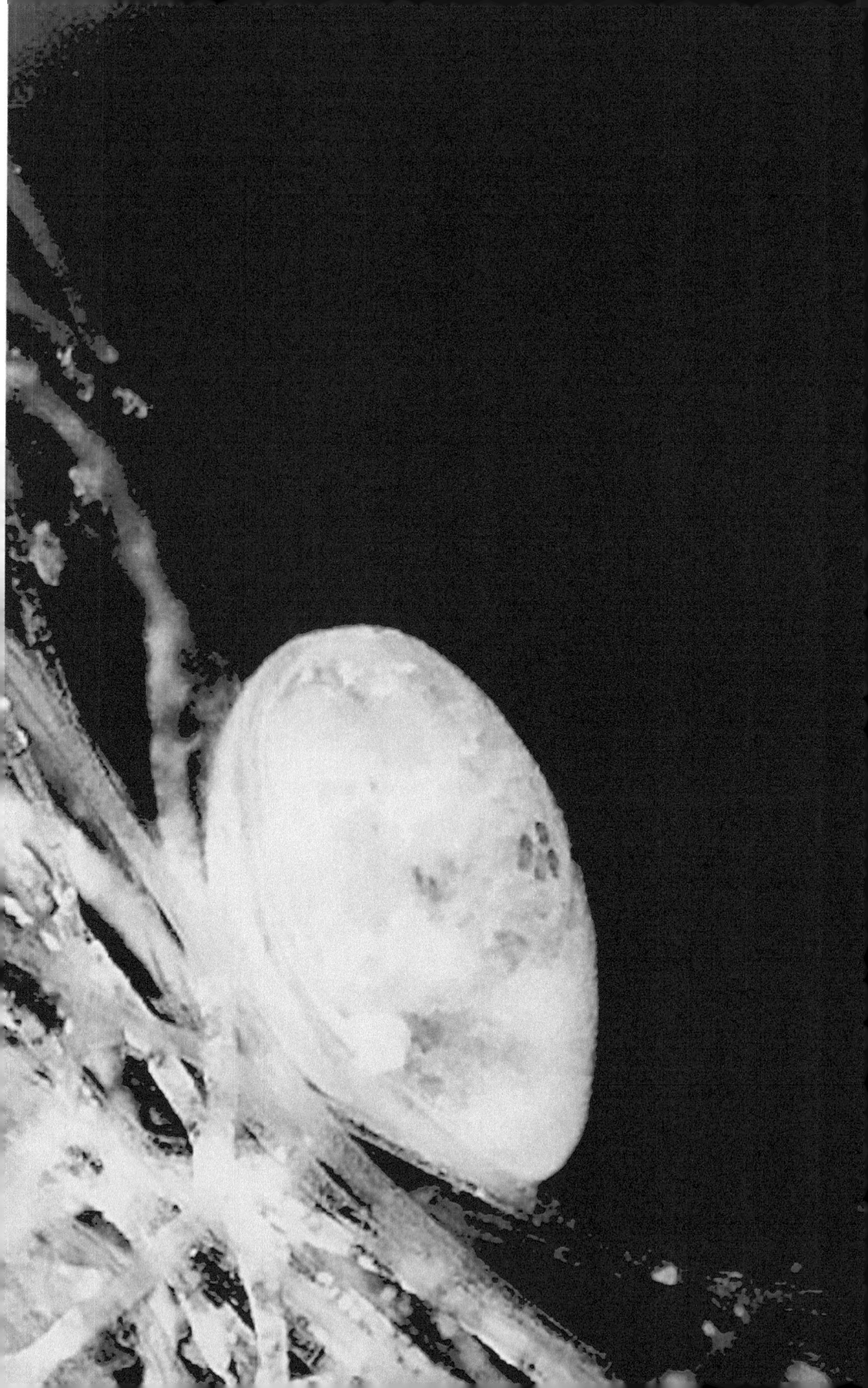

HEATHER TOSTESON

INTRODUCTION: WHOLENESS

I've been brooding over—and exploring broadly but intuitively—the experience and concept of wholeness for several years now, so the prospect of pulling some of those thoughts into a persuasive logical structure, rather than intuitive, pointillist jolts of recognition was daunting. So I stalled, rationalized, read more as an evasive maneuver. But just before leaving for an out-of-town overnight to see our grandchildren, I felt, with the help of William James, I was beginning to feel an evolving *communicable* coherence. I left my handwritten notes neatly stacked on the far side of my desk. My blue cloth-bound volume of his collected writings, 1902-1910, set a little closer to the corner. I was ready to begin—in all seriousness—as soon as we returned. In anticipation, on our way back from our visit, I read a favorite section of James' revelatory experience with nitrous oxide aloud to Charles in a Starbucks in Flowery Branch when we stopped for coffee on our return route.

But when we pulled into our drive, we saw that a very brief but intense storm the night before had ripped the tin roof off our house. Sheets of metal lay on the lawn and drive. Most specifically, the wind had attacked the roof right over my study. Large trees had broken in half or were uprooted and entrusting their enormous weight to their more securely grounded neighbors. There was no time to brood.

I raced upstairs to assess the damage. But the ceiling in my study was dry, the desk top dry. I pulled out my laptop, began making calls. Went down to reinspect the damages. It was only later, when I came back to the desk, that I discovered my notes—*and only my notes*—for this introduction were soaking wet. Nearly illegible. The entire desk was dry. The volume of James a foot away was perfectly dry. There was no sign of water on the ceiling above. But all *my* notes were drenched. I sat there oscillating between my symbolic/superstitious and scientific minds.

Charles came up to puzzle this with me. "I'm not sure what meaning you want to assign to this," he said, glancing over at the bone dry volume of James.

"I'll never be ready," I said. Or not in *that* way . . .

)()(❋)()(

So let's begin with my long love affair with William James' sensibility. Whenever I read him, I feel as if a weight has been lifted from me, that here is someone who shares my sense of the crucial interplay between life lived and life conceptualized—and who can *explain* it. This interplay is essential to the experience of wholeness—for we experience wholeness when our experience of life and our ideas about life come into some novel but faithful synthesis.

James sees all living creatures as living in an unbroken stream of sensory consciousness, one that, for humans, includes conceptualizations. However, our concepts are intrinsically divisive, essentially static. Their purpose is to divide the flow of life into discrete—and opposite—concepts. These concepts can be stacked up to create mental structures, but they can't *flow*, or metamorphose. This relationship between thought and sensory continuum is complex. We need both:

> *Each concept means just what it singly means, and nothing else, and if the conceiver does not know whether he means this or means that, it shows that his concept is imperfectly formed. The perceptual flux as such, on the contrary means nothing, and is but what it immediately is. No matter how small a tract of it be taken, it is always a much-at-once, and contains innumerable aspects (pp. 1007-8).*

> *Percepts and concepts interpenetrate and melt together, impregnate and fertilize each other. Neither, taken alone, knows reality in its completeness. We need them, as we need both our legs to walk with (p. 1010).*

Concepts *come* from life—but don't necessarily return to it. However, we can mistake the flow of ideas for the flow of life:

> *Conceptual treatment of perceptual reality makes it seem paradoxical and incomprehensible; and when radically and consistently carried out, it leads to the opinion that perceptual experience is not reality at all, but an appearance or illusion. . . . Briefly, this is a consequence of two facts: First, that when we substitute concepts for percepts, we substitute their relations also. But since the relations of concepts are of static comparison only, it is*

impossible to substitute them for the dynamic relations with which the perpetual flux is filled (p. 1023).

)()(✻)()(

You may well wonder what all this has to do with wholeness. Wholeness is both a *feeling* (part of that perceptual stream of consciousness) and an intellectual experience. It is a moment when these two worlds—life as we experience it and how we understand it—come into new resolutions that our conscious—conceptual—mind cannot reach. The recognition of wholeness feeds our relation with both forms of consciousness—but it also feels like gift. Thinking won't get us there.

But once we *are* there, new forms of thought—concepts—and sensations are possible. In that sense wholeness is like an emergent phenomenon. It presents us with a larger order that is unlike—and unexplained—by what comes before it. Like the difference between mind and brain. This larger order is able to influence, transform, what it emerges from.

When we experience wholeness, there is an aha sensation—we're *understanding* something, perceiving something in a new light. But wholeness comes not from solving a puzzle, but finding the puzzle itself redefined. This resolution has a mystical quality to it, which James describes beautifully, but which he would never—except under nitrous oxide—describe as his own sensibility:

> *It is as if the opposites of the world, whose contradictoriness and conflict make all our difficulties and troubles, were melted into unity. Not only do they, as contrasted species, belong to one and the same genus, but one of the species, the nobler and better one, is itself the genus, and so soaks up and absorbs its opposite into itself (p. 348).*

Wholeness is faithful.

Stories are one of the places that this *dynamic* can play out. A story, even our own life story, is an implicit concept that is constantly being challenged by the flow of life. The effectiveness, the *wholeness* of a story, depends on that over-story that doesn't exist on the page and in our implicit conceptual conversation with the story-maker . . . even if that story-maker is ourselves. Our sense of the effectiveness of a story comes from how much that over-story feels true-to-life-as-we-know-it (which is a sensation), especially if it does so in ways that also unpredictably enlarge our understanding of life.

)O(✷)O(

My own interest in wholeness expanded, a little paradoxically, from an interest in moral injury. What happens when the social systems we believe in and are loyal to betray us? What happens when in loyalty to the social systems we believe in we betray our personal value system? How do we recover from these devastating experiences? I was interested particularly in the experience of our volunteer army and the impact of the highly ambiguous Iraq and Afghan wars—and also of Guantánamo: in wounds of conscience and the loss of institutional trust. My interest then turned, out of emotional necessity, to helping behaviors, especially in World War II. How did people repair after such horrific experiences—or maintain humane integrity through them?

This extensive reading can be seen as driven by a deep and rather mysterious personal need-to-know and, also, a way to better understand our current troubling social polarization and distrust by providing a larger holding context for it. It did allow me to understand systemic dimensions of personal trauma—and also resilience. And provided a sense of proportion. When I think back on those pandemic years, and the social tumult that came with them, they can feel at a greater remove from me than these traumatic events from a more distant past, ones that I have encountered only in imagination. Imagination that holds a past tense. I also remember the quiet of my study, the puzzling but trustworthy inner drive to understand, the beneficence of full immersion, the trust in it. My mind and my feeling self *needed* to do this for reasons I couldn't explain but trusted implicitly.

)O(✷)O(

I share two of the stories that have stayed with me.

One image that stays in my mind comes from Mansoor Adayfi's *Don't Forget Us Here: Lost and Found at Guantánamo*, a disturbing and powerful memoir of his many years of imprisonment in Guantánamo from the time he was a late teenager until he was in his thirties. The story that I can't get out of my mind involves Moath al-Alwi's window.

The first military regime at Guantánamo was directed by the Army. It was particularly brutal. The most savage interrogations—and the fiercest resistance—took place during this time. Even though very young, Adayfi was an intransigent resister—and organizer. For nine years he fought, went on long hunger strikes, endured constant interrogations, forced feedings and years of solitary confinement.

But when the Navy came in to take a turn at management of the prison, rules were changed, and these young men were put in a communal setting. They still were imprisoned in high security, but they had common space. Adayfi describes lying out in the small common exercise area for a day just staring at the sky, which he hadn't seen in years. He also put his leadership and organizational skills to work, helping to set up classes for prisoners in an attempt to make up for all the time they had lost.

There was also an artistic explosion. Another prisoner, Moath, was a talented artist, and he began using cardboard and soap to build sculptures and even furniture. Here is Adayfi's description:

> Moath made his windows this way. He built the frames from cardboard with hinged shutters he could close. Inside, he made a sculpture with trees and birds, and behind them a painting of the sea and beautiful skies. This was his window to the outside world and the home he dreamed of having one day. They weren't just his windows, they were ours, and that included the Navy guards who helped cut the cardboard.

Adayfi's exploration of the impact—and origins—of the art-making is also interesting:

> As I assisted Moath and worked on my books, I learned that to be an artist you must harness your fear to take risks, question rules, and dare to cross boundaries. For years, our brothers in Camp 4 had all the privileges while we suffered, and they hadn't created anything. No art. No furniture. Fear of losing their privileges chained them. While there were some wonderful poets among the compliant brothers, few wrote anything down. The brothers like me who had resisted the camp admin with our bodies and had lived in isolation for years were now the ones most dedicated to creating art. At first, I just thought that we were hungry to claw back any part of ourselves we had lost during those nine years and art was our way of doing that. But I also wondered if maybe we had been artists all along, that self-expression was a part of us, and that our resistance was our way of expressing our humanity and showing the world a raw part of ourselves.
>
> As we had spread resistance, now we helped spread art-making. . . . Most brothers wanted to create art that told stories of their survival in this place. This defined us as artists: we found beauty where there was none and communicated our experiences to others.

When the command changed back to the Army, soldiers were ordered to destroy everything that these prisoners—and their guards—had spent several years making. The description of this destruction is heart rending. But the prisoners were left with the ineradicable knowledge that another way of being was possible—and that they *would* choose it if given a chance. This is also one dimension of wholeness—that our experiences of it remain with us, that they lodge in us and change us permanently just by having had them.

Another artist who captured my interest during this period of reading was the Israeli painter Yehuda Bacon, who survived Theresienstadt and Auschwitz, going in at thirteen and leaving at sixteen. When interviewed in his nineties about his experiences, the art he made from it, both immediately after and later in life, he described the difficulty of sharing the experiences, especially immediately after the war:

> *I had two reactions: silence and disappointment. Silence because people couldn't bear the testimonies and disappointment because people didn't improve personally. It took me years to figure out even how to talk, that there are things that can't be said or written. I saw that people were silent. . . . Maybe I spoke too directly. . . . I remember the first letter I wrote and sent to an uncle in Israel. I described exactly like a child, how tall the flames from the crematorium were, what the food rations were like . . . which uncle died, and so on . . . things a child thought would be important to say. That uncle suffered a breakdown, he was ill for two weeks. You can't talk like that. The technique of how to tell my story came much later.*

Bacon ascribes much of his own ability to absorb the experience to the kindness of a man named Premysl Pitter, who started several homes in Prague for children who had returned after the war. Pitter took in Jewish boys and also German children—who were now reviled—with no regard to race, religion, or gender:

> *Pitter was a wonderful person and I think he saved us from the horror of the past. It was the first time we trusted someone. We didn't trust anyone, why would anyone be kind to us? Everybody wants to hit and kill us. And he wasn't some missionary or propagandist who tried to persuade us to do one thing or another. His and his friends' kindness is what changed us. All the children who still live today remember him, both Jews and Germans can't forget him.*

Bacon also feels that the experience he went through can be bridged. His explanation of how, which touches on both artistic process and the mystical dimension, is a powerful description of the transformative effect of wholeness . . . and its persistence. Awe can be considered an essential part of the experience of wholeness because we are aware that we are in the presence of something larger than our own consciousness:

> *The very fact that a person regards another from within is effective. Every true thing has an effect. True in the highest sense, because it breaks something, it breaks the insignificance; the insignificant is the poison of the soul. You experience something again and again, but suddenly there is something, suddenly you see something and every language can convey it. I don't remember which philosopher said: every artist has experienced perfection at some point. Call it God, I don't know. . . . He who has experienced perfection in human relations, in a great love . . . . In something. And his whole life he then tries to capture that perfection or divinity, but he knows it's impossible, he can't grasp it and put it in his pocket. It's too big! The little leaf that is us can't be the tree, but he knows there is something whole, that is a tree and tries to express it. Any sincere work, like a prayer, gives us some part of that completeness. Artists might be more talented, but I believe that anyone has a gift for it. Whether you meet someone who is really exceptional or an ordinary person, that which affects us all is that we are all part of that great perfect completeness—this great divinity.*

)(❋)(

But let's return to *this* anthology—and how the concept of wholeness is intrinsic to our interest in the anthologies and listening projects Wising Up Press focuses on. Our choices of topics are always ones of close personal concern, almost all with an underlying experiential as well as conceptual origin. We're interested in what happens to our understanding of an experience when it is brought into relation to a concept or a series of concepts—how both are modified by the encounter. Take a story and publish it in an anthology on the theme of *goodness*—or one on *complex allegiances*. It may well illuminate both ideas—but in very different ways—and our understanding of both the story and the concepts will change.

We have said we listen for the "ring of truth" in the stories and poems we select—but we're also listening for those unexpected and liberating integrations that take place when they are brought into new relationships.

Listening for the intuitive divisions in the stories, memoirs, nonfiction, and poetry we selected for this anthology, we found three major ones. The largest section has to do with life course and our shifting sense of identity at different points in our lives. All our life stages invite different understandings—and inspire different experiences of wholeness, whether we are ten, twenty, forty, eighty. Our forty-eight talented contributors themselves range from their early twenties to their eighties—and, interestingly, don't necessarily write out of, or into, their current life stage.

There are interesting stories about developing identity, discovering identity (whether finding out your birth story or recovering parts of your past), encounters with illness, a relatively large number exploring longer developmental arcs, especially in women's lives. How we find our footing in the often radically different memory arcs of those close to us is another theme. We also have poetry and prose exploring the wholeness found in long marriages—and long lives.

The second major section focuses more on social context—how we understand and reconcile deep social contradictions in gender, negotiate socially in highly polarized times, how we understand and integrate changing standards of social justice.

The third section, which is primarily poetry, celebrates the more mystical dimensions of the experience of wholeness.

The images made for this anthology are intentionally abstract and are designed to invite us into the non-verbal, pattern-seeking dimensions of wholeness. We hope they invite you to read the selections themselves in similarly intuitive and evocative frames of mind, listening for new constellations.

References:

William James. *Writings 1902-1910*. New York: Hatchette Books, 2021 [*Some Problems of Philosophy*, "Chapter IV: Percept and Concept" and "Chapter V: Percept and Concept—The Abuse of Concepts;" *Varieties of Religious Experience*, "Lecture XVI, Mysticism."]

Mansoor Adayfi. *Don't Forget Us Here: Lost and Found at Guantánamo*. New York: Hatchette Books, 2021, pp. 309-310.

Interview with Yehuda Bacon, Holocaust survivor and artist. yadvashem.org.

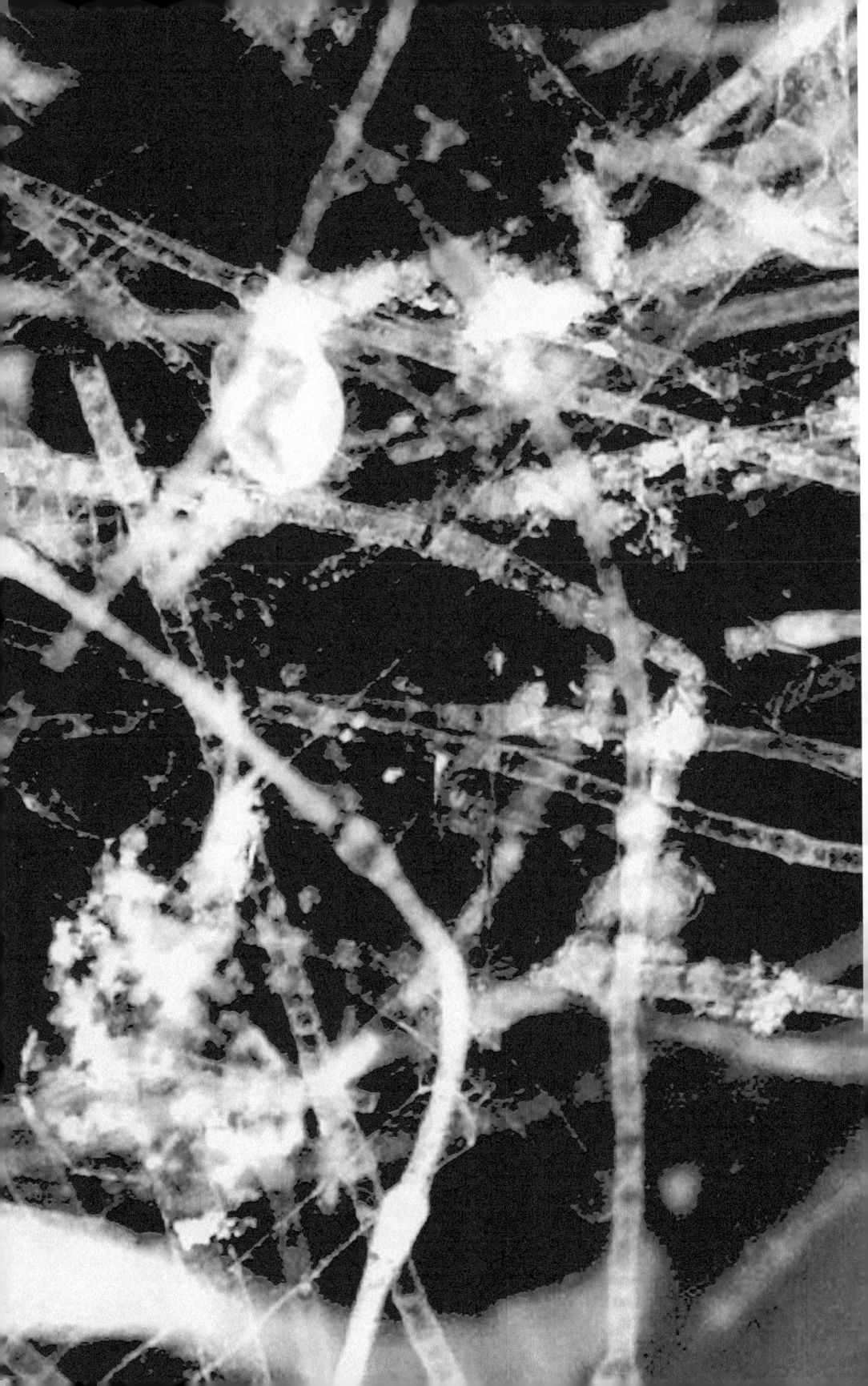

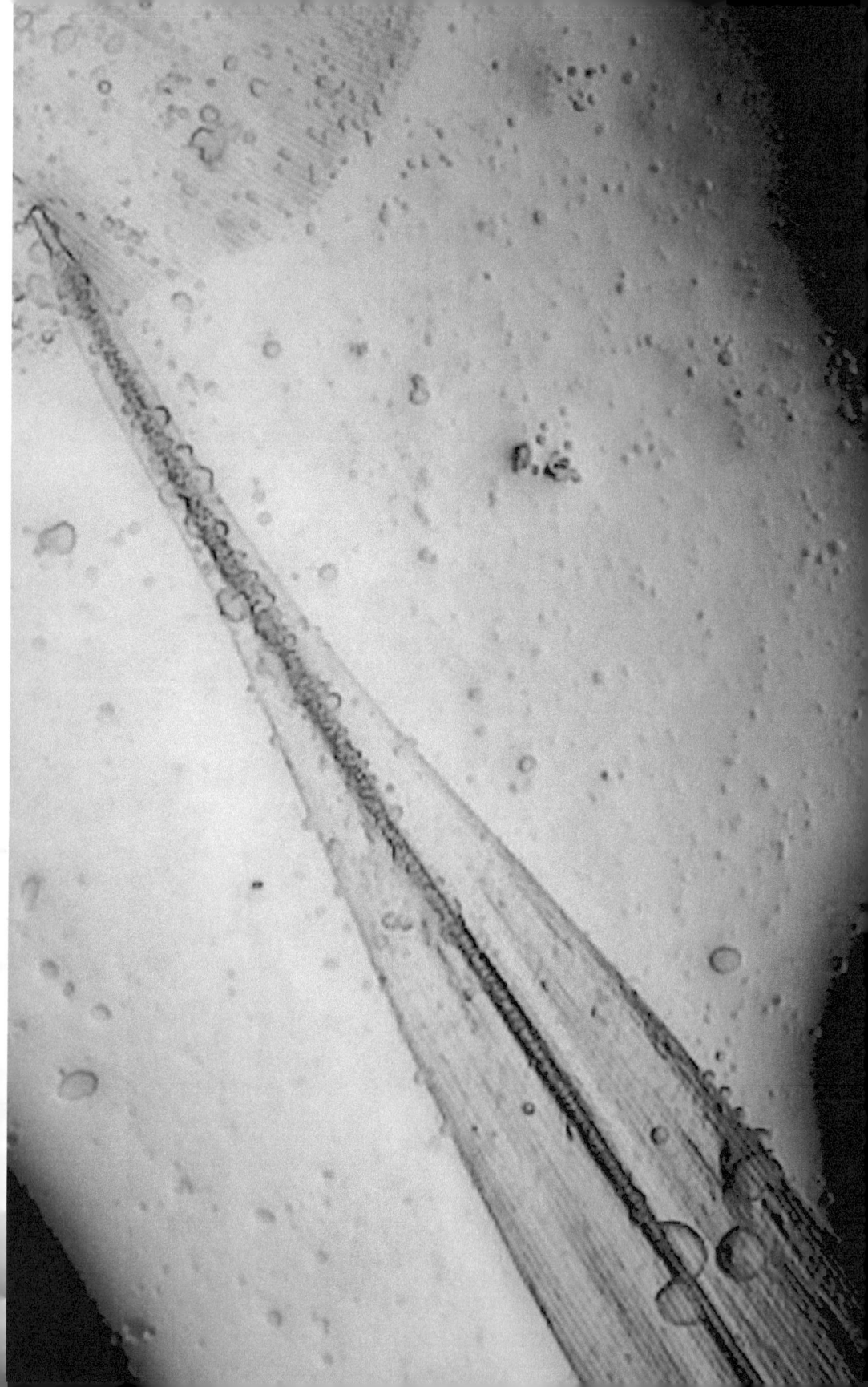

I
ARC OF LIFE

LAURA APOL

HANNA ON THE MONKEY BARS

When is she ever more beautiful than this:

shining, as hand over hungry hand
she crosses the ladder of sun
swinging herself forward
into day, willowy arms strong,
shoulders taut,

so in love with her own body
I can hardly bear it.

Now she grasps every bar, now every other,
her reach lengthening,
forward, back.

I have drifted naked in a bayou,
run marathons mile after mile,
burrowed toes into fine white sand,

but I have never loved my body like this.

She glides easy through this dance,
drops to the sawdust
and climbs to cross again, again, again.

My eyes follow as, clear-winged, she rises
and soars.

THE GIFT OF YES

I tell my mother I want to
go to the lake, waterskiing with friends,
instead of to Sunday service

and this time she does not say,
       Laura, you know how we feel about this.

She does not say,
       You can make up your own mind.
       But you know how we feel about this.

She does not say,
       My parents would never have let me go,
       but you can make up your own mind.
       And you know how we feel about this.

Instead, she says,
Yes. Have a good time. And here's some money
for ice cream—

and in that moment

her own father opens the car door,
her mother hands me suntan lotion and a hat,
her sister tosses me a towel,

and with her gift of yes, my mother
climbs in beside me in the back.

LIGHT, WATER, BONES

On the far bank, a willow weeps,
while in the river, its mirror
ripples with light. The cloud-blemished sky
meets a perfect dappling beneath.

Here are Plato's images in reverse,
the ideal in the darkening current:

a leaf, a branch, an evening bat.
Even the heron steps gently,
afraid to startle the flawless
heron at its feet.

Along the lane, the deer carcass
does not teach me about life or death,
but about the curve of ribs
whitening under the moon.

The lessons I learn
are soundless: the light, the water,
the delicate bleach of bones.

After years of listening,
perhaps in my next life
I will not need to learn to trust—

will come back faithful
to my own sense of smell,
wander like the possum, solitary
through the night brush and broken limbs,

burrow fearless as the sleek black mole,
far from this world's polished
surface, intimate with the wet
roots of things.

THEA HEARD

A GIRL NO ONE CAN TRUST

"That's how it's going to end up," my grandmom says to me. "You're going to be someone no one will trust."

My mom and my granddad and my aunt all nod. My little sister starts to, then stops when I stare at her.

Then I stare at each of them, one by one. "I don't care."

"Well," my mom says. "Now it's out there."

"Like a dead dog in the road," my granddad says.

"Where's the dog?" my sister asks. "Are you *sure* it's dead? Maybe it just needs to be taken to the vet." She looks very upset, her cheeks are getting red and her eyes are getting even bigger than usual. She's seven, four years younger than me.

"It's a metaphor," I tell her. I don't say stupid. "Grampa is speaking met-a-phor-i-cal-ly."

The grown-ups are all angry. It isn't the first time. They obviously think it's not going to be the last. I have to agree with them. It won't be the last. They leave me no choice. So I meet their expectations. I lie.

"You're right," I say. "You're absolutely right. Really and truly, I *am* sorry."

Sorry I exceeded my screentime allotment and lied about it.

Sorry I skateboarded down six blocks of the steepest street in my neighborhood. Without falling. Without losing my balance even a little bit. Even waving to the old lady gardening on the corner, the one with no memory.

Sorry I lied to my teacher when my dad left two years ago. I told her he died in Afghanistan fighting for the Taliban. He's not dead. I only wish he was. Because he treats us as if we are.

He lives with another woman—Cherie—and has another little girl: Cherie Amour. That's almost a redundancy. It's also a song whose chorus is lalalalalala.

Is unpredictable the same as unreliable? Is being a risk-taker the same as oblivious to consequences? Is being a child something you ever outgrow?

I mean, look at the way my granddad's lower lip juts out when he's mad, or the way my grandmom does that pout when she's disappointed, or how Aunt Darla opens her eyes so wide when she's pretending to be surprised or delighted. If they saw themselves the way I see them, I'm not sure they would recognize themselves. *I* see expressions I saw in preschool. But when they see me, they see a grown-up. A grown-up they *don't* like.

"I just can't take anymore," I heard my mom say last night. "There isn't the simplest thing I can ask—like not raiding the refrigerator at night, not cutting up the window screens to get out of the house when she's been locked in her room, spreading slime across that whole room. Or wearing a helmet when she bikes or skates. Or saying hello and thank you."

"We'd like to help you," my granddad said. "But I think she's worse with us. And your mom, with her arthritis and her heart . . ."

There was a pause. I think they were waiting for my aunt to offer. They waited and waited. She took a deep breath and let it out. "I travel too much," she said. "I wouldn't be able to supervise. And if I were around, it wouldn't work. We're not like oil and water. We don't repel, we grapple. Someone could get hurt."

"I just can't," my mom said, her voice cracking. She sniffed in with a really sad kind of gurgle. "I just can't do it anymore. It's a horrible thing to say. My own child. You look at her—and she's so beautiful. I know that's what other people see. But I just see that look in her eyes when she's decided she's going to do something—like climb the highest tree in the park—and I know I don't have what it will require to stop her. Not just one day—but every day. She gets something in her head, and she's just not going to let it go. And she has no fear."

She's wrong. I do have fear. I have fear as I listen to her. It is pulling my heart tighter and tighter in my chest. So tight it is almost impossible to breathe. I don't want them to let go of me. And I don't want them to hold me back. I want both of these. Equally.

That *is* the truth. I just can't see where that leaves me.

Between a rock and hard place there is a little space. It is *my* job, all alone, to find it. This does not feel like a metaphor. It feels impossible—and true.

WILSON R. M. TAYLOR

CROSSING THE LAGOON

Lucia looked out the window at the mists of the lagoon. The world was filled with faint sounds of lapping water and the muffled shouts of fishermen returning to shore.

A seagull shifted from foot to foot on the pier, shaking its wings dry with a shivering motion. The damp pervaded everything this time of year, clothes never fully dry on the line, windowsills always a dark, wet brown.

Lucia liked it. Her earliest memory was her mother running a warm bath for her in the depths of winter, the cracked porcelain of the tub, the way there seemed to be no barrier between her and the water.

"Hey, Lucia." Mr. Insigne snapped his fingers. "The lesson's in here."

Next to her Arturo snickered, and she blushed a little, but Mr. Insigne smiled. "Why don't you solve the next one for us?"

She went to the board, feeling long and awkward. She was wearing her mother's hand-me-down dress, the first that had ever fit her. Her mother's initials were on the tag. Lucia could feel it rubbing against the back of her neck like gentle fingernails.

She squinted at the problem. All those letters and numbers, together under the roof of the square root sign, waiting to be transformed. She solved it quickly.

"Arturo, why don't you try the next one?" said Mr. Insigne.

Arturo groaned. While he struggled Lucia watched the back of his head, then went back to staring out the window. The seagull was gone.

)()(❋)()(

After school Arturo walked with her to her father's shop, winding along canals and narrow side streets, the brightly colored houses slick with the remnants of afternoon rain. They glowed, more of a tourist attraction now than anything; in the old days they were supposed to help bring fishermen, wandering spouses, lost souls home through the dark.

At the shop Arturo continued on. "See you later?"

She nodded, and the bell dinged over her head. The one-room store was a cocoon of white lace, each thread tracing its orderly pattern across the canvas of a sash, a dress, a veil.

"Ciao, melagrana." Her father's voice came slow and raspy from the back corner behind the cash register. He rubbed a palm across his bald, stubbled head, face crinkling into a smile. "How was school?"

She shrugged. "Fine. Easy. We're always waiting on Arturo and Giacomo."

Her father glowed with pride. "You're headed for big things. But be patient—if I had patience when I was your age . . . " He chuckled. "Well, I wouldn't have this lace shop. I might have traveled the world."

She had nothing but patience, she thought to herself. She wished she had less of it.

"But I wouldn't have met your mother, either." He began telling a story Lucia had heard a thousand times, the story of how he dove into the lagoon and caught a jellyfish just to impress her mother, how she had been horrified and wouldn't talk to him for three days.

A few customers came in, but nobody bought anything. Her father sighed. "Time to close up."

As they emerged into the square the sky was streaked vermilion, clouds standing still above the slow death of the day; for a moment time seemed to stop. Her father pulled down the window grate, its metal groaning. People were gathered inside the warm glow of cafés, drinks cupped in front of them, cheeks ruddy above their coats.

Lucia and her father turned away from the crowd, down the darkness of their street. As her father unlocked their apartment she wondered if he was lonely; he hadn't seen his friends much lately. She tucked into the little red armchair with the fringed lamp next to it, feeling the familiar flash of sadness that appeared when her mother wasn't there waiting. She wished she could say something about it to her father, even in passing, but he didn't like to talk about it, and that time was long gone, anyway. She watched him humming softly to himself in the kitchen, cooking risotto. For a brief second she saw him clearly, his age, his round glasses slightly smudged. But then the frailty was gone; he was her father again.

"Check in the fridge," he said. "What should we have with our risotto?"

There wasn't much, just two cartons of mushrooms and half a bag of spinach.

"Spinach and mushrooms?" she said, expecting him to laugh. Instead he just nodded.

)(✳)(

After dinner she poured herself a glass of wine.

"Going out?" her father asked.

"Party at Serafina's. Arturo's dragging me."

"You'll be glad you went. You never know who you'll meet. Or who might surprise you."

"Not around here."

He held up one finger. "I have something to show you."

He retreated into his bedroom and came back with his ancient laptop. It roared like an airplane as it started up. He grinned, suddenly more energetic. "This might take a minute."

She went to change into jeans and a sweater, hanging her mother's dress carefully in her closet. When she returned he was holding the laptop triumphantly. "Look."

Two roundtrip train tickets to Rome. He was beaming. "It's your graduation present! We'll go on a little vacation."

"Papa, that's during the busy season—you'll have to close the shop."

"This is a special moment for you. Maybe we'll be seeing your university for the first time."

He was babbling like a child, but she could tell he was hiding his sadness. She thought of the quiet shop, the echoes of the lagoon, their apartment creaking, full of ghosts.

"It's where your mother and I spent our honeymoon," he continued. "Well, not the hotel. I haven't picked that yet."

She hugged him, thanked him, but as she walked back towards the square to meet Arturo, she realized he'd been saving up for it. And she didn't feel gratitude, or excitement, or even nervousness—she just felt guilty.

And confused, too. She didn't want to go away to university. He didn't really want her to go, either—they both knew. Why bother pretending? Was that such a bad thing? Why leave when this place was full of memories, when it had everything they could possibly need?

Arturo had two bottles of wine, his tobacco and papers, and some weed. He smiled at her, and she blushed a little, but he didn't notice, launching into a story about his little brother's escapades with their cat. Her confusion around her father and the trip began to fade. It was hard to think too far ahead around Arturo; they'd been friends so long it felt like they were part of an eternal present.

On their way across the square she spotted Mr. Lao ducking down a side street. He was an old friend of her father's. She pointed. "Remember him?"

"Oh yeah. We used to make fun of his accent." Arturo laughed, the sound echoing against the buildings.

She frowned. "That can't have been easy for him. Moving here." Shame welled up inside her; suddenly she wanted to cry.

"It was only behind his back. I hear Serafina's house is sick. Right on the lagoon."

"I've been," said Lucia. "Our mothers were friends."

"I never knew that."

"I haven't been back in ten years."

Serafina's house was sleek and modern, low-slung horizontal beams of metal and concrete framing a panoramic view of the dark water. The thump of rap music could be heard across the front yard, which seemed endless amidst the narrow canals and cobblestones.

To Lucia it seemed to say: *We're here to stay.*

To Arturo it was something else, an adventure, maybe; his eyes gleamed with desire.

Lucia felt a hint of jealousy. He was here for Serafina—it was unspoken, but obvious. The thought made her sick.

And when they emerged onto the back patio she remembered why she hadn't wanted to come. Everyone was dressed in black with a cigarette in hand, a war of cutting glances and tangled limbs like a Tintoretto. Arturo wandered off, and she found a chair near the water and a plastic cup for her wine.

Giacomo came up to her. "You look like you don't want to be here."

She laughed, caught off guard.

Emboldened, he pulled out the chair next to her. "Want one?" He extended a cigarette from the pack with a practiced gesture.

She hesitated. "Sure." She didn't normally, but she needed something to do, something to distract her. Everyone around them was laughing and flirting and drinking; she couldn't shake the sense that they all were pretending to have fun, that they all really wanted to be somewhere else.

But the thought vanished as the blood rushed to her head with the first drag. Arturo materialized, grinning.

"Wow, Giacomo, I can't even get her to smoke cigarettes. C'mon, you two. I've got a little present." He twirled a joint between his fingers. "Let's go smoke it with Serafina."

They followed Serafina upstairs to her bedroom, where a balcony overlooked the lagoon. The music was muffled now, coming from the other side of the house.

"Got a speaker?" asked Arturo.

Serafina nodded, moving like a flicker of smoke back into the bedroom, her hair flowing smoothly around her. When she came back Arturo sparked the joint and put on some music. The extra noise bothered Lucia; the sky was finally clear, a thousand stars twinkling above, and Arturo needed more. Or maybe he just needed to impress Serafina.

But Lucia could tell she wasn't impressed; the higher she got the clearer it became. Arturo was too of-this-place. Serafina was destined for big cities, better things.

She turned to Lucia, eyes half-hooded. "Do you remember that boat we used to go out on together?"

Giacomo, stoned, stared out at the lagoon as if he could see it there now.

Lucia could, its red wooden hull gleaming. "We used to pretend we were explorers," she said. "That the big island out there was a new world."

Serafina smiled. "Our mothers loved it. They always said we were so brave."

Lucia didn't remember it that way. She remembered her mother standing nervously on the shore, her hands held tautly on her hips as she strained her eyes to watch them cross the channel. She could see her there now, firm, shrinking, her gaze sweeping like a lighthouse.

The others were staring at her. She realized she was crying. Giacomo and Arturo looked at their feet.

"Shit," she said. She rubbed the heel of her hand against her eyes. "I'm so fucking high."

Giacomo pointed dumbly at the sky. "Look at the moon," he said, distracting them with what might have been chivalry.

"And the way it reflects off the water—the way it moves," said Arturo.

"The boys have to get stoned to realize it's a beautiful place," Serafina said to Lucia. She smiled in a bittersweet way. "It makes me sad to think about leaving."

Arturo changed the song. Giacomo grunted something about the rapper. Serafina sang along a little bit; suddenly there was warmth between them.

Down below the doorbell rang.

"Shit," said Serafina, sweeping hair behind her ear. "What's that?"

She went to get it, and the other three went out back, where the black-clad mass was moving restlessly.

"So early . . ."

"Too loud . . ."

"Fucking provincial cops . . ."

"It's Friday . . ."

"Way out here by the water . . ."

"Sound travels."

⟩⟨⟩⟨ ❋ ⟩⟨⟩⟨

They still had some wine left, and Arturo didn't want to go home. They wandered over to the square near San Martino Church. Lucia sat on the steps.

There was a plaque there, a memorial to fallen soldiers from the World Wars. "Look," Arturo said, as he'd said so many times before. "There I am."

He pointed to a name. Arturo Tagliapietra.

"And there, and there." Two more Arturo Tagliapietra's.

"Three of us, dead." He rolled a cigarette. "I'm the fifth. That's not good odds."

She looked at him. He was just annoyed Serafina hadn't asked him to stay. Lucia was pleased that she hadn't. "How were there two that died in World War I?"

"Father and son. The father got drafted, and the son was underage but he volunteered anyway, went chasing him. Junior and Senior. They say that Senior never knew that Junior died."

He lit his cigarette. "That's real bravery. We don't have anything like that anymore. Everyone wants to stay home, live in the same town their whole life, send their kids to the same school."

Lucia didn't mention that he would probably be going to university in Venice at the farthest, that of the two of them he was more likely to get stuck here. But there was something brilliant in the stars that defied truth, and he was dreaming, looking up. He handed her the cigarette. As the buzz enveloped her head she remembered the boat again, red boards tied against the damp brown pier, the benches looking up at her, the vessel waiting.

"Let's go," Serafina was saying as she climbed on board, black hair swinging, limbs chubby and stubborn as she grasped the oars. "They won't miss us."

Down a canal there was someone singing about love, and the sound seemed to come from inside of her, the words murmured like a long-forgotten lullaby: her mother there, her mother promising to never leave. And then the song was gone, back where it came from, into the mists of the lagoon.

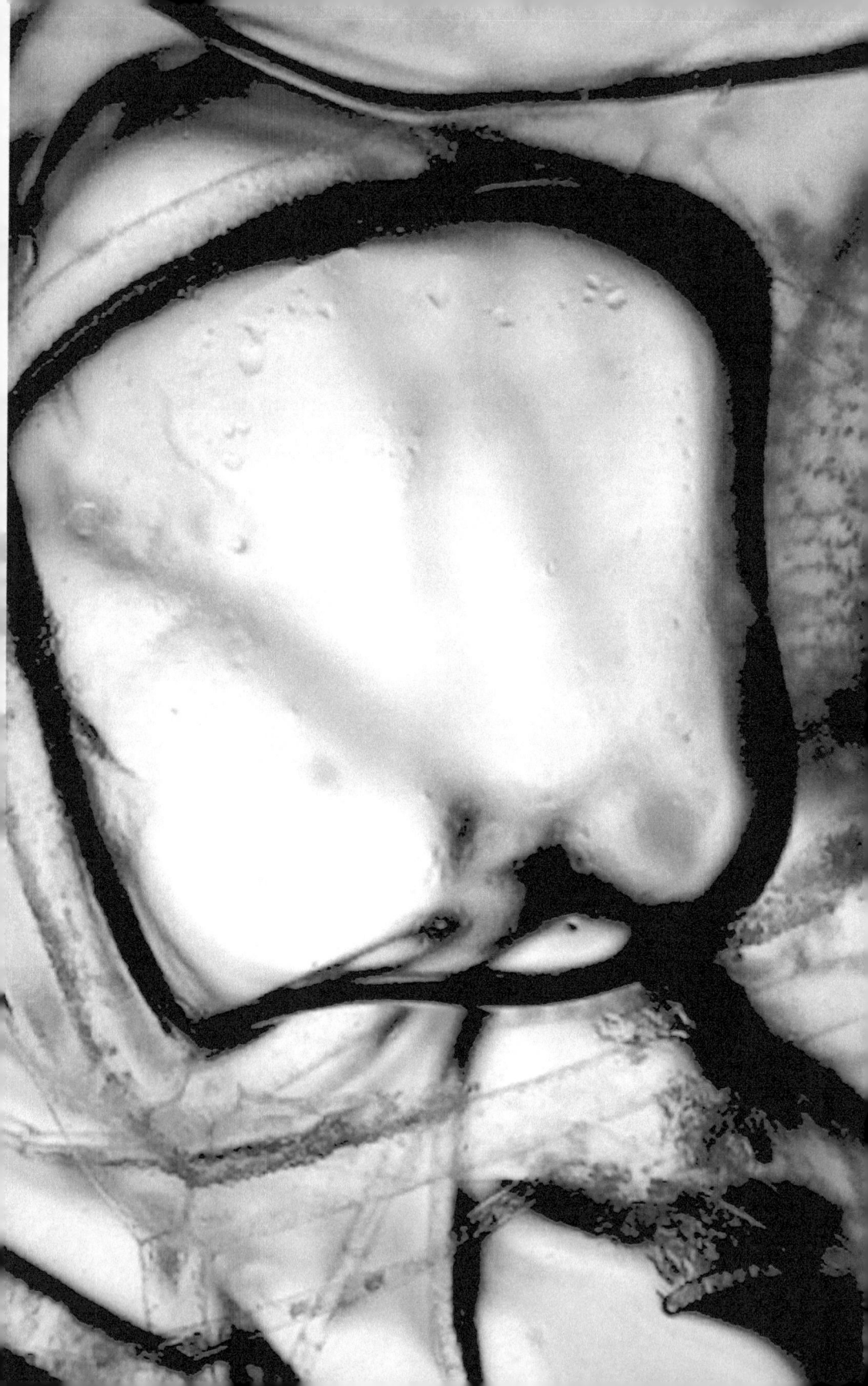

DEIDRA SUWANEE DEES

FRAGMENT:
NEGOTIATING IDENTITY IN THE SOUTH

I looked into the mirror today, smiling for a change, wondering what it would reveal. I noticed the ripples in the bronze-colored wrinkles beside my eyes delineating the signs of wisdom that only age can bring. As I work on my master's degree at Ivy League Cornell in Ithaca, New York, the mirror conveys to me that I will turn a year older this season. It is a reminder that I have traveled a long way from the reluctant womb that was a receptacle for my entrance into the South; the reluctant womb that turned away from me because I was a biracial birth followed by painful years of childhood neglect that ended in abandonment.

Because I did not have a fit mother as many other Mvskoke children had in our rural community of Uriah, Alabama, I have been coerced to find things out on my own that I otherwise would have known. I find myself realizing I have spent all my life doing this . . . and wondering if I will spend however long I have left doing the same thing.

How beneficial it would have been had I been taught the necessary life skills that come from a proper Southern woman, skills I have had to scratch and claw for—by humiliating trial and error—struggling and fighting every step of the way; indeed, fighting at times against the womb that bore me.

Anticipating an answer from the mirror, I asked:

> *How can I comprehend this all? If I die like my vanilla-skinned darling Selena in a deadly auto-train accident, or if I die like my chocolate-skinned dad in a tragic head-on truck collision, what will be the moral of my story? That I scratched and clawed for nothing? That my bronze-skinned life was worthless and good for nothing like the biological one who bore me used to say?*

While these are plausible considerations, the mirror reveals there is a force inside me—a strong life force—that compels me forward, and even fancies at times bronze images of *being somebody;* images of me rising above what Southerners see as unattractive mixed-race skin. The mirror shows me reflections of greatness which I have relegated to a cry for significance from my inner clay-stained child, the one who was neglected, abused and rejected; the one who—because of this—can never be whole. I have become strong, my bronze skin taut, by learning to live with the ever-present anguish of not being whole, while whole people have passed me by, enjoying their wholeness, unaware of my fragment.

ISABELLA OJEDA-AHMED

ALL THE PIECES

I have often wondered if I might be the only person in the world without a doppelganger. A natural consequence of adoption, I'm sure. How could I make sense of the brown face in the mirror without context, surrounded by pale unfamiliarity? As a child, all I had were three photographs of my birth parents and my brother, which I studied intently. I would place my thumb over each part of their slightly blurred faces in turn, trying to piece myself together from their fragments. My father's thick eyebrows, arched in surprise, or my brother's delicate rounded nose. The slight downturn of my mother's lips even when she smiled. But no matter how hard I tried to see family, I just kept seeing strangers. It's no surprise that I'm terrible with faces; I can't even recognize my own.

)()(✸)()(

We had arranged to meet at a Starbucks. Such a mundane place to have a life-changing encounter, and yet no other location seemed to make sense. *It'll be less awkward over coffee. Best to meet on neutral ground. Somewhere halfway between his place and mine.* These were all rational justifications at the time of planning, but now I stood in the middle of the sticky tile floor and wondered why on earth I had agreed to shatter my reality in such a public place. My stomach was a soda bottle, shaken hard. Anxiety fizzed up and threatened to burst through the lid. I glanced around the store apprehensively, praying that he would see me first. I didn't trust myself to recognize his face despite my husband's earlier reassurance: "He's your brother. You'll know."

I wondered how we would greet each other. *Hello* and *nice to meet you* felt laughably banal, but maybe they perfectly suited this bizarre coffee shop reunion. Should I go in for a hug, or was that too familiar? I had no plan, but it didn't matter anymore because there he was, standing up from a table in the back and waving me over, this man with the thick beard and gentle eyes behind black frame glasses. All of that rumination and speculation, and yet I never could have predicted the first words that came out of his mouth.

"You look so much like Mom."

)()(❋)()(

Late at night, in the quiet blue dark, there comes a soundless moment when your brain suddenly perceives itself. Awareness sinks deep into your skull, your bones—*you are real.* Sometimes, you welcome the reminder to be present. Other times, most times, you pray that sleep will take you first. After all, an existential wave is sure to follow, swift and all-consuming. But nothing in the world ever feels as true as that moment.

My brother's words sank in the same way, grounding me to the earth. Roots burst from the soles of my feet. Seeds of doubt had no room to grow. He had never met me before, but for an instant his eyes widened like he was seeing the ghost of our late mother. He spoke softly, his voice equal parts wonder and conviction. And even though I had examined those photos of our mother for years, trying and failing to see the resemblance, the man standing in front of me was her only other creation. I had no choice but to believe him.

)()(❋)()(

I can't remember a time before stories. My first story was handed to me through books and gentle conversations because my adoptive parents did not believe in keeping secrets. They told me that a selfless woman brought me into the world, but no matter how much she wanted to try, she lacked the means to provide a good life for me. So she looked through a scrapbook and chose the two of them to be my parents. "She loved you so much she gave you away."

I built my identity around this story and its unspoken expectations. I was obedient, grateful, eager to please; her sacrifice and their devotion would not be in vain. I lashed out in anger when a kid on the playground cruelly insisted that my adoptive mother was not my own, or when a curious friend asked that careless question—"Who's your real mom?"

That first story, so straightforward and reliable, began to fray at the edges over time. As I grew up, I pulled at the loose threads to see where they might lead. If she loved me, why did she leave? What would my life have been like if she had kept me? What makes a "real" mom? Gradually, a more intricate story materialized, shaped by my assumptions and misgivings. My birth mother, destitute and alone, must have been coerced by either the system or the circumstances into giving me up. My adoptive parents stepped in, doing their best to give me a life of opportunity I would not have been afforded otherwise. In that way, I had two moms: one who gave birth to me and one who raised me. But when I passed from the arms of one mom to the other, my physical self and my shadow diverged. A hazy curtain now separated the life I was living from its hypothetical alternative.

On the other side of that curtain, I could see a shadow play unfolding. I saw the contours of two silhouettes: my birth mother's and mine. I saw us at the beach, wading through paper waves. I saw us sharing meals at the kitchen table. We clashed, we sulked, we commiserated and wept. Her comforting embrace made our shadows eclipse. Mother and child together, two shadow puppets dancing before the light.

But shadow and self are not meant to be apart. From that central rift, more fissures will begin to form. With every birthday, milestone, breakdown, and heartbreak, I found myself ruminating on my shadow more and more. I couldn't build a puzzle without all the pieces, and the effort was breaking me apart. I struggled to forge an identity in that perpetually fractured state. What did it mean to be Mexican and Peruvian if no one had taught me our languages, histories, or traditions? Where did I get my tendency to overshare, and the instant red flush in my cheeks that always betrays my embarrassment? I wondered if I had inherited my artistic eye or just developed it after countless hours spent in museums. Did chronic depression run in the family, or was I just a self-pitying pessimist? In desperate times, I built my identity around the not-knowing. Maybe I was destined to be an unfinished puzzle.

)()(❋)()(

Now my brother sat in front of me, handing me the missing pieces one by one. As he spoke, I saw the image of our mother come into focus. A woman with a penchant for avoidance, full of secrets, only willing to open up while having a smoke. Smart, studious, and often sad. A woman with self-confessed poor taste in men. A cancer survivor, until she relapsed.

I saw that my brother and I had more in common than I expected. Our mother had cast us both aside in different ways. He talked about being left with family in Peru, wondering why she only visited a few times in the first ten years of his life. He found it difficult to view her as a maternal figure when she hardly attempted to be one. Confusion and resentment were familiar companions. In spite of everything, he insisted that he loved her deeply. I knew exactly what he meant. Sitting across from each other at a corner table, we struggled to comprehend how our mother died and left behind two children without telling one about the other's existence.

"I always wanted a little sister. I would ask Mom, and she would always say no," he told me. "Even in the hospital, when the doctors asked about a second pregnancy in her records, she claimed that she lost it. But this whole time—"

"I existed."

My words came out with a rueful laugh as I realized what this meant. Our mother was not that brokenhearted woman I dreamed about, the one who always prayed her child would return to offer forgiveness. She was simply a flawed and troubled human being who spent her whole life denying my existence to herself and everyone else. A pang of agony shot through an old, forgotten wound in my chest. I was her secret, her shame.

As my brother spoke to me about his upbringing, I kept thinking back to the first story I was ever told. Just another myth, unraveling. My brother and I were born into an accomplished family with high expectations and more degrees than both sides of my adoptive family combined. They valued education and hard work, not unlike the parents who raised me. They raised my brother when our mother shirked her duty, but when I was born, she never even gave them the chance. This story was not one of upward mobility, but of a family torn apart.

All that I had imagined, peering through the curtain at the shadows of my mother and myself, was a fabrication too. Exposed by the harsh glare of context, a new shadow play unfolded before my eyes. In this version, she treated me the same way she had treated my brother. I saw our family uniting to take care of us in the wake of her absence. Her rejection and detachment still inflicted a permanent wound, but this time we had each other. I could tell my brother saw our shadows too, and a part of him yearned to be on the other side of that curtain.

We must have sat in the coffee shop for hours. There was still so much more to discuss. We wanted to catch each other up on what our lives had been like for the past twenty-five years, but it was getting late and we each had a long drive ahead.

"In time, *hermanita*," he said wisely as we parted ways.

Reunion by definition implies a prior encounter, but my brother and I had never crossed paths, and my mother and I never would. And yet, it was the perfect word. Self and shadow reunited at the intersection of what was and what could have been.

)()(✲)()(

That day, for the first time in my life, I held all the pieces. I saw the stories, the dreams, the secrets, the desire to belong, the sting of rejection—all me. But I looked closer and found that they weren't puzzle pieces at all. They lacked the perfectly laser-cut edges, the predetermined knobs and holes. In my hands were countless fragments of pottery. All different shapes and sizes, some stamped with ridges and lines, others chipped and fading. I could not begin to guess how they must have fit together long ago. I wanted to cry, or maybe laugh, as I realized it would be impossible to restore them to their original form. Time had worn them down like sea glass, but at least I had them all. A pile of broken shards is just a vessel in a different shape.

BETH CHRISTENSEN

PART, PART, WHOLE

Libby

At first, they didn't want me to talk. They didn't seem to want to know anything about what I was thinking or feeling, or anything about what I knew that could actually help her. How could they even begin to understand her without understanding me? I thought that the absurdity of this was obvious: I had known her much longer, decades longer, than any of them. Why didn't they want me to talk?

Have you ever done a jigsaw puzzle, a really big one with a couple thousand pieces, and found out at the end of it that there are pieces missing? You look everywhere: under the furniture, in that little trove of toys and old socks that the dog keeps next to her bed, in your pockets (although why would you ever put them in your pockets?), between the sofa cushions—everywhere. If you can't find the missing pieces, your puzzle is never going to really be complete. It might be recognizable, but the holes will never cease to bother you. You might as well throw the puzzle away, but then you think, as soon as I throw it out, those missing pieces will show up. Isn't that how it always happens?

I'm one of the missing pieces. The picture of her life could exist without me, but there would be holes. Important, substantial holes that only I could fill. I had the general information, as did she by this time, as to what had happened. But I had more than that: I had all the human responses to that information that any normal person would have. I remembered the humiliation, the fear, the confusion. I remembered the experience of being chased by a shadowy man, and I remembered the feeling of him raping me when he caught me, as he always did. I remembered the sound of the heavy metal door closing, as one of the people who had possession of the keys (certainly not me) would close it, hard, so it would be sure to lock. I remembered the sound of that door closing as it echoed along the cinder-block walls of the psych ward. I remembered it as the sound of hopelessness.

It's not that they didn't believe in my existence. There were people, some of whom knew me, most of whom did not, who didn't think I was real, but *these* people had to know I was real. They had diagnosed me, after all. They had told her she had dissociative identity disorder, and that the many holes in her memory, the gaps in her story of herself where she just went blank, were actually occupied by me and a couple others who ran things when she just couldn't do it anymore. We operated the machinery of her mind during some of the worst times. We each remembered things that she could not yet bear to remember, and held the feelings that would have threatened her precarious hold on sanity. It was with the help of them—the therapists, the hospital staff—that we all began to become aware of each other, and for each of us to slowly come to know what the others knew. But we were only supposed to speak through her, using her voice, answering to her name.

This was not the same hospital, or the same staff, that had presided over my original incarnation, the cinder-block ward with the heavy metal door and the shadow rapist. In that hospital of long ago, I had been declared schizophrenic and the hopeless feeling that came over me whenever the door slammed shut was not unrealistic. I was told that my insanity was likely to be a lifelong condition. I knew that meant a lot of doors would be closing, and as far as I could tell very few would be opening.

No, this hospital, the new one, specialized in treating people like me, people whose rapes and other traumas had lurked in shadows for years, some of whose brains had created auxiliary staff to help with the overload. They knew that I was real, but they would only acknowledge me as a *part*. As I understood it, I was not considered to be a person, just as a steering wheel or a radiator is not a car. I, of course, felt otherwise. When I was in charge of the body, I felt whole. I felt young, energetic. I knew the body was forty-something years old, but when I was in charge it felt seventeen. When I looked in the mirror, I saw myself, not her.

To tell the truth, I didn't like her, not at first. She was old and fat and kind of frumpy. She didn't smoke and hardly ever drank. She drove a station wagon. As far as I could tell, she didn't do anything interesting or fun. I had dropped out of high school, but she made perfect grades in college and grad school. She had stopped playing the guitar and writing stories. She had stopped painting. There were at least a couple dozen oil and acrylic paintings of mine that had just disappeared; she said she did not know what had happened to them. She was colorless, faded, uninteresting. She definitely wasn't like anyone I had ever expected to become.

So, as I got to know her, I felt a lot of things; mostly I felt angry, outraged really. I was angry at her for creating this life without including me in the big decisions. I was angry with the shrink who had sexually abused her, and who had declared me schizophrenic. I was angry at how easily a man could snuff out the voice of a woman or girl, how he could render her irrelevant or even invisible just by making such a proclamation. I wanted to be allowed to express my outrage, something at which I was quite good.

I think it was my anger, more than my existence, that bothered them so much. Like most pissed-off teenagers, I wanted to be able to air my grievances. I had not developed much of a sense of propriety or manners or whatever the hell it is that keeps nice people from saying exactly what they mean. My kind and soft-spoken psychiatrist (the new one) told me that some of my expressions of anger had been inappropriate. *Inappropriate?* I was in a nut house, for crying out loud! I told him that appropriateness was relative to the situation in which one finds oneself. He tried to hide his amusement from me as he conceded that I might be right.

We worked out a compromise. I would be permitted to engage in discourse so long as I followed some of those rules of polite society that I still felt were woefully mismatched to the environment of any mental hospital, even this one. I was expected to keep my shit together. But I could speak in my own voice. I could refer to myself by my own name. I could finally, after more than twenty-five years, tell people what had been done to me and, more importantly, how it had affected me. I could be real.

What I couldn't say, because I didn't know, was how I had managed to slip beneath the surface for so long. Looking back on that quarter-century, I could see her life, like one of those home videos of mostly inconsequential crap, but I didn't see myself in it. I'm not stupid; I knew that she was me, or some version of me, but it didn't feel that way. For a long time, she felt like a stranger. It was when I started to be able to talk that the chasm between my experience, my self, and hers began to narrow.

)()(❋)()(

Sarah

As much as Libby wanted to make noise and be seen, what I wanted most of all was to disappear. I was ashamed, and so very sorry, that what I had done and the choices I had made, had ruined not only my life but the lives of everyone who came after. I tried my best to hide from her, and I was successful until sometime in 1999 when she was in her early forties and I was still fifteen. I would always be fifteen.

I slipped into her awareness unintentionally one night, that night in 1999, while she was asleep, and it woke her up. I guess the best way to describe the encounter was that she saw what I knew, like my memories and feelings had been hidden behind a kind of veil, and for a moment that veil had been pulled aside. I know it was overwhelming for her, and I pulled myself away from her awareness as quickly as I could.

But that was a bell that could not be unrung, and I guess she understood that she would have to communicate with me in order to understand how the abuse had happened in the first place. What I had shown her was just a little piece of what I knew. I had to find a way to explain to her how it was that I allowed him to rape me. I had to somehow tell her about feeling frozen in place when he started putting his hands on me, how I was unable to say, *no, don't do that, I don't want that,* and instead I just stayed there, and I didn't say no, and I didn't tell anyone. I had to help her understand how I allowed it all to happen, but the truth was that I didn't understand it myself.

Libby was all anger and outrage, but all I felt was sadness and shame. I knew that I was the cause of everyone's problems. I should have walked away. I should have said no. I should have told someone, but I did none of those things. I had allowed him to abuse me, not just once, but over and over for over two years. I thought it was my fault, for years I thought that, and I was just so sorry.

I wanted to die. I used to imagine myself just kind of melting, turning into a liquid that could ooze into the ground and just disappear, and everyone else would feel better. A long time ago, when he was still raping me, I almost did that. I went into a place that was completely dark and quiet, and as far as I can remember, I couldn't even hear my own thoughts. I found out later that they called it catatonia, but I always thought of it as death, because that was when I went deep under the surface, and I didn't come back up for many years. I think it was my job—my duty really—to die, and I screwed that up just like I screwed so many things up.

For some time after coming back to the surface, after I had invaded her consciousness and showed her what I remembered, I wished I could die without killing the others. That would be the perfect solution. I wasn't as smart as Libby, but I knew enough to know that if I killed myself, I would be killing them too.

So I was left with nothing to do but to share my memories with the others, these awful, sickening things that he did and my stupid inability to stop it. Do you ever have daydreams about what you would do if you could travel in time, stuff that you would go back and do over? Maybe you would apologize to someone you hurt, or study better, or rethink that stupid guy you went out with? Well, multiply that feeling a couple of thousand times, and that's close to what I was feeling. And even though I tried, I really tried, I couldn't shake that feeling of being the one who ruined everything.

)()(❋)()(

Beth

I have these holes in my life . . .

These words drifted toward me from a nearby table in a courtyard bar on a warm, sticky Sunday afternoon. I was waiting for an open mic poetry reading to begin. I had brought some of my own work, unsure of whether I would read, unsure of whether my words could have any resonance outside of myself. I wondered if my feelings of differentness, otherness, strangeness, were based in fact rather than simply in my own insecurities. How could anyone possibly ever know me? How could I ever truly know someone else? These seemed like impossible propositions at the time, and yet there I was, willing to at least take a chance on connection. Then I heard that tiny fragment of conversation: *I have these holes in my life.* I had the feeling, however briefly, of being understood by another human being, one I had never even met. I, too, had these holes in my life.

My life is my story, and my story is my self. Every bit of experience, sensation, emotion, and thought is somehow woven into this entity I call my self. It is always changing, as new threads are drawn into the weave and old ones fade and tatter, but it also has some stability over time. I am me, and the person I was, and the person I will become, must also be me. That, I think, is the most powerful and understandable way of identifying the self. It is me, all my past, my present, and my future. And when my life is over, the whole of me will have been completed, to be remembered or forgotten, maybe to be missed by some, but it will be the sum total of me. The story of my self will, at some unknown point, come to its conclusion, and its place in the infinite universe of innumerable selves will be set.

My life story, the tapestry of threads that constitute my life, has these holes in it. Some of them are relatively simple, the lost bits of memory we all experience. Was I six years old when I got my first bicycle, or was I seven? Who was my fourth-grade teacher? Why can't I remember my grandfather's funeral, even though I know I was there? These are the holes that pock the tapestry of every life, and we somehow manage to fill them. We might turn to others who can supplement the stories, or we might search old letters and photos for clues to awaken our memories. And even when we can't find a way to fill the holes, we generally assume that the missing information would not have a significant impact on our essential self. After all, even a moth-eaten sweater is still a sweater. Holes or not, we seem to develop a sense of who we are, the essence of which seems stable over time.

The holes in my life were bigger than those of most of the people I know. They represented vacancies that spanned years and held stories that had profound impacts on the progression of my self-story. Moreover, the holes seemed to disrupt self-continuity, so that the story of my self changed radically, even to the point of seeming to be not one but several selves. I was always trying to learn the role, take in the story of the new self and make it, sometimes with great effort, connect to the other self-stories. But despite these efforts, my self never felt fully formed. My past was, at best, a hodgepodge of fragmented and confusing memories, supplemented by the family folklore that I accepted, grateful and unquestioning, to patch the holes. My present was often a feeling of being in the wrong place, in the wrong life really, as if I had accidentally slipped into someone else's skin, and I knew I didn't belong there.

When I began to realize that some of the holes in my life story were occupied by other, partial selves, it was shocking at first, and I didn't want to believe it. But it also answered a lot of questions, big and small. Most importantly, it allowed me to begin the long and painful process of remembering and healing from past abuse. Sharing my adult life with badly wounded teenagers was challenging and at times tumultuous (to put it mildly), but over time I learned to accept, and eventually welcome, them as parts of my whole self.

As I discovered more of the truth of my life, as I filled in more of the holes, I understood why I had to hide these things from myself. I wished that a lot of what happened to me had not happened, but of course there was nothing I could do about that. What I could do was listen to what they had to say and feel what they had felt for so long, and as I did, the holes in my life got smaller, and the whole of me came into focus. And as ugly and painful as some of those restored memories are, the emerging whole is someone stronger and wiser than I could have ever been without the challenges of trauma and dissociation. I will keep remembering, and I will keep filling in holes, so when my story does reach its conclusion, the whole of me will be something beautiful and resilient. And on I go.

CYNDY KREY

PROMISES

after Jill Thompson (Ouija) &
Merriam-Webster Dictionary

rail
1. a fence or barrier
2. to revile

hatred beyond healing. My father
rips a handrail off a wall, descends into

brokenness
violently separated into parts

chained to a tree in the backyard. His parents
refuse to release him, until he swears
he'll never drink again. Promises

reverberating
as if in a series of echoes

disappearing down dark alleyways. Skipping
entire generations of

excuses
1. a note of explanation
2. to grant exemption or release

Two weeks after returning home
from combat-support in the Philippines,
his buddy dead-drunk at the wheel.

obdurate
unrepentent

as redwood epiphytes. My father stands
in a clearing with unkempt shoulder-length hair
and horrifyingly long, brown nails.
He is in a hurry. He

strides
takes long decisive steps

through the pines, conversing
with the trees, dragging
branches and wind-fall
onto the path in front of him.

He points across the

field
1. a large, unbroken expanse
2. the place where a battle is fought

You promise him, he can die out here
alone with his trees and lilies, where he feels

safe
free from danger, harm, or loss.

Behind his garage—
a deer laps from a rusted sink,
turns tail and is gone.

FINDING YOUR WAY

(After Adam Zagajewski's *Try to Praise the Mutilated World*)

Try to write yourself out of the corners
        where you live.

Fill the pages in your journal
        with images of heirloom tomatoes
        and decorative gourds.

You must write of blossoms
        and tendrils before they are gone.

Fill the bowl on your table
        with bright fruit and black walnuts.

You've seen crops destroyed
        by armies of locusts. Fields emptied.

You've heard the wind whipping
        down from the mountains.

You should write about being cornered.

Remember that moment between decision
        and indecision. Return to the window
        you considered jumping from.

Write yourself out of that corner
        and soar with the ravens
        over Cape Breton.

Forget about falling.

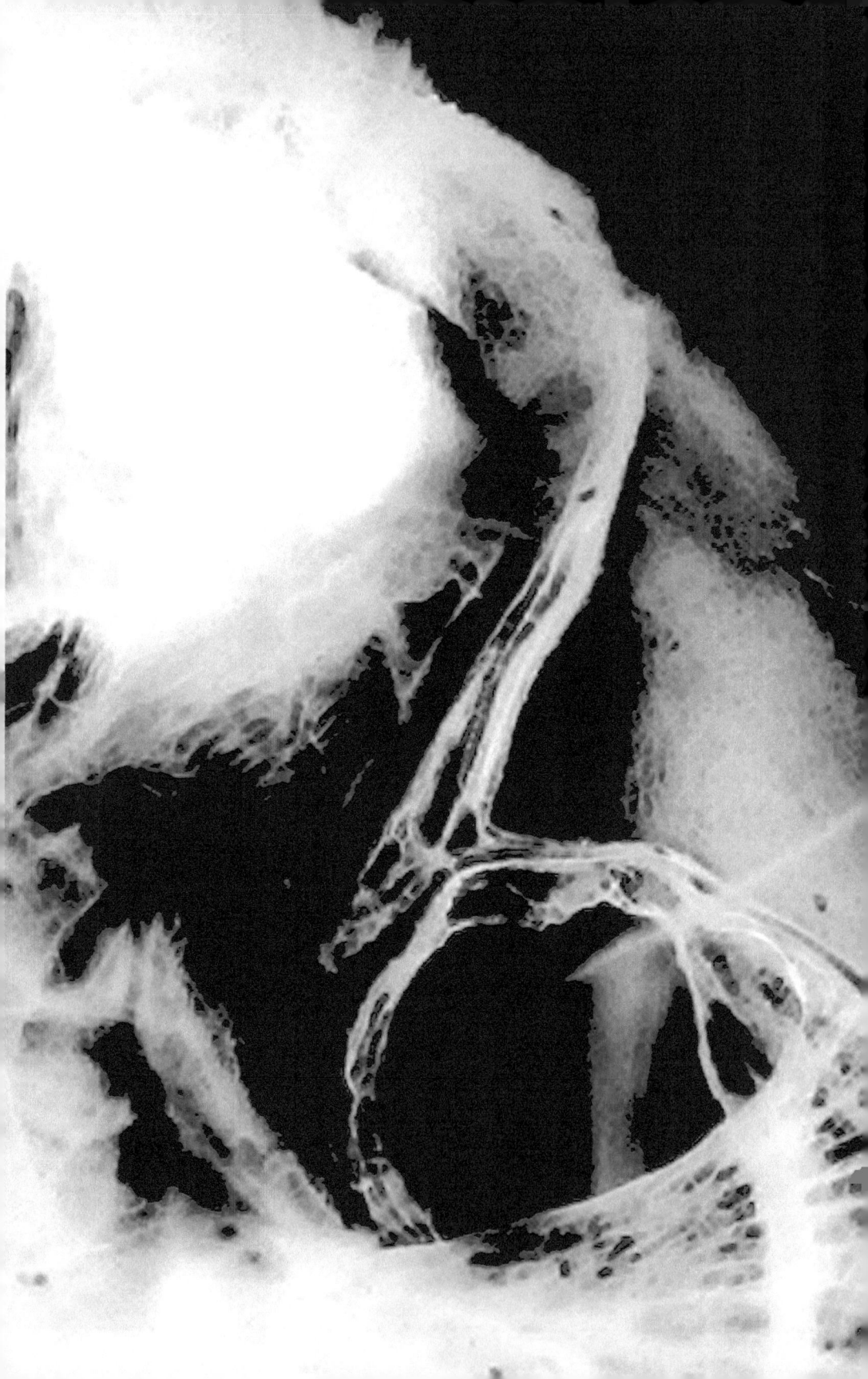

PATRICIA CANNON

WILD HEART

It was a Thursday
when I saw a row
of what resembled tombstones
suddenly appear
on the hospital monitor
hovering above your bed
and heard a voice like thunder:
"Code Blue. 10 Long. Room 1032."

The alarm incited the sound
of a medical team stampede
until they stormed into your room,
pressed the defibrillator paddles
against your chest,
and shocked
your wild heart
until it beat into
a lockstep rhythm again.

Days earlier, the surgeon
had cracked you open
at the space that lies
between your breasts, performed
a "quadruple coronary bypass,"
and then stapled
you back together.

But the distance
between the sound
of ambulance sirens
rushing toward you
would shorten into
one final sigh
when I signed
the DNR and DNI,
and your life force
disappeared into a flat line.

You didn't want
a memorial service
because you said
being inside a church
always made you cry.
Nor did you want
to be buried in one place
under someone's foot,
so I gave your ashes
to the ocean,
where the waves
carried you
far away
from judgment
far away
from shame.

When I drive across
the Golden Gate Bridge,
I will sometimes see
on my left,
a Claude Monet sunrise,
and on my right,
an Ansel Adams coastline.
Mother, the city views
are like my memories of you.
They move between
impressions and realities
that I have sewn together
into a multi-colored shawl
that I keep tightly
wrapped around me
as I move straight ahead
on the road to a new life.

INSPIRATION

Loneliness
began as a child
when she would place
with the utmost care
toy upon toy
on top of her small body
until she was covered
with the solitary sound
of her own breathing
certain that this
would shield her
from the wrath
of a human touch
that would first
wrap around her ankles
and then pull her down
into the watery deep
of haunting deceit
the forbidden country
where silence reigns
and innocence drowns
in salty tears and foamy sheets.

Then, as a woman
She would place
with the utmost care
book upon book
on top of her life
until she was covered

with a multitude of voices
certain that this
would shield her
from the warmth
of a human touch
that would first
wrap around her heart
and then pull her down
into the watery deep
of intoxicating heat
the borderless country
where love reigns
and exhalations
rise like sweet-smelling
clouds to the ceiling.

But her child
barely a year old
pressed against her chest
like life itself
with all its fragile hope
inspires her
to swim
toward her true voice
stranded somewhere
on the babbling sea
of her own fear.

JASON A. NEY

THE LIFE OF THE BLOOD

Usually when you cry, you send out a piercing howl, drawing in all of the air your lungs can hold and then ricocheting your screams off the walls of our home. But this morning, when I found you lying on the living room floor, bare-chested and covered in blood, your weeping had taken on a mournful quality, low and resigned.

I carried you into the family room and cradled you down onto the rug, doing the best I could to clean your chest, arms, and dripping nose. You had been sick for over a week, but this was a new problem. The Rocky Mountain air hasn't helped; your mom has been saying we should buy you a humidifier. As I cleaned you up, I thought about putting you into pajamas but decided against it. No need to dirty up any clothes until I could stanch the bleeding.

)(O)(✳)(O)(

A year and a half of pokes and prods in sterile examination rooms, of confusing numbers on medical documents that arrive silently in the mail. A year and a half of no real answers, of doctors telling us that everything looked normal, that we should be fine. Of fertility treatments that did nothing but drain our savings and our strength. Of prayers, some whispered, some shouted, some shoved out through gritted teeth, all asking the same question: *how much longer?* Of lying in bed at night, unable to sleep, hoping this would be the month the home pregnancy test would tell us, *yes, you've done it. Your child is finally growing inside and will be out in the world before you know it.*

Then, a year and a half ago, after sixty hours of labor, your mom gave one sweaty, mighty, final push, and I caught you, the answer we had so desperately sought.

And then the second pregnancy, a miracle on the first try. Then the lack of nausea, your mom pacing around the house and worrying because in the first trimester, a sick mom means a healthy baby. Then the bleeding that began during a Wednesday evening flight from Denver to Atlanta and the miscarriage over Thanksgiving, surrounded by too many members of your mom's side of the family, three thousand miles from home.

)(O)(❋)(O)(

Was this bleeding normal? Should I call her, explain the situation, ask her to drop everything at work and rush home?

The flow of blood wasn't slowing. I grabbed the suction device from the kitchen counter, braced your head between my arms, maneuvered the tube inside a nostril as gently as your thrashing head would allow, and drew a sharp breath through the other end. The tube filled with globs of dark red mucus. I emptied it into the sink and repeated the process in the other nostril, your screams shattering my eardrums.

By the time I carried you back to the family room, you had replaced your shrieks of panicked rage with a soft and plaintive weeping, the kind of crying typically reserved for adults. As I held you to my chest, you looked up into my eyes, and though you are still months away from speaking words we will understand, your inquiry—*how much longer?*—came through clearly.

I held you to my chest, saying nothing. I have to believe that only in this life will your question remain unanswerable.

YESSENIA GUTIERREZ

THE KIDNEY QUEEN

I.

I see them everywhere—sick souls everywhere. They're waiting for a cure to surround them with pleasure. I see needles being stuck in their arms. I see doleful eyes; I see long faces. The exhausted children look feeble and they are not satisfied. The sick souls that cannot be cured are the ones that suffer the most, but you and I are blessed today because we survive with dialysis. We rely on this to survive; without it we would not be alive. Because of this treatment we are safe, and we get to see another day. I see them everywhere. I see children with cancer everywhere and I see their despairing mothers searching for answers, anxiously praying to find a cure that will help their greatest treasures sustain and endure the strain.

II.

A kidney donor is hard to find
when the one you are waiting for has to die,
A kidney donor is hard to find
when the one you are waiting for has to be your same size,
A kidney donor is hard to find
I have waited many years,
and it has yet to arrive
They called me one day, but the organ was too big
But I don't lose hope that someday my kidney will come
and it will be the perfect fit
and it will be the greatest gift
Now I will start to live
There will be no more gloomy days
A kidney donor is hard to find,
But a kidney donor will save my life

III.

I am happy now.
I was upset.
I was enraged,
But I am happy now.
My heart & soul were full of hate.
Full of despair & agony
I didn't understand why this was happening to me,
But I am happy now.
It felt like something was missing,
I was alive but not living.
Nothing made me smile.
All I could see was troubles.
From the suffering & the pain,
There was a lot to sustain.
How could I not complain?
I needed a new kidney & liver to stay,
I fought so hard every day.
Depression took over my brain,
So, I started to pray.
God, please give me a break!
A miracle came, I was called one day
Both organs were on the way.
I am happy now.
I see myself as someone else.
I have good health now.
What I needed to live,
I have found.
No more crying, no more frowns
Because I am happy now.

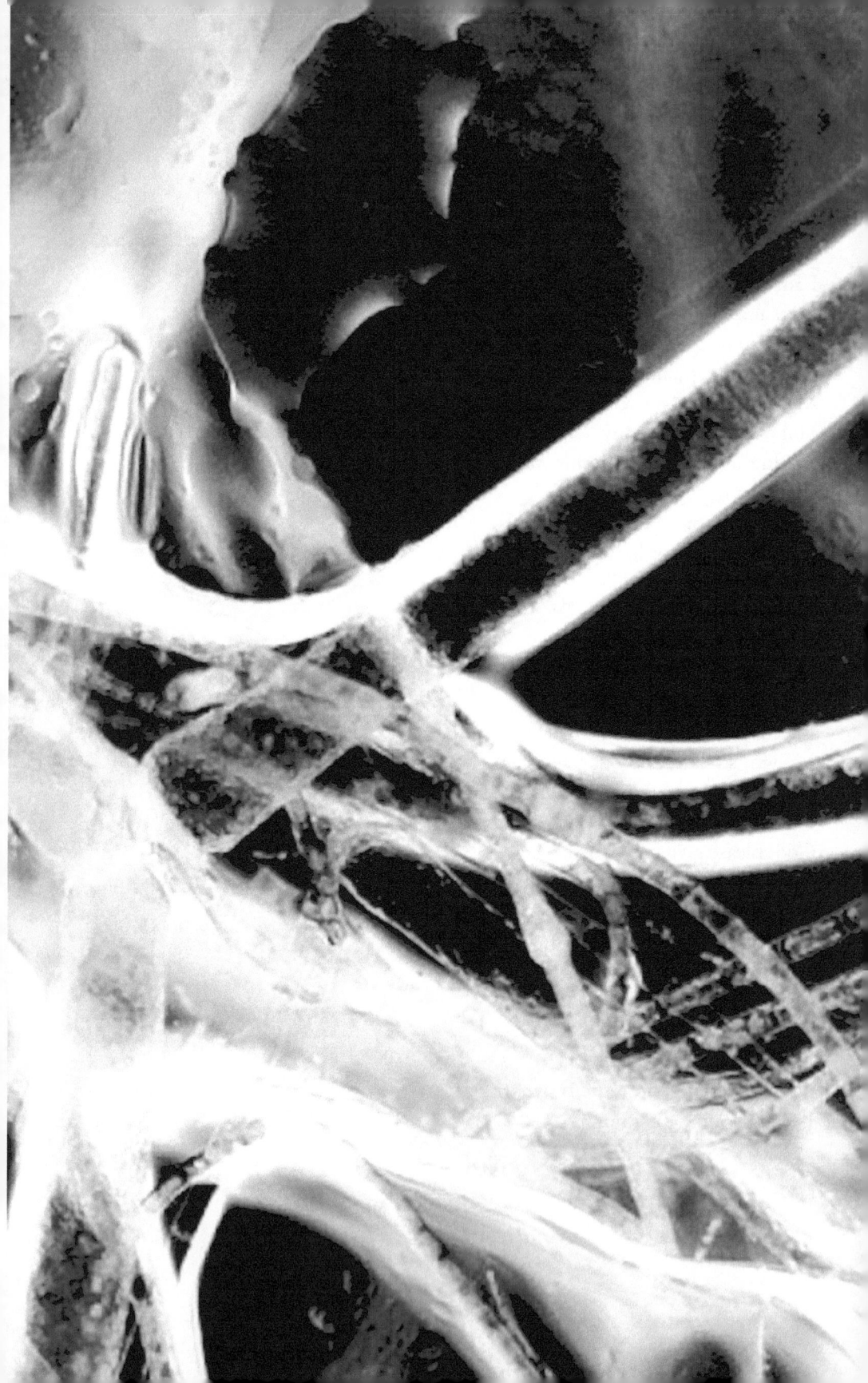

MAISIE MCADOO

AT WATER'S EDGE

Woe is me! Ah, woe is me!
I have seven bairns on land,
And seven in the sea.
               —from "The Selkie Girl," a Celtic tale

I remember those days, stuck on a small patch of beach, splashing in the same little waves, confined to a tiny space bordered by the baby, the snacks and the seaweed line. If I swam out any distance at all, I would hear urgent cries of "Mommy! Mommy!" and I'd have to return to address some small, imagined crisis.

I would gaze down the length of beach, out to the ocean depths, and ache to go there. I always came back to my true self in the water.

The ache was more than restlessness. I married too young. My first children came so fast. My husband was gone all the time. It was worse when he was home. I had three lovely bairns, but inside me something was terribly wrong.

That final morning, I woke with my teeth clenched. I heard the baby whimpering. and Ronan, the oldest, trying to talk to him. A little boy felt it his job to calm the baby, because he knew his mother was not able to do it.

Meara, my fierce second, was always agitated. I hear her now, her high voice escalating— "No, Ronan! Don't touch that! That's mine! I need it right now!"

I was afraid to get up. If I could have had a few moments to myself, I might make it through the day. But I heard Meara headed for my bed. The baby's wails increased. I felt a roar inside my head.

"Mommy, you didn't listen to my song. You said you would!" Meara planted herself beside me and stared accusingly as I struggled to sit up.

"Mommy, I'm so hungry. I can't wait any more," from Ronan, just behind Meara.

Screams from the crib.

I tried to smile. Any other mother would be glad to see her children in the morning. Another mother . . .

The night before, my husband had spent the evening criticizing me, accusing me of all manner of stupid decisions, moral wrongs, neglect of him and the children. He was furious that I was unhappy. He wrapped up by announcing that he was going away, again. "I have to go on business, Danu." He must have thought I was deaf and blind. His "business" was a very sleek young beauty. Everyone knew. My sisters knew.

I got up and tried. I did. I said I was sorry to Meara. I made breakfast, but the food tasted stale and Meara and Ronan wouldn't eat. I got the baby up.

I don't remember much of the rest of that morning. I know I yelled at the children. I said things like, "Shut up!" and "I can't stand this!" Waves of misery kept rushing through me. This is the great shock of motherhood: I cannot. I must. I cannot. I have to.

I called my older sister. She had two children of her own and had already done much too much babysitting for me. She had plans for the day. But she must have heard the desperation in my voice. She suggested we take our kids to the beach. She even called our younger sister and got her to come along, with her two little ones.

How I got us all there I do not remember. It hardly matters now. But I managed it, and if the world were fair to mothers, it would be seen for the great act of heroism it was.

But my heroism, such as it was, could not stand up to the things that were in store for me that day.

My sisters were kind and concerned. We lay next to each other on the sand, skin wet with ocean and perspiration, while I tried to tell them what was happening, straining to find the words to describe it. And the children kept running over, pouring sand or seaweed on us, arguing, asking for food. Mine, in particular, could not leave us alone.

My younger sister saw the bruises on my upper arm, with the distinct blue/black pattern of fingers and thumb. A look of pity crossed her face.

"Would you like to take a long swim by yourself?" she asked. "Let me take your kids to my place for dinner." She knew me well. I nodded gratefully and said goodbye to them. I watched them disappear.

And then I swam and swam. It felt wonderful, though I think I was weeping into the ocean. But I kept going for probably a couple of hours before I finally flopped down on the beach.

I was lying on my stomach, squinting into the setting sun, when I caught sight of a stranger approaching, unmistakably male.

He had a camera. I had the feeling he had already taken a couple of pictures before he approached. I think I felt anticipation. I was crazy then.

His red hair was striking, as was the way he moved, his concentration, his expressionless face.

I sat up to face him as prey would turn to keep an attacker in sight.

"Lovely," was the first thing he said, as he came close.

I don't think I said anything.

"Did I frighten you?" he asked. "I didn't mean to. My name is Douglas." He squatted on his haunches near me and picked up sand and shells as he spoke. "I come here often but I've never seen you in this cove. I'd remember."

"My sisters and I come here many afternoons," I said. "This is our secret place," and regretted it immediately.

He reached out and touched my hand. "I'll keep your secret," he said. It electrified me. Not his words but his touch, the coarse dryness, the hard warmth of his hand.

"I must go," I said, starting to get up.

He made no move to rise. "And where are you from?" he asked.

"I'm a sea creature," I said idiotically, but he laughed.

"Why are you here?" I asked.

"I'm an artist," he said. "I come here to take in the beauty of the beach." He rose. "Maybe you'd like to see my studio. It's just around that bluff there."

Somehow, we were standing in front of a small cement cottage. Had he carried me or had I walked? I can't recall. There was a little wooden walkway over the sand, and a door, painted blue, with a bench on one side. He must have taken my hand. I went in.

Light came in from a skylight. The color of the air in his place was cool and sheer. There was a paint-spattered worktable, three or four easels, and canvases facing one wall. There were photographs tacked above them. Under the skylight was a wide bed, draped with a quilt.

He started showing me the place, turning the paintings around and talking about them. I didn't know anything about art. "Thank you for inviting me, but I have to get home." I said something like that.

"No," he said, "stay awhile now. Let me see you," and he guided me to a spot under the skylight, holding my shoulders. "Let me have you," he said.

I felt a surge of desire and then it was as if I blacked out, the way my body gave way. I was aware only of sensation and hunger. He smelled intoxicating, his shirt smelled of wood smoke and paint and sea. I was drowning but I was happy to drown. I would have drowned continuously forever.

It was like rain after a drought. Everything in me came into bloom, filled up and turned a shining face to the sky. I cannot describe—I don't want to go on, but to recall my story I must understand that afternoon. As if a sea creature, too long on land, is returned to the ocean, or a land creature, close to drowning, finds at last a rocky perch. Breath returns, gulping breaths, then the most unexpected tranquility and relief and pleasure in everyday things.

Douglas rose, finally, and went to his easel. He turned it so he faced the bed and picked up a brush and palette. I watched him watching me. Like fish and visitor in an aquarium, we were locked together across a transparent wall. I turned my head in profile, and I remained there for minutes, maybe hours. I remained there, really, for weeks and weeks.

Of course, my family learned where I was: having a sordid affair with some mediocre local artist. It must have fit with what my husband thought he knew of me. I didn't care at all.

Douglas gave me a new name, Diana. I didn't use Danu anymore. He said I was his new model. While he painted me, I was to remain fixed, scarcely breathing. In the evenings, he would make dinner. We talked very little. I looked forward to lovemaking and sleep.

What was in my heart I cannot say. In the long hours of holding still, I thought of my children. They were with my younger sister. That much I learned. My husband ensured I would have no contact with them. I tried to send messages, but they were like notes in a bottle, bobbing on the waves. I never heard anything back.

Douglas moved us inland, saying it would prevent the sea from distracting me. "Distracting me?" I was incredulous. "The sea is like breath to me."

But Douglas said it wasn't safe by the water. "What if your husband found you?"

He sold several paintings of me for a good sum and bought a house. It had everything: bedrooms, kitchen, living room, windows. Trees hid it from the road. He made a studio for himself. He bought me clothes, though I didn't need a lot. His place became my new world. Bit by bit, I erased my memories. I was drying out inside those walls.

When customers came, Douglas was gregarious and charming. After they left, though, he would say that they bought his "less challenging" work, his landscapes and nudes, and couldn't understand his abstracts. I couldn't either. When gallery owners came, friends of his, I would put on my robe and go outside to watch the sky. Douglas complained I wasn't hospitable. But I didn't like these people for my own reasons. They knew I was his model and they felt free to look at me as if I were still undressed.

Douglas could be alive and pulsing, but he was also moody and remote. At first I liked that, but it became more like a wall between us. He didn't want to talk while he painted. He didn't want me to touch the paints. I was invited to see how his paintings came out, but honestly, I didn't care. It was just his vision of who I was. I never saw myself in them.

"Tilt your head up a little, Diana, no, down some, okay, good, hold still."

I held still because I had nowhere else to go.

)(❋)(

When our daughter was born, she arrived with a bit of luminescence. Her birth kicked something open in me. The presence of this new child, her tiny feet and fingers blue-ish with the transparency of her skin, was like an invitation of spirit. She seemed ethereal, made from something other than the usually sturdy stuff of babies—half anima, eyes roaming, hands opening and closing, touching me.

Douglas named her Elizabeth, after his mother. When she was barely a week old, I took her outdoors. It was late March and windy. The big sky over the woods was marbled with fast-moving clouds. "Look!" I said to Elizabeth, "Sky!"

And then Douglas's voice pierced the wind, calling me, insistently. Worried, I rushed back to the house.

"Are you mad? The baby will catch her death of cold," he said accusingly.

"She is well wrapped up," I answered, with more assurance in my voice than I'd felt in months. I was an experienced mother. The child was fine.

"Come in. I don't like this," Douglas said, holding the door open so I had to duck under his arm. "You do things without thinking." Douglas was often in his own world, lost in his painting. But this was something I'd learned about him. He was frightened by things he couldn't control.

I shrugged and went into the house.

By then Elizabeth was hungry and I began to nurse her and sing to her.

Douglas didn't come in. I heard his footsteps fade and knew he would be gone on one of his long walks. I could have taken Elizabeth out then. Instead, I lay down beside her while she slept and watched the sky. It was as blue as my beloved ocean.

Elizabeth's arrival also stirred recollection.

Like all babies, my daughter pursued independence. She learned to roll over, to crawl. When she was 10 months old, she started teaching herself to walk, pulling herself up the leg of the table and dipping and straightening her knees. When I had seen this several times, I offered my two index fingers and let her toddle where she wished. I did this with part of my mind enthralled and part of it shut down, so as not to remember the others.

When I was pregnant with our second, Douglas's paintings made me look like the Madonna. He all but painted a halo around my head. But that was him again. There was no saintliness in me. That pregnancy stoked the old misery. Instead of feeling like I was giving birth it felt like something was eating me from the inside. This baby absorbed my blood, my senses, my strength.

Indifferent, I let Douglas name this one too, Eric. I nursed him while Elizabeth played on the bed next to me. I watched the top of my baby's head firm, closing its soft opening. I spoke nonsense with them. But that was about all I could do. I could not take them adventuring, could not open the world for them. I felt heavy and drained. At night, when Douglas was asleep, my eyes remained open,

This new baby provoked more recollection, dim like watercolors but occasionally with spots of vivid color. There would be murky depths, grey and brown, with bright white shapes darting through it. I saw red and blue creatures in the water and heard the calls of whales. After all this time, I saw my sisters' faces.

I resolved to tell Douglas what was in my heart.

I rehearsed a beginning: "There is something wrong." But I couldn't find any words after that. How to say that I felt ripped apart?

Then one day, casually, one of Douglas's clients called someone "a fish out of water."

That's it! I thought.

Elizabeth was sitting up at the table in her booster chair, and I was feeding Eric in the highchair, when I told him. "I feel like a fish out of water, Douglas." He was startled at first; then he laughed. "I would say so, Diana.

I'd say that's pretty obvious to everyone."

I stared at him. "It's not a laughing thing," I said.

"What is it, then, Diana? Am I supposed to return you to the ocean?"

"Yes," I said.

"Shall I throw the kids in after you?"

"They can't swim yet."

"Oh, I see. Well, you might drown them in your misery first."

I didn't know what he meant but I knew his look. He was angry, "They will learn," I said to him.

"Maybe you should learn to drive," Douglas shot back, "before you start giving swimming lessons." He picked up his plate and marched to the sink. "You haven't tried to do anything."

I didn't answer, but feelings battered me. I squeezed my jaws together. Maybe color rose in my eyes, because when Douglas came back for the platter, he stared at me for a moment with a curious expression.

"There is something wrong." I said to him. He turned his back. "I am not whole." He remained facing the sink.

When he finally turned, he exploded. "What the hell do you want, Diana? I've given you everything!" His face was red and his head was trembling. "You haven't tried to meet people or fit in, I can't do it for you!" His fists came down on the table, starting both children howling.

A final wave of memories broke over me. My husband's anger exploded like that. I had fled from it, let myself be "rescued" by a seemingly gentler man, taken to a place where I could not be found. But only part of me went. Where were the other parts? Where were my other children, where was my furred and soaking skin?

I stood up, keeping the table between us. "No, Douglas," I said, "you haven't given me everything I want."

"What fucking thing haven't I given you?" And he began to come around the table. I lifted Elizabeth from her chair and reached an arm for Eric until he pushed it away. "What are you in need of, Diana?"

"I have to leave here."

"If you go, you go without the kids, hon. Because you're crazy and I could prove that to a judge in a heartbeat."

And then the last memory hit me. Their voices were even similar: "You go without the kids."

Douglas stormed off on one of his "walks." When I was sure he was gone, I slipped into his "off limits" studio. A palette knife was lying on an easel. With no more thought I took three paintings of me propped against the wall, the ones where I was pregnant with Eric, and cut long gashes in them. In the closet I found the older paintings and sketches of me and sliced them into strips as well. Then, calmly as could be, I returned the knife to its place.

I went back to the house, packed what I could carry, and left with Elizabeth and Eric.

I walked three miles to a bus station, and we took a long bus ride to the water's edge. Once there we walked a long way again, down the beach, to a remote spot I knew. We stopped at last, Elizabeth beside me, Eric in my arms.

The sun was high and bright and the beach cliffs were blooming with ice plants, grasses and scores of sand crabs. Elizabeth screamed with laughter at the touch of the cold water, and Eric clutched me with fascination and apprehension.

The wind blew stronger. We climbed out to the end of a rock jetty that stretched into the water. And there, beyond the breakers, I saw three wet brown heads. I thought I might.

They played and dove and came to the surface as I watched. It was the happiest I'd felt in ages. But then they pulled themselves onto the rocks and stretched out in the sun. I called urgent warnings to them, "Beware! Beware!" but my voice was lost in the wind.

I drew Elizabeth and Eric to me. What if I could change their jackets to sealskins? "Come," I'd say. "We'll swim out. Would you like to meet some other children?" Is there anything that could make them go with me?

What if this wind, filled with sand, could polish our bodies to sleekness so we could pass through the seaweed and floating driftwood until we reached the open ocean. What if we could live there?

The sea's vastness can hold anything. I will teach my new children to swim. They'll meet the others, Ronan, Meara and the baby. One day I will tell all of them my story. They will understand. "You had no choice, Mama." I don't know if children ever understand such a thing. But they might come to respect it. And they might find a way to patch the rips and tears. Children can give us a second chance. One day, one day, I could be whole.

MARIAN MATHEWS CLARK

JOURNEY OF ALOHA

No one could have predicted it. The two of us. Married. In fact thirteen years after our wedding an acquaintance said, "I was shocked when you and Kauila got together. But now that I've gotten used to it, I'm sad you're getting a divorce."

We were a mismatch from our first semester at Graceland College in small town Lamoni, Iowa, where Kauila had flown in from Hawaii, and I'd taken the Union Pacific from Oregon. That fall of 1963 we weren't in the same classes and didn't run in the same circles. I switched from physical education to English after landing in an honors rhetoric class, while he hid out in history but wanted art, unacceptable for a *man* in his family. Coming from a high school class of thirty-two and afraid I wouldn't measure up, I studied constantly. He spent a lot of time shooting pool and went on probation after that semester.

I'd heard he was a Romeo, but didn't actively dislike him until that spring when, in French class, I sat by his dejected ex-girlfriend who'd not known she was ex until she arrived from Hawaii and found him dating someone else. Every day she looked forlorn and after a couple months, flew back home. Hesitant to kiss a guy, I considered him a cad.

The next year there was the tragic car accident where Kauila and a bunch of guys were returning to campus in a snow storm from a late-night snack in Missouri. He was driving when a semi hit him, and his best friend was killed. It was rumored everyone was drinking, a no-no at our church college. But when he didn't get expelled, I suspected there was more to it. I wouldn't find out till later that he was the designated driver because he *wasn't* drinking.

No, I didn't learn much about him until the fall of 1968 when we ended up car-pooling to Mt. Ayr High, twenty-five miles from Lamoni, where, after earning my master's in counseling, I signed on as the school counselor. Kauila called to say he'd been hired as Mt Ayr's art teacher/assistant football coach.

Would I like to share rides? Though I didn't look forward to being around him, it was better than driving that narrow two-lane by myself. So I said okay.

Even on our first trip to Mt. Ayr, I was surprised at how easy he was to talk to. And in the following weeks, I found myself telling him that though I was encouraged that students were confiding in me about their problems, I struggled with teaching my freshman English class where a few kids seemed bent on disrupting instead of doing anything remotely English. And it was especially upsetting when for my pet peeve assignment, four of the twenty-five—including my best writer—targeted the class.

Kauila told me he didn't drink because his father drank too much, that he'd died in an industrial accident Kauila's senior year at Graceland, leaving his mother who'd moved with him to the mainland the year before, on her own. She'd bought a house in Lamoni that Kauila was sharing with her. He was still struggling with the reason his pre-med friend, not him, had died in the car crash and why, when the doctor pulled his arm out straight during his draft physical, it dislocated his shoulder, keeping him out of Viet Nam.

Whatever the reasons—luck or destiny—I was glad he'd stuck around. It wasn't his looks I fell in love with, though with black wavy hair and dark brown eyes he was undeniably handsome. But it was something in his gentleness alongside that karate strength. I came to admire him as a teacher and his ability to relate to marginal kids who didn't trust anybody. He didn't look at them askance, maybe because he'd been in their shoes.

And he could be a charmer. One evening when he dropped me off at my apartment, I said "Mahalo," trying out Hawaii's *Thank You*. As I stepped from the car, he said, "Good night, Miss Oregon." I gave him an "Oh Good Grief" look, but smiled whenever I thought of it.

Our second year in Mt. Ayr we started spending time together. That spring he was accepted into University of Puget Sound's MFA Ceramics Program so would be heading to Washington the next fall, and I was considering moving west to be near my parents. By then we'd decided we were serious. When he asked me what I thought we should do, I said without hesitating, "I think we should get married."

When we told our families, his didn't blink. His four siblings had married *haoles* which he said meant 'foreigners' but usually referred to whites. But my folks struggled at first, especially Dad, ensconced in his all-white logging town. And my WWII uncle wondered if I was desperate. How could I marry Hawaiian, Irish, English and heaven forbid Portuguese and Chinese

Kauila? But my cousin Linda said, "I don't care what he is; if you love him, that's good enough for me."

After word leaked out about us in Mt. Ayr, the principal called me in. "I've been married to my wife from Germany for years," he told me. "We have a lot in common. Like you and Kauila. If you two decide to get married, I'm behind you." Yes that from small town Iowa where, when Kauila's brother learned he'd signed a contract at Mt. Ayr, said, "Are you crazy? I stopped there to get gas a couple years ago, and they refused to serve me."

)()(❋)()(

I never told Kauila about the Bethel High incident. Maybe I was afraid he'd think Paula Brown was braver than I was or worse, that I was ashamed of *us*. It was 1970, sitting in the teacher's lunchroom, one month married and two months into my job as a freshman counselor, that I froze when long-time algebra teacher Mr. Harris said, "I don't approve of these black students dating white students. If God had intended for us to mix races, he would have made us all the same."

Why didn't I speak up and say "My husband's Hawaiian?" But it seemed defensive somehow. Or maybe I was just scared it would be another way I didn't fit.

While Kauila was bonding with fellow potters in Puget Sound's ceramics studio, I was an oddity at Bethel. Most of the teachers thought a high school counselor's job was to be a disciplinarian. Even the sophomore counselor who'd taken me under her wing called students in and scolded them about their grades.

When history teacher Mr. Gleesan beckoned me out of my office in the middle of a session and said, "Don't you ever again pull a student out of my class for an appointment," I was rattled. But I nodded, and after he huffed off, went back to listening to the boy who'd witnessed his step-father shoot his mother and sister, then fled, with a load of guilt. Or maybe that day it was the girl who spent breaks between classes outside in the smoking area, pretending not to see the drug deals go down, scared of the consequences if she were targeted as a snitch.

I should have trusted I could tell Kauila anything because that night when I told him about Mr. Gleesan, he was angry and said, "Do you want me to talk to him?" But I figured if I didn't fight my own battles, I'd be dubbed a coward. So I kept my head down and stayed clear of the teacher's lounge where Mr. Gleesan always said with a sarcastic smirk when I walked in, "Oh, there's Mrs. Clark, and she can solve *all* our problems."

No one at the table in the lunchroom that day had met Kauila except for the shop teacher. At Mr. Harris' comment that blacks and whites shouldn't date, he'd looked uncomfortable then said, "Well, I don't think Asian-white is *so* bad." But Mr. Harris shook his head. Any mix was too much for him. Then Paula Brown, the new health teacher who I'd only exchanged nods and hello's with, said, "I think anyone should be able to date and marry whoever they want to." What she believed. Just like that.

When the Faculty Rec Night came around, I didn't want to go but thought spending time with my colleagues might be a way to connect. I was relieved when Kauila said he'd go with me.

That evening, while I played badminton, Kauila joined a basketball game. When I glanced over at him a couple times, it seemed he was enjoying himself. But on the way home, he told me a drunken jerk on his team kept calling him Tonto. "Throw me the ball, Tonto." "Over here, Tonto." He was annoyed but said the guy was an idiot and let it go. He'd dealt with worse.

The next day at lunch the shop teacher said, "How did your husband feel at Faculty Rec when Coach Collins kept calling him Tonto?"

Before I could say, "He didn't like it," Mr. Harris said, "Does your husband have long hair?" That day I looked him in the eye and said, "No, he has brown skin." I don't remember who said what after that but do know I've never forgotten Paula Brown and the attitudes that shook me out of my oblivion. And how Kauila was my ballast as I made my way.

✖◯✖❋✖◯✖

"You can't be serious," I told him. *"Move back to Iowa?"* Just when I was adjusting to Bethel High—no one else had summoned me out of my office with an edict—Kauila got a call from his former art professor at Graceland, encouraging him to apply for an art instructor position that had opened.

I was settling into life on the West coast where we'd spend occasional week-ends with my parents. Though Mist, my hometown of fifty, offered no entertainment and had only a general store, Mom's chicken tamale pie and Dad's tours into the woods where he pointed out old growth and bear droppings, gave us a break.

Thankfully we never ran into the neighbor whose son had gone to Pacific University.

After she'd read our wedding announcement in the paper, she'd told Mom, "There are a lot of Hawaiians at Pacific, but Bob promised me he'd never date one." Though she probably would have gushed over Kauila as she had his mother at our wedding, I hoped to never see her again.

I hadn't thought of working at Graceland and had no idea it had been Kauila's dream. In fact I was surprised during our year in Washington what I was learning about him. I was struck by how well-liked he was and a stand-out in his program. His thesis was big pots, four-foot vessels that he threw in several pieces then forcibly coaxed together when the clay was ready. I was a bit envious of him, following his creative dream when I was floundering with mine.

And to be fair there was a lot he'd found surprising about me. It wasn't until our honeymoon that he discovered how inept I was in the cooking department. He suggested we wash and cook the rice that friends had dumped in our suitcases and buy sea food to go with it. When I said, "We can't eat that. There's throwing rice and cooking rice and this is throwing rice," he was incredulous. Needless to say, he did most of the cooking after that.

Though it was becoming obvious how much he wanted to return to Graceland to work with his old professor, I held out, mostly because I wondered what I'd do if we moved. I'd never assumed it was Kauila's job to support us while I floated along, as I'd always intended to forge my own path. But when Graceland offered me the alumni publications job which I'd not applied for, the die was cast.

I'd always written—poems to my cats at an early age and in seventh grade "The Hair Cutting Little Man" about a weirdo who broke into the Miss America Pageant and cut the contestants' hair—but I'd never had a writing job.

So that first year back in Iowa, while Kauila was absorbed in teaching art and karate classes, throwing pots for art shows and founding the Polynesian Culture Club, I taught a rhetoric class, edited the student catalog and acquired interviewing and article writing skills in producing the mag-paper we mailed to alums.

In the next few years we bought a house where students flowed in and out. We were Grand Central Station especially to students from Hawaii who cooked and danced and enjoyed hanging out. And Malcolm Lutu, who worked for a summer as a body guard on *Magnum PI*, brought me an autographed photo of Tom Selleck. Yes, there were great moments. But though I enjoyed the students, Kauila thrived on the constant flow which I sometimes found exhausting.

)()(❋)()(

We did have our getaways. He'd said, shortly after we married, "I'll travel anywhere with you on the mainland except the South." I didn't have to ask why. He'd told me about the diner in Missouri his senior year at Graceland whose waitress took the orders of everyone on the track team except his. And his foray into Texas where cops shined a light in his van while passing him, then hauled him in. No, we wouldn't go south. So we ventured west:

To Colorado for an art show where we were stuck for hours in a blizzard on Loveland Pass. When we made it off the mountain to a gas station in the middle of nowhere, it was dark, we had no place to stay and a punctured radiator. The owners drove us to and from a motel half an hour away, welded the hole in the radiator and filled the car with gas. And all for $35. We were perplexed by their generosity, until they smiled at Kauila and said as we parted, "We've really enjoyed meeting you. We moved here from Oklahoma and miss our Cherokee friends."

To San Diego where we met my parents at Mom's sister's retirement village. When Kauila swam across the communal pool, two old codgers on the other side said so he could hear, "He's just chicken shit." He climbed out and told my aunt, "Everything's fine." But when I told my dad what they'd said, he was angry. "Kauila's one of the finest people I know," he told me.

To Canada for the Calgary Stampede where our friend Gerald Sitting Eagle asked Kauila if he wanted to earn a fast fifty bucks to open the rodeo. He told Kauila, "All you have to do is jump on a buffalo, ride for a few seconds and when you hit the ground, run like hell." Kauila said *no thanks* but danced with his Polynesian Culture Club in the opening ceremonies. Not much of a dancer nor Polynesian, I ironed costumes. Our travels bumped us out of our comfort zones which cemented shared memories and exposed our challenges.

)()(❋)()(

Back in Iowa, I was caught off-guard. After two years as director of alumni publications, the director of counseling position came open. Though I didn't plan to write alumni bulletins forever, the counselor who was retiring had a PhD. With a master's, what wouldn't I know that I'd need to? What issues would students have that I'd not dealt with?

After a couple weeks, when Kauila asked why I'd not applied, I told him," I don't have a PhD." He shook his head then told me, "It's what you've studied for. And you handled all kinds of problems as a high school counselor. What could it hurt to try?"

So I decided to apply, was hired and experienced things in the coming years I didn't know to anticipate. Like the fall of that first year when the Dean of Students assigned me the task of showing a VD film in the men's and women's dorms. I was afraid a bunch of guys could be a challenge. Luckily, my work-study student Jimmy Devito was captain of the football team. When guys hooted at images on the screen, Jimmy shouted, "Hey! Listen up!" And they did.

As Lamoni, a small isolated community, didn't have a hospital or offer mental health support, finding places for students who needed more services was a challenge. During those years, I drove a student who continually threatened suicide to the State Mental Health Facility, admitted a student who began identifying as Jupiter to a hospital in Des Moines, traveled to the small hospital in the neighboring town to visit students who attempted suicide. I attended sexuality, drug and alcohol abuse and pre-marriage workshops, taught "The Changing Roles of Women" winter term class, and finally got permission to have Planned Parenthood visit campus.

The downside was that my job added another challenge for Kauila and me. How could I share my career life with him, when the problems I heard were confidential? And sometimes when I met him for lunch in the student union, he'd be chatting with a student who'd been in my office the day before to confide she was pregnant and considering an abortion, or had just been dumped by her boyfriend, or was thinking of dropping out. Would she be offended if I pretended not to know her? Or would she feel betrayed if I smiled and acted friendly?

My job was consuming, but Kauila wasn't standing still. Besides spending a month in Japan on a pottery tour, taking winter term groups to Hawaii each year, and traveling to art shows around the country, he'd decided to pursue a doctorate of education at the University of Kansas which required a two-year leave of absence from Graceland.

He moved to Kansas and worked as a TA in the KU ceramics department while I continued my counseling job and rented out rooms in our home to Graceland students to help pay the mortgage. I thoroughly enjoyed my roommates but it was a houseful, and on week-ends when Kauila drove home, there was never alone time.

After the first year he asked me if I'd go on leave and join him in Kansas. "We could be together," he said. But I'd started taking night classes at Drake University toward an MA in English. And I was thinking of pursuing a doctorate of arts where I could use the stories and essays I'd been working on for the creative dissertation.

Yes, we were both up-to-our-eyeballs busy. And there was the issue of kids. I suggested we each work part time, cut back on activities, share the parenting. But he said he'd still be involved in art shows, teaching, Polynesian culture programs. Definitely not cutting back. I'd be a stay-at-home mom, at least for a while. He knew that wasn't me. I knew it, too.

❎❎❖❎❎

Kauila never slowed down and I didn't trust Makani. It was summer, the end of our twelfth year together. Kauila was gone. Again. This time to DC where he was staying with Makani and acting as his intern for the National Endowment for the Arts.

One day Makani called out of the blue and said, "What do you know about Kauila and Raina?" I said I didn't know anything then called Kauila. "What's going on with Raina?" I asked. He seemed surprised—maybe his first taste of not being able to trust Makani either—and said, "She's a friend from Tahiti. An intern I've gotten to know. Nothing's going on."

"Just another admirer?" I told him and could hear the annoyance in my voice. After we chatted briefly and hung up, I thought "Here we go again. Magnetic Kauila with followers wherever he goes." Yes, at times I found his fans unsettling. Once, when we were eating lunch in Graceland's student union, a woman walked over, introduced herself and started gushing about a talk he'd given, how amazing it was and how amazing he was. When she left, he thanked her but seemed tired. "See," he said as she walked away. "I didn't do anything to encourage that." Yes, I saw. And most of the time, I believed it.

I didn't want to be around Makani but knew our marriage was teetering so decided to fly to DC for a visit. That evening, after Kauila went to bed, Makani said he needed to talk to me. I followed Makani into the living room, wary, sat across from him and waited. I was used to the *big presence, head held high* Makani who, when he walked into a gathering, commanded attention, often without a word.

That night, though, he was a *no persona,* smaller, quieter Makani. So when he said, "Marian, we have to let Kauila go. He needs to go home, work with Hawaiian people, and we can't stand in his way," I sensed he spoke some truth. He said he was frustrated, wished he were the one going back, fighting to restore Hawaiian culture, working with young people who were floundering. But he said, "It's not mine to do. I come from privilege, and Kauila's grass roots, grew up poor among our people. They trust him. I don't like it, but I know it's my job to teach him Hawaiian language, dance, the old culture that I've learned through the years."

I studied him a few moments. He looked humbled, and his words seemed to come through him, not of him somehow. I nodded, but he wasn't finished. He said, "You have to find what's yours to do. I'll help you however I can. And others will, too, along your way. You'll know it when you find it. But don't wait too long."

)()(❊)()(

A few days later, back in Iowa, I was in a fog. Where was I supposed to go? Before I'd left DC, Kauila and I had *the talk.* We agreed we were headed in separate directions but how difficult it would be, getting a divorce in Graceland's close-knit community. I couldn't imagine staying there in the wake of it. Nor could I return to my home town even though my parents were there. I loved Mist when I was okay. But when I was sad, it was *the ends of the earth* lonely.

All I could count on was that we would be at Graceland another year during which time I'd need to find my way. I was sad but relieved we were talking openly and kind to each other now that we'd decided to divorce. Yes, I was grateful but still didn't know how to stay open to the *it* Makani said I would recognize.

That fall I decided to finish my MA in English and enrolled in a Faulkner night class at Drake. One evening the professor, who paced the floor as he lectured, stopped and looked at us.

"So what compels someone to become a writer?" he said. "Well, some writers grow up in an unusual landscape. They leave that place and looking back, write to make sense of it, bring it to life." He paused. "And some writers are people with contradictions warring inside them that they try to integrate, heal in a way through their writing." Then he went back to pacing.

And there it was. Me, from my odd little burg that I'd left but that was tucked inside me, forever. Haunting. Me, with a soul full of conundrums I was always trying to unravel. Though I'd always written, I'd never thought writing was a feasible pursuit. Now, maybe a possibility. So thanks to Makani, I released Kauila. And in doing so released myself.

ЖᛰЖᛰЖᛰЖ

I can hear him now. "You live in your head," Kauila told me our first year of marriage. Though I didn't know what that meant, I denied it. But oh, was he on to me. And during our thirteen years together, he said more than once, "Can't you ever just accept things?"

I argued that I did accept things, unless they didn't make sense. For instance, why would we spend our tax refund on his friend's stereo when ours worked just fine? How could he even consider buying a chopper? I'd taken charge of our finances and knew adding a motorcycle to our expenses was a bad idea. And how long was his friend Lonnie planning to store his enormous antique pot-bellied stove in our TV room? Lonnie had said, "Just a short time." Though Kauila's generous spirit was nice in theory, I'd been living with the huge stove for three years, not my idea of *short*. Yes, some things needed to be questioned.

And it's not that he never questioned me—or tricked me for that matter. After our divorce, I moved to Des Moines where, as a TA, I worked on my doctor of arts at Drake and applied to fiction writing programs. I applied to Iowa and to Arizona, my fiction teacher's alma mater. Arizona offered fellowships, and he assumed, that with a recommendation from him, I'd be a shoe-in. I didn't get into either, so called Kauila, desperate. "We're struggling to sell our house, and as a TA, I don't make enough for another year at Drake. But if I get a second job, I won't have time to continue taking classes. What am I going to do?"

He was quiet a moment, then said, "Well, I think you'll do what you always do: You'll get scared like you are now. Then you'll get really mad and figure something out." When I didn't answer—not realizing that was my pattern—he said, "Or you can just give up."

"I'm not giving up," I sputtered.

He laughed. "I didn't think so," he said.

So I fluctuated between scared and mad. Then I continued taking classes and applied for a part time job, working for a widower who needed a nanny for his eighth-grade daughter. When I called and asked Kauila if he thought I could manage the cooking, he hesitated, then said, "Yes, if you stay conscious."

His final writing prod came the next year when, much to my surprise, I was admitted to The Iowa Writers' Workshop. Though friends encouraged me, I was afraid to go. So once again I called. "What if I just lucked out, getting in?" I said. "And what if the other admits are all published writers except for me? Maybe I should stay at Drake and finish my degree."

This time he was sterner. "Listen," he said. "I've heard you talk about Iowa's program for as long as I can remember. You have to go and demythologize it. Find out what it's really like."

So I took a deep breath, packed my things and made the move.

)()(※)()(

It was a decade later when we crossed paths at Graceland's homecoming. I'd driven from Iowa City where I was writing and working as an academic advisor at the University. Kauila had flown from Hawaii without his wife and boys to visit his brother, now a Graceland recruiter. I was surprised he'd been able to get away with all his commitments—serving as the Hawaiian board chair for the National Association of Community Health Centers, throwing pots for a Buddhist temple, making a living.

We ran into each other in the art department and ended up discussing—well, sort of arguing—about church. He was disgruntled with our church's attitudes and outreach in Hawaii and no longer saw its purpose. I defended its existence for people like my elderly parents who found a family in it. Finally he said, "When I go to church, I'm frustrated . . . " and I interrupted.

"Wait. You go to church?" I said and told him I was taking a break, hadn't been in several years.

He shook his head. "It's so us," I said, and he agreed.

The next day on my way out of town, I stopped to say good-bye to Kauila and his brother's family. He walked me to my car. "About yesterday," he said, "You always make me think."

I laughed. "That drove you crazy when we were married," I said. "All that questioning."

He smiled and said in the kindest voice," You can't help it. It's who you are." That was the last time I saw him.

)(✼)(

He knew it was coming. He'd had triple by-pass heart surgery and was on dialysis after all. When I heard that his pottery had brought high prices at a friend's estate sale, I emailed him. He asked if I still had the porcelain vase that won recognition at the Iowa Arts Show. I emailed him photos of it, as well as his lamp that lights my bedroom.

He emailed, "It's nice to know I still hold a presence in your life."

I emailed back, "No doubt about that." Two weeks later he was gone.

I miss him. Cousin Linda would say, "No matter what happens, I'm always here for you." Makani would say that I have to let him go.

What would Kauila tell me about growing old alone in this strange scary world, still trying to make sense of things? Maybe to stay conscious? I take a deep breath and look around. At my Skechers by the door that I'll slip into when I go for my walk. At my laptop, waiting for me to get to work. At my cat Lucy's toys strewn across the floor. And then I spot it on the mantle. His quaint little bottle whose glaze ran askew making it oddly, unexpectedly beautiful. Ah Kauila. Mahalo.

JAMES WYSHYNSKI

WOMB

Waves from that amniotic ocean crashed
against you every time your mother rose
from her chair. In that dark salt water,

you birthed yourself, cell by cell, thought
by thought. Don't believe them, those who
talk up the quiet, the calm and safety, who

hold it out as a harbor. Instead, fill a tub,
add salt. Kill the lights and lie back.
Never again will you face yourself

with nothing between you and you.

AT THE CARWASH

The moment comes, past the *your-car-is-soaking*, when the windshield
is dotted—a geography of bulbs spread out like the Midwest
from a night flight. Make of these not cities or even single,

lit rooms, but souls shrunk into a diorama of rapture, an experiment
in salvation's viscosity. Let the overhead vacuums swing into action,
huge cones stuttering under the current, before they begin

their appointed task—specimens whole one second, comfortable in their
bodies, the next sucked into a higher atmosphere. Others take the shape
of comets as if wrestling with their appearance in the *Book of Life*. Now

they too are gone, lifted outside recognition. Here are the unchosen laid out
on a slide dissected by sight. What to make of this? Explore this darkfield
illumination. Go past drop, atom, muon—what of those who stay, who

turn down nirvana? Do they remain to lift others up? Where in the world
are you now, you scientists of intercession? Who will launch these in orbit,
spin them into a new mercy? *Drive forward.*

CATASTROPHIC MOLTING

They return after years at sea, feathers
worn through from coping with wave
and wind and shore themselves

on the frozen beach, little to insulate
them in their middle age between who
they've been and who's left.

Standing, they start at what's needed:
arching their beaks to yank out
what's without use—the stiff, small

blades that remain, and the down
below them, its fluff a confetti
of spent dreams and broken vows.

This unraveling must be done
alone, in snow gusts that question
every vertical. That's the easy part.

Then they must dig their webbed toes
into the ice and wait and watch the moon
wax and wobble through its full

orbit until their new suits fit
their worn frames and they debut
their new look into the sea's grand foyer.

INTERIOR DIALOGUE

The bobber, red and white, plops into the cup
of lake and settles into its saying:

I am Buddha's belly, you see only half-white,
red, depending on the wind's lilt, but below

the worm twists blind—hurt as a held-out hand.
The line that snakes between us is thin,

translucent and like your life's thought,
only scrapes the lake's surface.

Turn to those three hawks above, reading the wind,
to that flock of geese landing at the lake's far end.

When you turn back, I will be gone. The tug
in your hands will lift a new life out of you.

JEN WEBB

WORLD WILDLIFE FUND

He is taking a census of animals, out every day with his clipboard and his pen, talking to the bees. He has found his calling, he tells you, here at the end of human history. It's not good for his health, says the therapist, he is feeding his despair. But when you delicately pass on that advice: Better to know than not, he says, so you bring him whiskey and sit beside him on the settee, stroking his back, watching the world wind down.

THE LAST OF THE FUTURISTS ARRIVES
IN THE SUBURBS

A crane has landed just beyond our house. Yellow struts, polished grips, straight-backed as a bishop. We quarter the block, checking every angle and fall of light with photographers' eyes, and its great neck inclines, politely. *It's a Futurist's folly*, you say, and watching it watch the space where it has no task to perform, I concur. Its great arm sways slowly, following the wind, and birds cluster nearby, talking amongst themselves. As though the mechanical age were over. As though nothing vast need ever move again.

ON BEAUTY

Beautiful is an empty nest, feathers and pellets left after the children have flown; it's the trace of sun disappearing or stars considering their daily rounds, the strains of songs long forgotten, the bluster and flurry of mud pools where women play guitar and sing songs that bear the genome of more ancient tales. Beautiful is the fall of numbers across an equation, the brackets that contain sets and break all rules, the immortal cockroach making his thoughtful way across the kitchen floor.

ON LOVE AND LOVERS

My lover is a seagull. Stealing my chips, screaming in my ear.

My lover sets out in early morning, alpenstock teamed with tam-o-shanter, his earbuds fully charged. And yes the river is in flood but he remembers fording it as a boy, unharmed. He takes a swig from his hip flask, plants one foot in raging water.

My lover is a seal. Lolling on the shores of a loch, or balanced against Atlantic tides on a rock off Robben Island. His satin coat. Impervious gaze. Distance.

My lover is the sea, reaching out fine pianist's fingers to caress my legs, or raging with passion against night-time sand. Carrying me off to the zone of no way back.

My lover is the sky, looking down as I float face up in the sea. If I could give myself entirely. If finally I could be.

THAT "FORMAL FEELING," EMILY

The Rorschach sheets are face down in front of you. Flip the page, says the therapist, and you do, and drone responses into the mic. Bird. Mushroom cloud. Song. And pause, while she writes down notes and you close your eyes, remember that this is another day when the car did not spiral out of control, after another night when the cats did not bring in dying rats and place them at your feet. Hope that in the meeting you must chair later today the zoom link will not break, and quorum will be reached. And then tonight you will drift toward your bed along a passage of Ambien, my voice murmuring through the earbuds that I am waiting for you in your sleep.

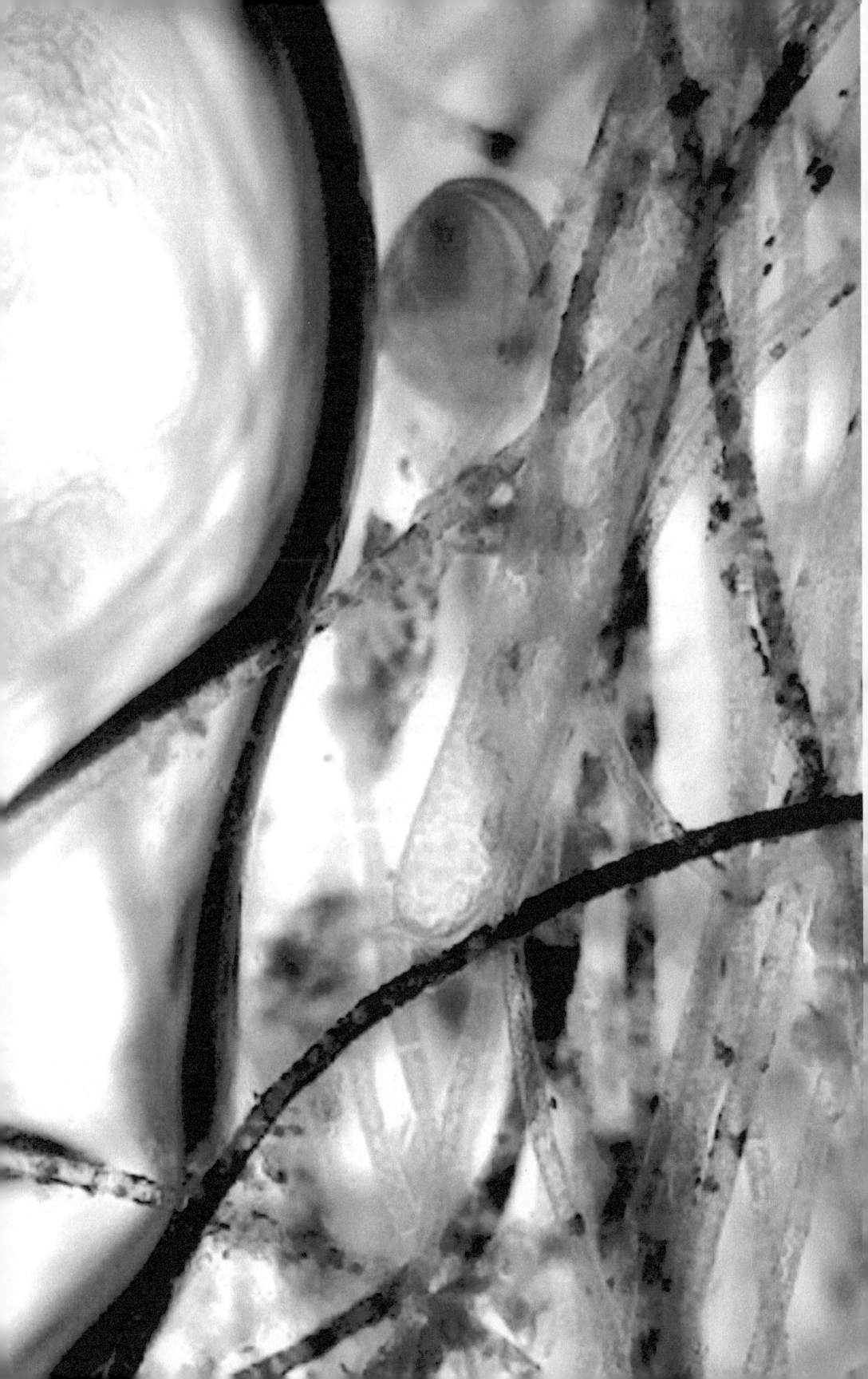

RANJANI RAO

THE OPPOSITE OF PERFECTION

It's a warm evening in Singapore, as most evenings are. There is a full moon somewhere, hiding behind the trees, or amongst clouds that move languidly overhead. I unroll my purple yoga mat in an open field inside the Singapore Botanic Gardens, a UNESCO World Heritage site. The springy grass tickles my bare feet as I sink onto the mat and look up at the slowly darkening sky.

In this gorgeous place, I am just one spoke in a circle formed by a dozen or so women, gathered for our full moon circle meditation. We meet here once a month, a diverse group ranging in age from 30–70 years, who have arrived here from different countries, speaking multiple languages, and holding vastly different life experiences that have marked us, made us who we are and brought us together on a tiny island that lies one degree north of the equator.

Stephanie, my colleague, and good friend, lays out a handful of battery–powered candles at the tips of the long–stemmed roses arranged in a circle in the center. The yoga mats form another circle around the roses. Soon we will begin our meditation in the presence of the full moon as our witness.

How did I get here?

Not just to this circle of moon sisters, but to this bubble of a city–state in Southeast Asia which has now been my home for a decade.

When I first left India for the United States as a twenty-two-year-old newlywed, my hands bore faint stains of bridal henna. My eyes held visions of a happily ever after in a foreign land where I believed all dreams could be fulfilled. Not once did I imagine that in the distant future, I would once again leave India for an unfamiliar country with a new husband, boldly hoping to unite a new blended family of four, with each of us bringing one child to our union.

But all that is not on my mind as I look up at the night sky with crisscrossing silent clouds that shield the moon. The air is warm and still. A few birds chirp as daylight dims. Only the faint glowing tips of the candles mark our space in the darkness. I close my eyes as Stephanie leads tonight's meditation.

There are many reasons why I attend the monthly moon circle. But the most important reason is because I feel a sense of wholeness in this space out in the open in the presence of a full moon that watches without judgment.

The circle is a simple representation of the cycle of life, a system without hierarchy. In this safe space I am finally able to honor my journey to this serene moment–the result of many detours, delays and debacles. So many decisions, some taken lightly, some with great thought. So many paths traversed, some filled with joy and others with pain.

The decades of life have been eventful, although not always kind. Every time I felt I had arrived; I knew that there was more ahead.

)()(✳)()(

When wishes come true

As a young bride, I was convinced I was the luckiest girl in the world. The most important decision of my life had been made. In India, getting married is considered as being "*settled*". A single person is a square peg who sticks out and makes everyone uncomfortable. By getting married, you become part of a unit that is considered complete, a stable building block of society.

My parents had introduced me to an almost–perfect potential spouse, a young man who lived and worked in the United States. At our first meeting, I expressed my desire to pursue higher education. He didn't object. I agreed to the wedding.

As a student, a recent immigrant, a bride, I was fascinated by everything: wide open highways, ATMs, free public libraries. I lived in the Washington DC metropolitan area. I joined tours of the Capitol and the White House and took pictures outside the Jefferson Memorial when the cherry blossoms were in full bloom. One cold December night, dressed in a saree, I walked in the first snow of the season (and my life) to the Lincoln Memorial.

Life was perfect.

What more could I want? I naively believed that if you stayed positive and visualized the life you desired, things would slide into place.

My miscarriage was my first jolt of reality, an introduction to loss of a magnitude that I was not prepared for.

It wasn't my fault.

It wasn't anyone's fault.

Yet, the unfairness of it hurt. The soothing words of the gynecologist who assured me that first trimester miscarriages were common didn't help.

Loss changes us. My husband and I changed. Then drifted apart.

We turned away from each other to find solace in our own ways. I edged closer towards a successful PhD dissertation. He turned to his work. The space between us widened into a deep chasm.

Although I went through the motions each day, all I could sense was the gaping, baby-sized hole in what should have been my perfect life.

I felt empty.

Emptiness feels unpleasant precisely because it is unnatural. It is said that nature abhors a vacuum. Our quest for the next thing does not always arise from boredom or envy. Fulfillment is an innate need, not a passing fancy. Like hunger, which arrives not long after a satisfying meal, the laws of nature are fixed and unchanging.

A PhD in the U.S. had seemed like a pipe dream while growing up in Mumbai, yet I had always assumed that one day I would become a mother. My yearning stemmed from being raised in a culture that revered motherhood. "*Have children and all will be well*" was a mantra that I had breathed in since birth.

Once I become a mother, I would be whole. I was convinced that a baby was exactly what we needed—a common focus to help us bond, to love, and to point the way back to each other.

The funny thing about life is that it grants you many of your wishes and then warns you to be careful what you wish for. After three years of despair, in the span of a few weeks, I was inundated with good news; a fantastic job opportunity necessitating a cross-country move to California followed by confirmation of a viable miracle pregnancy that had occurred after a second miscarriage, a period of infertility, many prayers and intense medical intervention.

The pregnancy was stressful, but as I entered the third trimester, I finally allowed myself to relax. My dream of motherhood was now within reach. When I held my tiny wriggling baby in my arms, I couldn't stop smiling. My baby and I were finally together. The three of us were a real family now. I couldn't ask for more. Or could I?

Motherhood changed everything. My priorities, my ambitions, and my attitude. It magnified my perception of life in myriad ways. I was simultaneously elated and exhausted, content and worried, ecstatic and flustered. But there was something about having a tiny life that depended on me that provided an undercurrent of calm in my otherwise chaotic life. As I leaned into motherhood, the fragile bond with my husband frayed further. He was a devoted dad but a distant spouse.

We focused on our child but seldom looked at each other. During my period of infertility, weighed down with self–pity, I begged and made empty promises to various gods—*please let me be a mother, I won't ask for anything else.*

But I lied. I wanted more.

As parenthood took over our days and nights, I felt even more distant from my husband. I wanted a loving, cohesive family. Yes, I had won the motherhood lottery. The gods had been kind, but what now? I was still human. And humans had desires.

Unending desires and dreams and aspirations tumbled into my consciousness. Had I bartered my hope for a happy married life for the chance at motherhood? I felt greedy and ungrateful for all that I had—a good job, a great kid, a wonderful group of friends. Yet something was missing. What was it?

I was lonely.

Of course, there were perfect moments—holding my toddler's hand on the beach at Santa Cruz, watching a snail cross the walkway on a sunny morning, marveling at a rainbow after the rain. Yet, I was dissatisfied with the way things were.

Perhaps I needed a change.

)()(✻)()(

The opposite of perfection

When my husband suggested that we move back to India, I hesitated but ultimately agreed, hoping that by returning to a familiar culture, our relationship would improve.

The opposite happened.

Two years after our move, I walked out of the home I shared with my husband and his parents.

Why? Because changing a location doesn't fundamentally change you or your relationship dynamic.

As Ernest Hemingway wisely observed, "*You can't get away from yourself by moving from one place to another.*"

Soon after my fortieth birthday, my mother died, my marriage of eighteen years collapsed and for the first time in my life I was forced to determine my own path. I was not a wife anymore, but I was still a mother. I had a job but no training to live on my own. I had to rebuild myself.

My job provided the foundation for a fresh start. Beginning with the intensity of graduate school to the ongoing satisfaction of a scientific career, being involved in interesting and meaningful work had sustained me. But it had not helped during the low periods of my life.

I had experienced emptiness in a marriage followed by the loneliness of motherhood. Now I was enveloped in sadness. For the breakup of a long marriage. For the loss of a future as an intact family. At the prospect of my child being labeled as the product of a broken home.

Being sad was understandable but being submerged in it was not an option.

In all my dreams for a child, I had never imagined a scenario where I would be a single parent. But here I was, employed but without a support system to keep my child safe while I went to work. Forced to figure out a way for us to be both solvent and safe, I had to let go of my career aspirations and forge a new path.

Wasn't life supposed to get easier with the years? You were supposed to acquire things—a degree, a job, a house, money, family, and other fabulous experiences. It was all eventually supposed to add up to a wonderful whole—a successful life. That was the plan.

Yet my path had been defined by bumps, and gaps and holes. There had been effort, accomplishments, happiness but also emptiness, loneliness, and sadness. Instead of acquisitions, my life trajectory was defined by subtraction. Frankly, my life was not perfect. In fact, it was the opposite of perfect.

)()(❋)()(

In search of wholeness

Purnamadah Purnamidam
Purnat Purnamudachyate
Purnasya Purnamadaya
Purnameva Vashishyate
Om Shanti Shanti Shanti

At the yoga teacher training course at an ashram in Kerala, I learned this prayer. Although various translations are available in English, one interpretation is as follow:

> *Wholeness is complete.*
> *The world is born out of wholeness and thus is also complete.*
> *Even if we remove everything from what is complete, it will remain complete.*
> *Om, peace, peace, peace.*

As I struggled with the daily demands of life in an ashram that required a 5 a.m. wake up for morning meditation followed by a rigorous schedule of asana practice, Bhagavad Gita classes, Vedanta lectures and other activities, I came to slowly understand that my life, although seemingly chaotic when observed minutely, was still an integral part of the whole. Of the cosmos. Of the universe.

Wholeness was not a destination or a prize. It wasn't a puzzle to be assembled. Wholeness was acceptance. Wholeness was a state of dynamic equilibrium. Wholeness was knowing that everything was unfolding in the right order at the right time. Wholeness was attained by staying awake to those momentary flashes of perfection that lit up the most difficult of days. Laughter, rainbows, tears, friendship, fun, loss, community—every moment was part of the whole. It wasn't perfect. It just was.

Had I been striving for perfection all this while? Marriage. Motherhood. Making a living.

Had I mistaken standards that others had imprinted on me as must–dos for my own life? And when I strayed off the beaten track, had I concluded that I had been a failure?

Chasing perfection was a recipe for unhappiness. Wholeness on the other hand, had always been within reach. I had been whole the day I welcomed my baby into this world. I had been whole the day I signed the divorce papers in court. I had experienced wholeness the day my siblings and I immersed our father's ashes in the holy Ganga.

When I met the man who later became my second husband, I didn't expect him to complete me or fulfill my wishes. This wasn't a cynical conclusion but a practical approach, one that has enabled me to enjoy this marriage. We were each imperfect but still whole. A large part of our individual pasts was unknown to each other, but we were OK with that.

When we made a commitment to each other, we knew that there was no perfect happily-ever-after. Together we would face challenges; some anticipated, others unexpected, but we both wanted to share the ups and downs of our lives with each other. When we merged our families, I got another daughter to love and nurture in addition to my own, who was now a teenager.

✕✕✸✕✕

My life is like the moon

As Stephanie guides us into a deep state of relaxation, I allow myself to follow her cues. Some memories rise, linger for a bit, and fade away. Various scenes float in my mind's eye, not all make sense. I watch them all with an indulgent sense of detachment.

The unknown future ahead looms with uncertainty. Will we remain healthy as we age? Will our children find happiness in their professional and personal lives? Will we continue to remain in Singapore or move to another country as our priorities change? I don't know.

In life we are always moving. Towards something or away from it. There is always something incomplete, something unfinished. But amidst all the movement, there is a window when I feel whole. Like this moment. Suspended in time, under a full moon.

But the moon always changes; it waxes and wanes. It disappears altogether and appears again. Is a crescent moon perfect or a full moon? You can see more stars on a new moon night compared to one when the moon is in its full splendid glory. Which one is perfect?

The moon is never the same, but it is always beautiful. All I need to do is look upwards on any given night. With or without clouds, stars, or even the moon, I can always find my tiny place in this vast world.

My presence, although insignificant, is important because it is part of the whole. Perfection is not a prerequisite for wholeness. Perfection is a myth, a state that is always out of reach. But wholeness is what we can have. All we need to do is surrender to this imperfect moment. Now.

GABRIELLE LEMAY

NIGHT PEEPERS

So tiny, they could party on your thumbnail.
So shrill, their starlit cries could break you.

You peer out your cabin window
into the night, aim your weak flashlight
there, then there—and at once

there they are: pot-bellied, leggy little bags
of nightlife, perched and swaying
on fragile lily-petal thrones.

Drawn to your light, they leap straight at you,
land with a *pat* on the window glass,
then slide slowly down till they tip over backward

and fall away somewhere out of sight.
When at last their wild song makes your eyes go dim
and your dreams quicken, the stars begin

their own slow slide down the night sky,
winking, flashing, trailing silvery rivulets
that pool on the forest floor in mysterious rings.

Later, should you waken startled in the dark,
you can slip off your gown, go outside
and dance barefoot in heavenly light.

And you can sing.

NIGHT TRAIN

I've dozed off with the little bedside lamp on again,
Brahms turned down so low a late train
clacketing and moaning up the east side of town
has broken through. I love that sound.

I've traveled alone by cross-country train
almost 70,000 miles so far,
hurtling across Midwestern flatlands in the dark,
leaving big Eastern cities far behind—
the quaking concatenation of sleeping cars
rocking and shaking so fast and hard
it's a circus trick to get to the after-hours diner
for a Coke, some crackers, a bit of
flirting with the porter.

Two a.m., the noise in the train is deafening.
The Coke has flooded the pull-down;
cracker crumbs are everywhere.
I fall back asleep, dream of horses.

I wake to sun-spattered foothills,
rolling swaths of meadowland, canyons
so deep I can't look. Up ahead, a long
tunnel through a mountain; to the left,
an upslope clad in pines; way down to the right,
a fleeing *manada* of parti-colored mustangs
kicking up so much dust they can hide in it.

I own the memories of all of this:
Moffat Tunnel, Feather River, Book Cliffs.
The sulfurous aura of Great Salt Lake.
The hoot of the train as it races like a flame
through the night.

The engineer hunches forward,
stares down tracks that never change.
They stretch into infinity, which is
where we're all headed . . . perhaps some of us forever
reaching for the controls—but most of us merely
huddling together as the light fades, holding hands.

PROM NIGHT

Just the one lantern in the kitchen window;
too warm to need the woodstove yet.
Rain on the roof a steady murmur.
Night will bring him soon.

I nuzzle the back door screen; breathe in
rose, juniper, bergamot, hay, a far
campfire sizzling out—horse heat: the blood-bay
stallion's running down

from the high field; hooves pound like fists
in time with my heart. Marcel's
truck crawls up the drive; six mares canter
down behind the bay: they are all wanting.

Sun sets quick as a tail-flick. The rain lifts:
Marcel enters, glides his arms around me.
We slow-dance in place, listen as the horses
snort, gather, settle under trees

for the night. We move to the window
and look out at them:
moonbeams slash down clean,
paint their satin backs platinum.

I can't get enough of him. I suck in
his breath, tongue; press him to the window glass
that fogs with our heat.
He snuffs out the lantern.

A late train lets out a piercing *whoo*—
old tracks cut through hayfields here like shears
through sweet velvet. The ground shakes; couplers clang
at the curve where the train must brake.

The roan mare with one blue/one brown eye
goes loco—swoops her long head side to side,
spins, bucks, rushes down the field
to where the creek has flooded its banks—

to where lilacs frame her stage center, blinded
by glittering mist: prancing, squealing, gorgeous
in her terror—her brand-new snow-white colt
whirling as one with her,

pinned to her side like a corsage.

LISA HOCKSTEIN

A LOVE STORY IN EIGHT SHORT ACTS

June 7, 11:35 p.m.

"Hello?" The man does not turn on the bedside lamp. He holds his cellphone in his right hand and covers his forehead with his left.

"Did you sleep with my wife?" The voice is gravelly.

"What?" He props himself up on his left elbow.

"Did you sleep with my wife?"

"What? Who is this?" He glances at the screen of his phone. He doesn't recognize the number.

"Did you sleep with my wife?"

"Hey, whoever you are, I don't have time for this." He ends the call and places the phone face down on the bedside table. He leans back onto the pillows. He knows he won't get back to sleep for a while. He has left his phone on every night since his wife ended their marriage three months ago. His wedding anniversary is in two days. He takes a deep breath to slow his racing heart.

June 14, 11:35 p.m.

"Hello?"

"Did you sleep with my wife?"

"What, again? Who is this? What do you want?"

"Just answer the question: Did you sleep with my wife?"

"Listen, I've never slept with anyone's wife!"

"You listen! My wife isn't just anyone's wife."

"No, of course not, I didn't mean to imply that. I'm just saying—"

The caller hangs up.

The man lets his hand fall to the bed, where the phone screen casts a triangle of green onto the bedcovers, like a nightlight.

June 21, 11:35 p.m.

The man answers the phone call without saying hello.

There is a bit of a stutter on the other end. "Hello? Are you there?"

"Yes, I'm here. What do you want?"

"Did you sleep with my wife?"

"No. No, I did not. Look, I'd like to sleep through the night without you calling me." He hears muffled, distant words and the hard crack of something inert hitting the floor and bouncing. He flips the mouthpiece up to the level of his ear until the noise stops. He sighs, then lowers the phone back to his lips. "What's your name?"

"Don't you try and change the subject."

"I don't understand. Why do you call me at this time of night?"

"I want to know: Did you—"

"I know, sleep with your wife."

"So you did!"

"No, of course not!"

"Ha! No use trying to deny it now." He hangs up loudly.

The man sets "Do Not Disturb" on his phone before placing it face down on the table. He works his body under the covers. He sits again, picks up the phone and removes the "Do Not Disturb."

June 28, 11:35 p.m.

"Hello!" he says. He is almost relieved to hear the phone ring.

"Who is this?"

"You called me!"

"Oh. Oh, yes. There's something I wanted to say." He doesn't say.

"Is it about your wife?"

"Yes, that's it! Did you sleep with my wife?" The question has the same intensity as the first time.

"No."

"But you said her name just now!"

"No, I didn't. I don't know her name."

"You bastard!" He snarls and hangs up.

July 5, 11:35 p.m.

"Hello?"

"This is Ben calling."

The man turns on his bedside lamp. "Hello, Ben. How are you doing?"

"Why does everyone keep asking me that?"

"No matter. I just thought I'd ask."

"I'll do the asking."

"All right, then, go ahead."

Many seconds pass. He hears the relentless sequence of someone dialing numbers into a rotary phone, something he hasn't heard since he was a boy, then the sound of the phone handle trying for and missing the cradle three times before it ends the call.

July 12, 11:35 p.m.

"Hello, Ben?"

He hears an exhalation, then nothing.

"Are you there?"

"I've forgotten why I called."

The man turns on his lamp and puts on his glasses with one hand, though he doesn't know why he needs them. "Are you calling about your wife?"

"Yes, my wife." Ben's voice catches. "She's a very beautiful woman." He begins to cry softly.

"Yes, she is. Very beautiful."

"You know, too?" He stops crying.

"Yes."

"Everyone wanted to sleep with her!"

Behind his glasses, the man closes then opens his eyes. "Yes, but you are the only lucky one who did."

When, after a minute or two, there has been nothing more, he hangs up and snaps off the light. He lies still until sometime later when he realizes he is wearing his glasses. He removes them and places them close by, next to the phone.

July 19, 11:35 p.m.

"Hello?"

"Hello, it's Ben here."

"Good, it's you." He sits up and waits.

"I remember why I dialed you."

"Yes?"

"I dialed to tell you that I am the lucky one." He hangs up.

The man remains sitting upright and smiles in the darkness. Then he places his cellphone on the far end of the bedside table and slips under the covers.

July 26, 11:35 p.m.

There is no phone call. The man sleeps.

ELLEN BIRKETT MORRIS

WHERE I'M FROM

After George Ella Lyon

I am from stacks of books on end tables,
from second hand smoke and shiny red cans of Coke.
I am from apartments, each the same only
because they hold our worn couch
and the brown and white afghan
knitted by my distant grandmother.
I am from John and Elizabeth,
a bright spot in an unhappy union.
I am from afternoon television,
Bewitched, *The Flintstones*, and *Scooby Doo*.
I am from frozen pizza and bags of greasy fast food,
and from my mother's goulash and raspberry trifle,
made after working long shifts at the hospital.
I'm from her warm kisses and lingering hugs
and the lonely marriage that echoed behind them.
I'm from trips to the library and afternoons at the zoo.
From *Ramona* and *James and the Giant Peach*,
from Jo, Meg, Amy and Beth.
I'm from an angry man who'd shout at the world,
then put on the record player at night and smile
as my sisters and I danced and sang along.
I'm from plays performed in the neighbor's backyard.
From fly swatters and homemade strawberry ice cream.
I'm from candy bars out of vending machines and
laundromat popcorn. From games of hide and seek
at sunset and sleepy mornings reading the funnies.
I am from cerebral palsy and early birth,
from stiff lower legs and falls on the concrete.

From schoolyard taunts and funny best friends.
From sisters who looked out for me and laughed with me.
I am from dewdrop diamonds on the grass and
honeysuckle nectar on my tongue.
From tall trees and blue skies.
From big dreams, some of which came true.

REEL TO REAL

I love how he loves my broken body. How he faces me on the floor, smiling, as he helps me put on my support hose, ties my shoes, tells me today will be a better day. The way he holds out his hand as we navigate uneven pavement. The way he kisses me gently, caressing my arthritic neck as if it was made of glass not bone. How he pats my behind as I struggle to get up the stairs, saying he enjoys the view. How slowly he makes love to me to make sure every movement brings pleasure, not pain. His love feels unique, yet I know this quiet tenderness is played out in rooms across the world. A gorgeous reel of geriatric sex scenes that will never be seen on screen.

KESHAWNA MOONEY

A PREDICTABLE CRISIS

Ernestine had started thinking the only way to really determine if she wanted to leave her husband was to have an affair. But when she woke up that morning, and looked over at Jerrold, a brown starfish floating in a sea of blankets and throw pillows, she thought that was a preposterous idea. Not just because she didn't need another man to leave him—though it would have been nice to have a reason—but because he looked so innocent sprawled out the way he was that she felt almost tender toward him. He would be a helpless fool without her.

Before they met, some fifty odd years ago now, it pained Ernestine to remember, she had been senselessly, out of her mind infatuated with another man; a smooth crooning musician who left one night to play a gig with his band and decided Ernestine wasn't enough reason for him to return. She was inconsolable before her mother lifted her chin and told her to quit all the crying. "A man is like a train. Miss one, catch the next," she said with a wink. And catch the next is what Ernestine did.

Jerrold was the next man who came sniffing around, and when he asked her to marry him she said yes only because he was off to Vietnam. She thought if he was going to run off and die, then maybe letting him think he had a girl waiting for him back home was something nice she could do for him. But then the dullard jumped off a wall carousing with his fool buddies and got both feet broken. Having no use for him, the military discharged him and within the month, before she could give it proper consideration, or much thought at all really, they were husband and wife.

Even though Jerrold's drinking was a third partner in the marriage, he seemed to really love Ernestine. He wasn't a mean drunk. If anything, he was more affectionate, following her around everywhere, pawing at her at all hours of the day. So, it was no surprise when their son, Paul, came along. Jerrold was so happy he quit his drinking for a time, and it wasn't long before their daughter, Lisa, followed. Ernestine settled into her little life almost effortlessly. She spent so much time cooking meals, scrubbing stains, and shuffling children back and forth, forty years had passed before she looked up and realized she had been feeling empty for a long time. She wasn't sure if that was Jerrold's fault, and when she saw him sleeping like this she always felt sorry for blaming him. He wasn't her first choice, but she didn't mind him most of the time. But then again, peeling herself away from the wall on her side of the bed, doing her routine frontwards crabwalk to climb over him rankled her insides enough that she thought she might like to be without him for just a little while.

She moved into the kitchen for her morning phone call to her sister, Irene—a habit they developed in their early twenties when Irene was newly married and Ernestine was a new mother and both had lots of questions to ask and household predicaments to complain about. Now at seventy and sixty-seven, with Ernestine being the senior, the habit had endured this long, Ernestine thought, only because Irene's husband went and crashed himself up after a night of drinking, leaving Ernestine to look after yet another person who depended on her. Ernestine stood at the wall telephone, a relic of times past, lighting up and puffing on a cigarette which was just one more thing in her life that had gone out of style. When Irene answered with her raspy, "Hey," Ernestine took a puff of her cigarette and blurted out, "I'm leaving him, 'Rene."

"Yeah, what he done now?"

"Nothing, that's the problem. I'm sick of looking at him. I'm a get me a new man. I ain't found him yet but I'm going to go ahead and find one. Let Jerrold fend for himself for once."

"You know that man would die without you," Irene sighed. "Hell, he'll probably die soon anyway."

"With me right behind him, and then what?" Ernestine chewed her lip and flicked her cigarette into the sink, cradling the receiver between her ear and shoulder. She heard the thump against the side door meaning the paper had arrived. She noticed there was a note attached to the blue bag telling her it was going to be the last one and that next month she would have to "find them online," whatever that meant.

"Everyone moving on to somewhere," Ernestine said quietly as she pulled the paper out of the bag and threw it on the counter.

"Check the numbers," Irene said.

Obediently, Ernestine unfolded it and flipped through the pages. She flipped until she saw an advertisement that took up half the page. "If you suffer from depression, chronic pain, so on, so on," she mumbled to herself, reading the ad, "LSD trial might be right for you, so on, so on. Our pivotal phase 3 . . . well I don't know what all that means. Seniors especially encouraged to apply. Hm, they're looking for volunteers to take LSD. Maybe I'll go on down there and see what that's about."

"You lost your mind old woman?"

"What harm could it do? They're doctors." Ernestine thought she might like to find out what all the fuss was about back in the old days. If an affair wasn't in the cards, going on a head trip before she left the earth might have to do. It wasn't like she had been on any other kind of trip in her whole life.

"You better be careful thinking of doing something stupid like that. Don't you remember them people hallucinating and killing their whole families and jumping off buildings and stuff?

You trying to see God, you better get to a church."

Ernestine had never been in anyone's church and definitely didn't want to start now. If God was as disappointed in her life as she was, then surely it would be a flagellation she had no interest in exploring. No, she was looking for a religious experience without the religion. Something to make her remember what it felt like when the possibility of life was promising, when she had endless paths laid before her, ripe for her picking. Though hers wasn't the hardest, lately she couldn't help feeling like she had chosen the wrong one. Standing there in her old-fashioned kitchen, talking on her wall phone, with a cigarette hanging from her lips, she looked around her time warp of a home that might have been funny if it wasn't so frustrating. It wasn't just that she was getting old but that she seemed to be simultaneously frozen in a time that only reminded her of what used to be, not what could be.

"And you better hope those people let you go home instead of holding you for illegal experiments," Irene prattled on.

Ernestine didn't want to be talked out of this. "I'm going now, 'Rene."

"Aww don't get sour, I'm just looking out for you. What about my numbers?"

"Get your own numbers!" Ernestine yelled into the receiver before slamming it back on the wall.

)()(❋)()(

Ernestine stood outside on the line and craned her neck to see ahead of her. She felt so nervous that she almost walked right on by. Although she wasn't the oldest one there, that wasn't what gave her the confidence to stop. Surprisingly, the thing that stopped her were the young people with thick framed glasses. She hid a smile behind her hand thinking that in her day, the only kind of person you'd spot in glasses like that would be a blind old biddy. Now, she supposed, it was fashion. As she stepped on the end of the line she cut her silent giggles short when she realized that she might be considered a biddy. She folded her arms indignantly across her chest at the thought. She was so incensed at her own thoughts that at first she didn't notice the old man in front of her turning around not so surreptitiously with a shy smile.

"What's brought you down here today?" the man asked.

Ernestine blinked, seeing him for the first time and said gruffly, "The ad."

He leaned in close, conspiratorially. "Me too. I guess they wanted seniors, huh?"

Something about that statement alarmed her. The nervous excitement that only moments before was a slight tickle in her throat, immediately morphed into full blown paranoid fear. What if Irene was right? Maybe they were trying to recruit seniors, thinking no one would miss them. Lord knows Jerrold and her children wouldn't realize she was gone until they needed something from her, which was always. The thought both comforted and terrified her.

"They'll let us out of there after it's done, right?" she asked. The man looked quizzically at her, and she asked again a bit more hysterically this time. "They'll let me out, right?!" Her hands were clenched at her sides and the man put his hand on her shoulder.

To calm herself she thought maybe she should focus on him. She looked at his button down dress shirt tucked neatly into his pants. He had a bit of a paunch but who didn't at their age. If she was serious about having an affair, he might do. He would be as good as any, even if he wasn't particularly good looking. He was bald on top, and Ernestine studied the smooth skin on the top of his head. She tried to imagine this strange man's naked body on top of hers and for some reason she felt embarrassed for him. Just when she thought she could try getting used to the idea, she looked at the man's face and realized the hand on her shoulder wasn't to comfort her but instead to steady himself. Suddenly he went stiff and fell over flat on the ground, his body landing with a sickening thud on the pavement. She leaned over him and, not being able to bend down on account of her bad knees, nudged him with her foot. She peered into his peaceful face and wondered what else he had planned for the day, for the rest of the month, rest of his life. Whatever it was, it was all off now. Ernestine reached over and tapped the young lady in front of his prone body and asked if she could call the police or alert someone. The young woman looked down, gasped, and ran to the front of the line. More gasps spread through the small crowd. People turned around, some eyeing Ernestine suspiciously as if she had something to do with it, others with fear probably worrying she was next.

A moment later, in another stroke of pure Ernestine luck, a young man came out, faced the line, and announced loudly, looking directly at her, "For the time being, we need all seniors to please step off the line for safety reasons." Ernestine looked down at the prone man again and thought, "Leave it to this old clown to go and ruin it for everybody."

)()(❋)()(

Once a month Ernestine would do her best to get to Paul's apartment to clean and make sure he had enough to eat. Most of the time Lisa would find her way over too, using it as an excuse not to call or visit Ernestine any other time. She suspected it was because Lisa's husband didn't like her, but Lisa denied this, telling Ernestine she was paranoid. Ernestine wasn't convinced—why else would Lisa volunteer to come all the way to this side of town dragging two sulky preteens with her? At ten and twelve years old Ernestine's grandchildren were polite enough, if a little sullen. She wasn't sure she even knew what their voices sounded like, but she tried to keep her complaints to a minimum, occasionally glad she got to see them at all.

It was difficult getting to Paul's and he never offered to come and pick her up from the station, let alone help her up the four flights of stairs she needed to ascend to get to his door. He offered once when he first moved in and, not wanting to be a bother, Ernestine had said she would find her way. Now all these years later he still expected her to find her own way. She guessed it was okay since Jerrold usually picked her up, stopping for a bit to chat with the grandchildren, making it an unofficial family affair.

Since Paul, never having married, spent all his time on his contraptions, Ernestine always tried to make sure he was taking good care of himself. Ernestine didn't know exactly what he did, but she imagined he was an inventor of sorts. He had a habit of getting lost in his creations, forgetting other people existed, especially his mother. Maybe that's what it's like to be an artist, Ernestine thought. She liked to think he got that from her. When she was younger she thought she might like to be an inventor. She was always coming up with new uses for things. There was that time she made the razor blade contraption to remove those fuzzy bits from clothes the kids didn't wear anymore before donating them. She was absolutely put out when she saw one in a store, looking much fancier than hers. She moaned for days about some noname stealing her idea until Jerrold got sick of hearing about it. Then there were the sponge stamps she used to like to make because she thought they were cute and because she found out sponges were the wrong thing to use for dishes. But those she just ended up chucking at Jerrold whenever he complained about her cooking because they were the closest thing to hurl at him without hurting him too bad. By the time she reached Paul's age, which didn't seem all that long ago to Ernestine, she had given up on making anything at all.

She knocked on Paul's door before letting herself in with her key. She called out to him and got right to work inspecting his refrigerator and cabinets. "Just like his father," she muttered under her breath. These men would starve without her. Ernestine always made sure everyone else was fed before she was, and this reminded her that she hadn't eaten breakfast. Not one to leave a stone unturned, Ernestine flipped up the butter dish in the refrigerator and found a candy bar in a plastic baggy. She wasn't surprised this was the only edible thing in the place. Still waiting for Paul to remember that his mother had stopped by to see him, she pulled it out and took a small bite, telling herself she'd buy him ten candy bars later. It wasn't very good. Crumbly and cardboard like, she didn't bother to savor it, stuffing the last half whole into her mouth.

When Paul finally came out he was holding something asking her if she "wanted to see something cool," which Ernestine thought was a ridiculously childish question at his big age. Not to mention that she thought the thing looked like garbage trying really hard not to look like just what it was. No, he didn't get this from her. She wouldn't take credit for this and if he kept on disappointing her like this then she really wouldn't have anything to live for. She sat down slowly on his couch, trying to think of a word that wouldn't be too discouraging. Failing at that, she changed the subject.

"When is your sister getting here?" And it seemed as if she blinked and there was Lisa, standing right in front of her. She couldn't tell how much time had passed but she looked around at her children and her grandchildren and got the sudden urge to announce her displeasure with Jerrold.

"I'm leaving your father," she said.

"Don't joke," Lisa said sensibly.

"We don't love each other no more." Ernestine wasn't sure that was true, but it felt true in the moment.

"What do you mean Daddy doesn't love you?"

"What would you do without taking care of Daddy?"

"She could get a hobby."

"She could get a hobby without leaving Daddy."

"How? The old buzzard takes up all her time."

"I think it's pretty evenly split between the two of you old buzzards."

"Ma doesn't mind helping me. What else has she got to do?"

Ernestine's eyes darted from Paul to Lisa not sure which one of them was saying what, but she felt like she should join the conversation.

"I am in this room!" she shouted as she got to her feet. And then she was yelling, her voice hoarse with emotion. "I'll get a hobby, alright. And it'll be a sight better than whatever claptrap nonsense you got going over there." She gestured wildly at Paul's device.

"Ugh, Grandma, don't say claptrap."

Ernestine turned to look at her granddaughter. Yes, it definitely seemed like the first time she had ever heard her speak but she felt like time was moving too quickly to think about that.

"This'll happen to you too," she yelled, pointing at Lisa. "And your ugly little children, looking just like their empty-headed daddy, will pretend you're not even in the room when they say for you to just lay down and die like you all are doing right now."

And then she burst into tears. She wasn't meaning to cry, but she couldn't stop herself. She suddenly felt sorry. Sorry because all she had ever been was someone's daughter, someone's wife, and then someone's mama. Sorry for raising her daughter to be her daughter, then a wife, and then someone else's mama. Sorry that Paul never married but grateful that he wasn't ruining someone else's life with all his hopeless machines and sloppiness.

Through her tears she saw the picture of the Earth on the back of Paul's closet door. She stopped crying, sniffling like a child. She chuckled to herself and, just as suddenly as she had started to cry, was struck with the need to tell her children right away that there was a lot of life to live. Even at their ages. She desperately needed to tell them before it was too late. And then she remembered they were standing right in front of her. The fifty-year-old man-child and the haggard, beaten down wife and mother, both looking like their useless father. When had her children gotten so old? She needed to say something, but all she could manage was, "Don't disappoint yourselves, kids."

Paul and Lisa smiled nervously at her. Then both of Ernestine's grandchildren erupted into laughter, frightening her back into her spot on the couch with a flop. She watched as Paul walked into the kitchen in slow motion, saying in a low deep voice that she was having a breakdown. Had he always sounded like that? And why had she never realized that her son looked kind of like a cartoon villain.

"Ma, did you eat my candy bar?" he said in that weird deep voice. It was oddly loud to be so deep. Almost booming, like what God might have sounded like if she had half a mind to even think about what he would say to her.

"You better not come and talk to me," Ernestine said to the ceiling. "If you show up, you better come clean about all the lies you told. Ain't no way you created the heavens and Earth without a woman!" She thought she heard God ask where his other half was, and she was ready to shout that he probably ran her off because he stole all the credit.

But it wasn't God after all. It was Paul, still talking slowly in that booming voice. "Where's the other half?" he asked. Ernestine stared at him. "I think she ate the whole thing," he said to Lisa. They looked at her with a mix of accusation and fear.

"You don't need it," she huffed defensively.

"I thought that stuff was supposed to mellow you out," one of the grandchildren said.

Who was talking now? Ernestine was tired. She thought maybe she'd close her eyes for just a second but just like that, Jerrold was there, hustling her into the car, telling her she was embarrassing everyone.

The drive home was a silent one, other than a mumble from Jerrold about the two of them maybe taking a trip. Although it wasn't quite the religious experience Ernestine had in mind, she was stimulated. The feeling was so strong that she almost agreed to the outrageous idea of a trip. There was a time she thought she might like to travel the world, even if it was with

Jerrold. But with this inspiration came clarity and the very idea of having to plan a vacation that wasn't all too different from her regular life sounded exhausting. She decided she did, however, need to make a move. She was so sure of this that as soon as they walked through the door she started to pack. She didn't know why but she went to the kitchen first and started packing up all the cleaning supplies. Then all the food. She didn't know what she was planning on doing with any of it, but she knew she didn't want Jerrold to have it. Jerrold, for his part, didn't give Ernestine a second glance until she finally got around to packing clothes. The first piece of clothing she pulled out of her dresser—a sweater—she wouldn't even need since not only was it too small for her, but it was the wrong weather for it.

Jerrold looked over at her and without a word grabbed the sweater from her hands and stalked back to the dresser. Ernestine grabbed the arm of the sweater. Jerrold tried to jerk it back but it was stretchy and he ended up yanking his arm over his head, wincing at the sudden movement. They did a slow tussle back and forth that still managed to knock the wind out of both of them, leaving them both wild-eyed and breathless. Ernestine was the first to let go. She turned her back on him and went to the kitchen. While she began to unpack the food and cleaning supplies she had hastily thrown into black trash bags, Jerrold folded up her sweater and put it neatly back in the drawer.

)(❋)(

Ernestine's birthday came and went without any more talk of her leaving Jerrold. Since the incident at Paul's, the kids hadn't let her out of their sight. They had started to accompany her on her grocery shops, lying about needing this or that. When she went on these shopping trips she would look in the freezer cases at the old woman staring back at her. She didn't feel as old as she thought she looked. Her only problem was that tender ache of boredom that she was starting to accept as her permanent companion. The confirmation that she was a woman of a certain age who had never done anything spontaneous, never done anything worth talking about, and now needed her children to chaperone her in the supermarket.

She started making it a habit to buy the smallest, most runty looking of the meat, the most wilted vegetables. She selected crushed boxes of pasta, dented cans of beans, talking to them in baby voices as she picked them off the shelves. Saying gently to the smallest chicken in the poultry case before getting the butcher's attention, "Don't you worry little one, you're coming home with me." The handsome butcher would give her a kindly look under his manicured brows and ask her if she was sure she wanted *that* chicken. He was nice. She thought just for a second that she might want to kiss him just so she could tell someone, anyone, that she had done it. Her children would be mortified. Irene would never believe it. She wasn't sure what Jerrold would do. She imagined him stalking down to the supermarket and socking this good looking guy once or twice in the face. What a ridiculous thought, she giggled to herself. Now if she had told Jerrold she was going to clean the man's house then that might have led to something. It was like that time she thought she might want to get a job but all she knew how to do was cook and clean and so she applied for a job at a doctor's house for when his wife was away for work. Jerrold made a big stink about washing another man's underwear.

At the time Ernestine foolishly thought he was jealous.

At home she would gingerly place her dented cans and crushed boxes in the pantry. Gently washing the runty chicken and wilted vegetables, tenderly cleaning them in the same way she used to bathe her children. She hardly ate a thing, just sat at the table watching Jerrold chew, feeling disgusted with him, and disgusted with herself for being disgusted with him.

One night, while she was washing the dishes after dinner, she could feel him hovering in the kitchen. He stood there for so long she was tempted to turn around.

"Stine, I'm leaving," he said to her back. She kept right on washing dishes but knew instinctively that there was someone else. She tried to picture the woman. All she could imagine was herself as a young woman, a girl really, willingly choosing the path with Jerrold on it waiting for her. Then she pictured Jerrold sprawled out the way he always was in the morning—sprawled out on that dusty road and her as a young woman gracefully stepping over his old butt, the somewhat cloudy, path brightening up and straightening out.

"And before you go on about it," Jerrold cut into her thoughts, "I got me a grown adult woman. No child half my age, okay?"

She didn't say anything but thought a woman half his age might still be an old woman.

"Well, if you ain't got nothing to say, I'll be on."

So, he was leaving right away, then. When she heard the door shut, she sat down at the kitchen table and, realizing she had been holding her breath, let out a long sigh. Relaying this story to Irene later, when asked what she was thinking in that moment, Ernestine would say she was glad he was gone; that if Jerrold had expected her to beg him to stay he was a fool; that she had chased him out the door with just the clothes on his back. But she didn't think any of that while sitting there at the kitchen table. Whether or not she considered it disgraceful, Ernestine tried to conjure up the image of a woman over seventy deciding she might want to run off with a married man at her age and actually doing it. All she could think in that moment was she might like to meet a woman like that.

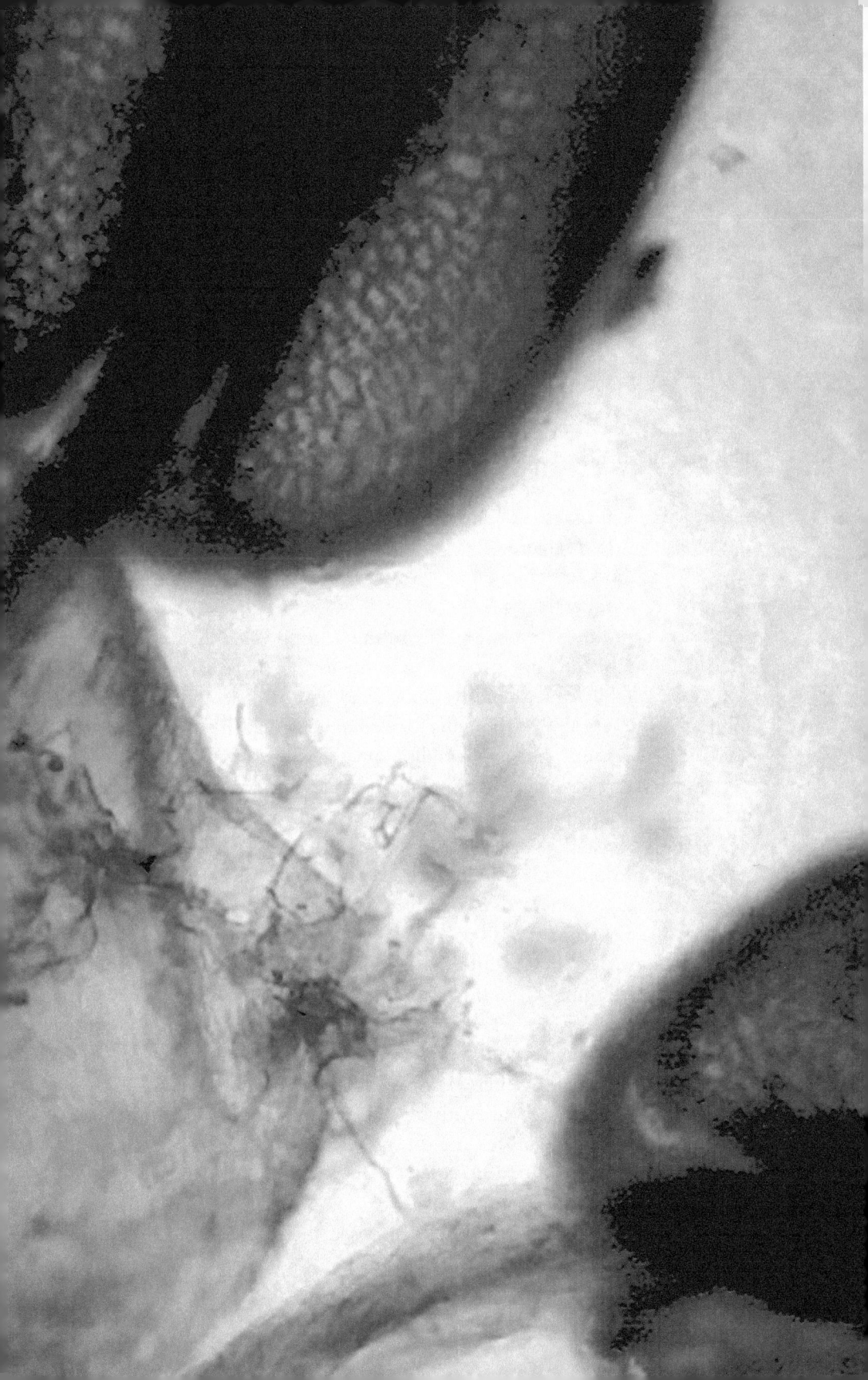

GEETHA NAIR G.

TESTING TIME

"Your father isn't really your father. You're my love-child." Vasuda was holding out the next spoonful of unsweetened porridge when the words erupted from her mother's oats-smeared mouth. The spoonful landed on the plastic sheet that covered the invalid's bed. The empty spoon reared up like a question mark in her hand.

"What did you say just now?" Vasuda asked the semi-reclining, wasted figure in front of her.

"You heard me," came the reply in the beloved voice she had grown up hearing. "And he too knows it. Now give me my porridge."

Vasuda fed her mechanically. Shock had sent words spinning out of the room. Slowly, very slowly, thoughts formed in her mind. Black thoughts that scudded across the blankness, heralding fire and thunder.

What could have caused this monstrous truth to erupt from that cropped gray head; a full-grown ogre to knock her down, tear her thudding heart out of her chest and swing it in the still air? That it was the truth, she had not an iota of doubt. One does not lie about such matters to one's beloved child. Especially when death is already a presence in the room, darkening the window like a perched bird of prey.

Suddenly, rage flowed into her. She lunged at the wasted body on the bed; she wanted to fling it to the floor, and stamp on it until it grew still. Was this her mother? Her mother, who all her remembered life had been kindness and honor personified, who even now spoke only to ask after her husband's health or her daughter's welfare. How could she? How dare she!

Vasuda straightened up with an effort, biting down on the violence within her. "Why did you tell me this now? Amma, Amma!" she asked the inert figure, her voice vibrating with despair. But Amma had already covered herself in her customary blanket of silence.

He was sitting close to the television set, intent on the talk-show that was screaming from it. Vasuda looked at the bald patch on the back of his head, at the long, sinewy arm flung across the sofa back, at the glimpse of the white dhoti touching the floor. Father. My father. The calm and efficient man of the house who had nursed her tenderly through childhood ailments, who had taught her the maps of the stars, to whom she had cuddled on cold evenings while he read some book or the other.

"Your father isn't really your father."

The words kept beating thudding against her ear drums. Had he always known that she was the cuckoo in his nest? Her thoughts went back to her thirty years in their tranquil home, cocooned in the wholeness of their family. She saw the years as a globe, radiating love like light. Of course, she had always known that he loved her less than he did her elder sister. But Janaki had a deformed body, could barely walk, and Amma had explained to her that parental generally love flowed more strongly towards the less blessed child. She had accepted that and felt grateful that she could walk, run and play as she pleased.

"Let's have dinner . . . ," she said. She could not bring herself to add "Appa" to her words. The clock struck eight loud notes. In this house the clock ruled every activity. 8 p.m. was dinner time. As she served him the brown potato curry he relished, she watched his fingers on the chappati. Fingers that resembled Janaki's, not hers.

She looked at his face, the broad forehead, the small bright eyes, the small nose and the thin lips. The mirror above the wash basin showed her a narrow forehead, large eyes, a long nose.

"What are you looking at? Haven't seen your face before?" he laughed. "Sit down and start eating."

After dinner, she went into her mother. She needed to know the truth urgently: who was the man who had fathered her? But Amma was already sleeping the comatose sleep of the drugged. The caregiver they employed for the nights was seated by her bedside.

She went back to where he was locking the front door and sliding the bolts into place. Yes. Everything was beginning to fall into place.

She remembered the two kittens she had found in the backyard one morning. She had brought them to the veranda where Janaki was sitting. They yearned to keep the two furry balls as pets. But Janaki and she knew he disliked house pets. Yet they made an attempt. At first he had been unyielding but had finally melted when Janaki dragged herself to a corner to weep, one plump kitten at her feet. How delighted they had been, she and Janaki! Janaki. How could she have blinded herself to the fact that it was because of Janaki's Bessie that she too had been permitted the joy of Bunty?

He had reined in his grief when meningitis took away Janaki in her sixteenth year. But when it was time to lift the plantain leaf on which her thin body lay, he had fallen back, crying aloud, "My child, my darling child! I lived for you; how will I live without you?"

It had shocked and pained her then that he should break down so in public, her strong Appa . . .

Now those words uttered eighteen years ago seared her as if the strong breeze from the pyre had flung them at her. How often he had stressed her lifelong role as Janaki's protector and companion when their parents were no more! Had his beloved Janaki been her raison d'etre? Had that been the reason why she had been allowed to live as a part of the family, why she had not been aborted, or thrust into an orphanage? Also why, after Janaki's passing, he had been luke-warm in his interest in her.

Why had he not arranged her marriage the way fathers did?

Of course she would not have left her home with her Amma so ill and her Appa so helpless. She had declared she would not leave her mother whose health was worsening day by day. But surely he should have counseled her, told her to make her own life? He hadn't uttered a word. Now, at thirty, she could see she was aging. Didn't he care ? Why should he?

In her room, Vasuda switched on her laptop, as always. But tonight she sat staring at the lit screen. It was preposterous, said a part of her mind, Appa not her father? Impossible. And yet. How could she live with this unconfirmed knowledge? Knowledge is pain, she remembered reading somewhere. This knowledge was loss as well. A single line had gifted her an enormous bundle of loss. It had wiped out her past life, had darkened and shattered that lit globe that had been her home.

She could not exist this way.

She had to know.

Her fingers raced over the keys.

   A DNA paternity test can prove a father-child DNA match. You must be wondering now, can anybody get their DNA tested, is it that easy. And the answer to your question is Yes, anybody can get DNA tested and it's easy. It's simple all you need is to provide the blood, buccal swab, nail or hair samples of the family member with whom you want to do the test.

Alternate Friday mornings were set aside for nail-cutting. As usual, he folded the square sheet of paper onto which the nail parings had been made to fall and deposited the little packet in the waste bin. Vasuda picked it up a few minutes later.

At ten o'clock, Vasuda left home. The renowned clinical laboratory where her dear friend worked was just across the road.

Step one of her mission accomplished, she got back in less than fifteen minutes.

It was one of Amma's bad days. They had been getting more frequent of late. She would not speak a word or allow herself to be fed. "Tell me, Amma, tell me it was a cruel lie," Vasuda entreated her silently. She looked down at the inert old woman and suddenly hatred rose like bile in her throat. She reached out her arms to squeeze out what remained of life within her.

Then her arms dropped to her sides. "Amma! Amma!" she cried. There was no response.

"I am going crazy," Vasuda whispered to herself.

Several times, when she found her mother's eyes open, she asked her the question. Again and again. "Is it true ? Is it true? " Each time her mother stared mutely at the wall opposite her where hung a photo of her little daughters at play on a green lawn.

She avoided her mother's husband as much as she could. He sensed there was something wrong but said nothing. At night she swallowed a couple of her mother's sleeping pills in an attempt to shut out the void within her. It was as if her past—her babyhood, childhood, teenage days, youth—had all been erased, totally lost in some dimension. So this was what the loss of a certainty did to one. She remembered with a bitter smile a popular flippant saying: "Motherhood is a matter of fact. Fatherhood is a matter of opinion." But that had been before DNA tests.

One more day to go and the results would be in her hands. The next morning too her mother's condition hadn't improved. The doctor would be calling soon. Vasuda rushed out. Her friend was waiting with a smile and the just-arrived results.

"They match, of course. You crazy girl!" she said.

Vasuda read it in black and white. She was her father's daughter after all. But why had Amma lied to her? Relief made her slump onto a chair. But she was up in no time, racing home to her Appa and Amma, her losses restored.

The doctor was at Amma's bedside when she returned. Appa was next to them, his beloved balding head bent earnestly towards the young doctor's words. Her mother's eyes were open, her face alert.

The doctor turned to her, "She has slid into another stage of the disease which involves . . . "

His words were cut short by her mother's impatient exclamation. "Ramesh Uncle, go on, tell me more about your trip to Rameswaram!" Amma's bright eyes were fixed on the young doctor's face.

"Delusions," concluded the doctor.

As Vasuda sobbed, her father's arms enfolded her in a shining band of love.

JEANETTE MILLER

MY MOTHER, MY CHILD

The rectangular Amana freezer in my parents' basement opened from the top. Over a hundred plastic boxes were stored in it, layers of frozen food stacked in containers, the names of fruits and vegetables, the year they'd been frozen labeled on their plastic lids with a black marker. One container of peaches read 1976, deep frozen for twenty-four years! "We'd better throw this away!" I announced as I brought the container upstairs to Mom who was sitting at the kitchen table playing solitaire.

"No, don't throw it away. Those peaches are still good!" she declared but the peaches had turned to a dark brown mush. I suggested a plan. I'd transfer the edible food from the basement freezer to the one on the first floor where it would be easier to get to for both Mom and Dad and, if the food wasn't edible, I'd throw it out. Mom resisted. I'd proposed a solution to a problem that she didn't consider a problem. "Don't throw any of that food away. It's all still good!" she commanded from what seemed the throne of a queen bee, her chair, its seat covered in orange, embossed plastic.

The next day I carried eighty containers of frozen food up the stairs to the kitchen table where Mom was sitting after breakfast. Diagnosed with macular degeneration, she was legally blind. *I'll convince her by telling her why this food isn't all still good*, I said to myself.

It took two hours to read aloud the date written on the lid, then describe the contents of each plastic box: freezer burn, dark brown or gray, unnatural color, a mushy texture, thick ice crystals or an open lid that had allowed juices to ooze in a sticky gel to the freezer floor.

"Okay, okay, throw them away," she conceded as she pushed against the table with both hands to exit her chair. "But don't throw away any of those containers!" This meant I was to wash all of them.

I separated the edible, frozen food into categories and carried it to the upstairs freezer. I'm a Virgo who couldn't keep myself from organizing it into categories: Bread. Meat. Fruit. Vegetables. Pecans (brought back from snowbird winters in Arizona). I labeled the lids in large letters with a wide, black marker so Mom could see the names and tossed over one hundred empty plastic containers into the kitchen sink.

A child during the Depression, having enough food represented security, an insurance against wanting for my mother. For as long as I could remember, food was her primary expression of love.

I walked down to the basement again and pulled the Amana's cord from its outlet, my declaration that I wasn't still an obedient child, removing a substantial portion of my mother's identity from the large metal box with motor and lid. She and I had grappled to the core of the mother-daughter thing and, at its center, was food. I would be lying if I said I didn't feel guilty.

Mom was delighted when I told her I was retiring from my job at the mental health center as lead therapist to take care of her and Dad but, when I added that I was also looking forward to having time to write, she blurted, "Why in the world would you want to write?"

Jealousy tinged Mom's voice but not about writing. She had no idea of what it meant to want to write but it was clear she envied that I could perform domestic tasks she could no longer accomplish. Laser-like darts of anger directed at me came from her eyes. I could feel them even when I wasn't looking directly at her. Shopping (especially shopping for groceries), cooking, cleaning, and managing the checkbook had been her turf. "Do as you're told," she'd order. *She wants to put me back in my place as a little girl again.* I was in a position where, even though I didn't want to, I was usurping hers.

When Dad had hip replacement surgery, she couldn't comprehend the list of meds he was to take. She couldn't grasp instructions for after-care read aloud to her by the discharge nurse. Mom had no choice but to turn to me. The jealous darts again. *I didn't ask for this wifely role either.*

In *Memoirs of a Dutiful Daughter* Simone de Beauvoir writes, "My mother's whole education and upbringing had convinced her that for a woman the greatest thing was to become the mother of a family. She couldn't play this part unless I played the dutiful daughter. *If I weren't the dutiful daughter, I'd quit this job* I told myself.

One morning, as I was changing the bedsheets in Mom and Dad's bedroom, I spotted, on the sewing machine near their bed, a framed photograph nestled in a pile of clothes that needed mending. An Art Deco frame held an 11" by 14" photo of a woman, her face surrounded by a bob of dark, wavy hair. Holding up the frame, I turned to Mom, "This is a good picture of Aunt Grace."

"That's not your Aunt Grace," Mom mumbled. Jealousy? Anger? in her voice. "That's your father's old girlfriend."

My jaw dropped. I'd be hurt and angry too if, after seventy years of marriage, the face of my husband's former girlfriend seemed to focus her gaze at the portion of ceiling directly above the bed where I slept. Dad told me he and Mom slept in separate bedrooms because her snoring kept him awake. She said the same thing about him, but maybe there were other reasons they didn't sleep together.

At age eight, a girl with questions, I approached Mom at her stove and asked, "Where do babies come from?" As she stirred something in a pan, Mom answered, "God has a way." Dismissing the idea of a bearded, male god dressed in a white robe who handed off an infant to waiting parents, I imagined a stained-glass window like the arched ones at church, rays of light streaming in. I didn't ask for further explanation. Sex and babies as a mystery of light was enough.

When I was thirteen, Mom gave another Biblical explanation for the blood on my upper legs. She left the stove to rush down the hall to stand in the doorway of my room when I shouted, "Mom!"

"What's wrong?" she asked, her voice raised and impatient. "Did something happen at school?" It was clear that she'd rather be cooking than talking to me. When I pointed to the blood on my legs, she proclaimed, almost shouting, "Oh, you've got The Curse!"

"What is 'the curse?'" I asked.

"All women get it. It's The Curse of Eve."

Mom left my room and returned carrying a long piece of elastic and told me to put it around my waist. Attached to it was another piece of elastic with safety pins on it to hold a thick, gauze pad in place between my legs. I stepped into the elastic belt and fastened the pad at both ends with the safety pins. It was a Friday, the 13th. It must have been bad luck to have been born female, I thought. To change my luck, for days I searched the lawn for a four-leaf clover, found one and pressed it into my diary, the one with a tiny lock and key, and hid it in my underwear drawer.

)()(❋)()(

After two years of care-giving, I made an appointment to talk with a woman who did past lives readings. Maybe she could explain why I felt consumed taking care of Mom. Had I been a caregiver long ago in a past life? Or a nurse? Or maybe I'd refused to take care for someone who needed me.

Natural ground cover, not grass, thrived between rocks and under tall evergreen trees in Edith's yard. She asked me to leave my shoes on a mat just inside the door and led me to a room where drawings and paintings of saints, mandalas, and totem animals adorned the wall. Edith offered me a cup of tea and a wingback chair facing a floor-to-ceiling window overlooking the pine trees.

Edith was candid. She didn't have the stamina to do a past life reading that day. Would I settle for a guided visualization? Even though we'd just met, I trusted her. I settled back into my chair but, before she began to guide the visualization, she exclaimed, "Look who you've brought with you!" A female deer had approached the window, standing so close to the glass I could look into her eyes. The deer wasn't frightened. She paused, walked away, then returned to nibble on a plant and walked away again. Edith thanked her for visiting us.

Carlos Castaneda, a student of shamanism, wrote that the animals who come into our view are trying to tell us something. This deer's direct gaze was the message: don't be afraid to look directly at what comes before you.

Edith asked me to close my eyes, then guided me into an elevator that took me to another dimension and asked me to exit. I found myself in an old theater. A woman, substantial in size, wearing sturdy, thick-soled shoes, a wool overcoat, and a headscarf was standing on the well-worn stage floor, her back to me. To her left was a girl who was looking directly at me. She was me.

Edith asked, "How old is the girl?"

"About five years old," I answered. "She's not smiling but she's okay."

Edith questioned, "What is she doing?"

"She's playing with a yo-yo," I replied.

The girl brought the yo-yo up and slowly let it roll down its string. It never touched the floor. Then the woman and girl disappeared. A rush of tears. Edith handed me a box of tissues. She didn't say a word.

At first, I thought the woman on stage had been my grandma Peterseim. Then a long silence. Mom was shaped like Grandma. "It was my mother," I told Edith.

"From now on you will never see your mother in the same old way,"

Edith assured me. That this would be a good thing I heard in Edith's voice. I wanted to be able to spend more than a couple of hours with Mom without getting a severe headache.

Driving home from Edith's, I asked myself *Why a stage?* My answer: Mom, in her own way, had been a stage mother. When I acted the part she'd scripted for me, a girl who didn't talk back, who didn't have her own opinions or want a life apart from the life her mother wanted her to live, I pleased her. In band I played clarinet, the same instrument Mom had played in high school. Like her, I sang in chorus and quartets, and, like her, I craved attention from boys.

I added more and more activities, hoping to gain Mom's praise. I played the lead in school plays and made the honor roll. Just before football half-times, I changed out of my cheerleading sweater and purple felt skirt into a satin, feather-trimmed costume I wore as a baton twirler in marching band. I was voted homecoming queen after learning that a ready smile for everyone made me a promising candidate who could win votes. I performed.

Monday through Friday of my senior year of high school, during lunch period, I walked the three blocks home to be on time for the soap opera, "As The World Turns." Mom and I watched it together, the plot driven by the search for a husband by the women playing leading roles, this endeavor fueled by emotion. I hid my emotions and kept my own counsel in my room.

After my appointment with Edith, the atmosphere in my mother's kitchen felt lighter. The tiny zigzag of lightning that often crossed under the skin on my forehead to signal a headache disappeared.

One morning Mom told me about the book she'd just listened to on her audio player. It was the story of a wealthy professional man who drove an expensive, foreign car who moved from New York City to a small Midwestern town and fell in love with a town girl, deciding never to return to the big city. *Is this the story you wish you'd lived?* I thought but didn't ask. It was too loaded a question. It would lead to a litany of disappointments she often shared about Dad.

One day in May, after the usual Sunday dinner that I served because Mom could no longer manage it, Mom's speech was slurred and slow. She couldn't get up from her chair, even by pushing against the kitchen table with both arms. My son and his wife thought she was having a stroke. Dad was silent. I drove Mom the seventeen miles to Mercy Hospital in Iowa City where tests were run. She hadn't had a stroke. Her heart was alright. There was no systemic illness. Her diagnosis: weakness. Her body had simply stopped supporting her. I couldn't hold her up to walk. She outweighed me. The ER doctor advised that it was time for her to go into a nursing home where she'd receive a higher level of care than I could provide.

As I turned Dad's Buick north from 5th Street toward Pleasantview, Kalona's only nursing home, Mom pointed to a house on the corner. "The woman who lives there owes me ten dollars," she pronounced. The debt was over forty years old. I silently rebuked my mother. *You are about to go into a nursing home, and you're worried about the ten dollars some woman owes you?*

A friend suggested that Mom was using this debt remembered as a distraction from the reality that she was going into a nursing home, but I remembered the time I told Mom I'd had coffee and a cookie at a Starbucks's. The cookie cost $1.79. "I could have baked a dozen cookies for that amount," she announced. Turning the corner on 5th Street, turning the corner in her life, it really was about the ten dollars. As our car approached the nursing home, Mom turned to me, "Are you the one who's signing me in here forever?"

"No, your doctor signed you in," I answered, knowing that Mom believed that doctors had God-like authority, but I was hurt and angry with her for blaming me. At the same time, I felt I'd betrayed her. I hadn't been able to take care of her until her life ended.

From her bed in the nursing home, Mom reviewed her life. "I wanted to go to nursing school but Dad wanted me to stay home." At ninety Mom was blaming my father for preventing her from realizing her dream. Months earlier she'd shared the same regret but without blaming him. Her high school grades in math and science hadn't been high enough to gain her admission to the rigorous nursing program at The University of Iowa.

A photo in our family album pictures me dressed in a nurse costume, wearing a stiff, white starched cap, and holding a baby doll. I am a living projection of my mother's unfulfilled dream.

When I was eleven or twelve, my parents began to call each other "Mom" and "Dad," not just to refer to each other when talking to my brother and me. My dad became my mother's dad and she, his mom. "Dad, I'm going to the grocery store" and "Mom's sleeping too much."

One morning shortly after Mom went into the nursing home, Dad told my brother and me that he hadn't been able to sleep the night before. Then he stunned us with a surprisingly intimate disclosure, "You won't believe what Mom told me yesterday. She said, "Your mother wanted you all to herself so you could take care of her. She didn't like me and didn't want us to get married. And Betty! Did you know that she had an abortion?" Dad turned to me, then to Jim. "My mother liked Mom. Betty didn't have an abortion. Where is Mom getting all this?"

I thought *Mom's doing her darndest to get Dad to declare (with gusto and preferably on his knees) that she was the most important woman in his life, more important than his mother, more important than Betty, his first girlfriend. and she's trying to portray Betty as a bad girl, one who had sex before she married.*

Jim brought an end to the resulting silence with a witty remark that resonated with truth. "Mom listens to too many romance novels!" he proclaimed, breaking the silence that had prevailed for over sixty years, keeping the four of us in check. And I spoke up, for the first time, to Dad about his relationship with my mother. "There isn't a man alive who could sustain an intense romance like the men in those romance novels Mom's listening to."

Dad's face showed relief, but he didn't say anything. I suggested that he respond to Mom in words. He could tell her that she WAS the only one or he could say something, not just sit there. "I did tell her that my mom liked her," he replied, confusion still registering on his face.

Just as I can roll Mom back to Room 17 West in her wheelchair, I can take her back to her childhood by reading her excerpts from this memoir. She's prompted to recall memories that well up in stories, some I've not heard before. She doesn't want to BE HERE NOW. Her past, remembered, is a happier time. Yesterday she told me, "I want to go home to my folks." This request differed from other requests to go home. It wasn't the wish of a little girl who wanted to return to the house where she was born. It wasn't a wife wanting to go back to the ranch house her husband built in 1950.

I touched my hand to hers and asked what she meant. Again, "I want to go home to my folks." "Do you mean you want to die?" "Oh, yes, I . . ." she responded and then not another word. Two nursing aides had entered the room, "Oh, Pauline, don't talk like that!" I asked the girls to sit down. "Why don't we let her say what she needs to say?" I went on, this time from my soapbox. "We Americans don't handle dying very well. Mom wants to talk about what's really going on with her." "Yes," the girls nodded but I don't know if my words made a difference.

My mother's hands move back and forth in watery slow motion as if she were an infant suspended in a womb. Unable to stand or walk at ninety-six she nears the threshold of her death, traveling now in time, not in distance. She greets my brother as "Dad." My father died two years ago. "Dad, I'm not putting in a garden this year. I sold all the Mason jars." Sometimes she sees my brother as *her* father, "Dad, will you walk me to school?" Often, she's Baby Pauline, who wants me to spoon feed her breakfast. I oblige when I can't talk her into maneuvering the spoon herself.

Mom's death seemed near. Hospice was called in a second time. Three months earlier her doctor had thought Mom would die soon but she rallied against death, perked up, wanted to feed herself, and tried not to fall asleep during visits. This lasted only a few days. Often, she didn't want to eat at all. She'd clamp her mouth shut so the aides couldn't put a spoon in it and, sometimes, in a burst of defiance, she spit out her food.

On a Saturday morning in May of 2017, Jim arrived at the nursing home at 8:30 to be met by a nurse who told him she could barely detect Mom's heartbeat. Twenty-eight minutes later Mom died so gently and quietly that Jim, sitting bedside, couldn't tell when she took her last breath. He was at the post office getting the mail when I phoned to say I'd drive to Kalona to visit Mom on Monday. "No, I was about to call you. She passed this morning."

"You did it, girl!" I whispered to the sky. "You went home to your folks just like you wanted." The day before, I'd talked to a photo of her mother to relay a message, "Grandma, your daughter wants to come home."

SHERRY SHAHAN

JOINING MY MOTHER FOR BREAKFAST
AT A DOWNTOWN MOTEL

Where I'm sure I've forgotten some holiday.

A man who looks older than god sits across from her in the motel's breakfast room. They split a maple-glazed donut like she used to do with my father. I'm introduced to Fred who appears to be bewildered and shuffles off.

"They have plain yogurt and hardboiled eggs," my mother says.
She thinks I should be on a diet. "I'd rather have your pimento-cheese in a jelly jar."

Brochures are strewn across the vinyl table. "Free Underground Donut Tour." "Spicy Chicken and Beer Pub Crawl." "Food of the Gods Immersion Workshop."

"Where did you get these?" I ask.

She rolls her eyes like she's my child. "The lobby, where'd you think?"

The cook rings a bell and calls her by name. "Bea? Your egg-beater-no-salt is ready."

Everyone seems to know her.

"Do you really have a room here?" I ask.
"Is that any of your business?" she asks back.

My mother is eighty-seven and still drives. A two-door-hatchback-fastback.

Minor dents, hubcaps intact.

A man in a hairnet swings by with her plate. "Enjoy, honey!"

My mother pretends not to hear. She squeezes a packet of ketchup over her eggs, takes two or three bites, folds her napkin into a neat square.

"Eating like a bird is a misnomer," she tells me.
"You're right."

"Because birds eat seven times their body weight a day," she says anyway.

I follow her into the ladies' room where she dumps a basket of Tampons into a purse large enough to hold a six-pack of toilet paper. Today she only takes one roll because it's single ply.

"Not a word," she says.
"Tampons are good for nose bleeds," I say.

I laugh because she laughs.

The café has emptied out. My mother makes one last sweep, eying a surveillance camera, lingering by tiny tubs of cream cheese and peanut butter.

"Why pass up a good deal?" she asks.

I know how she thinks. Free isn't stealing. It's thrift.

My mother says, "Do you think I'm losing it?"
"No, it's me. I'm losing it."
"I said it first!"

I walk my mother to her car while she tells me about Happy Hour. "Five to seven. Complimentary wine and unsalted pretzel sticks."

"Is it a date?" she asks me.
"It's a date!" I tell her.

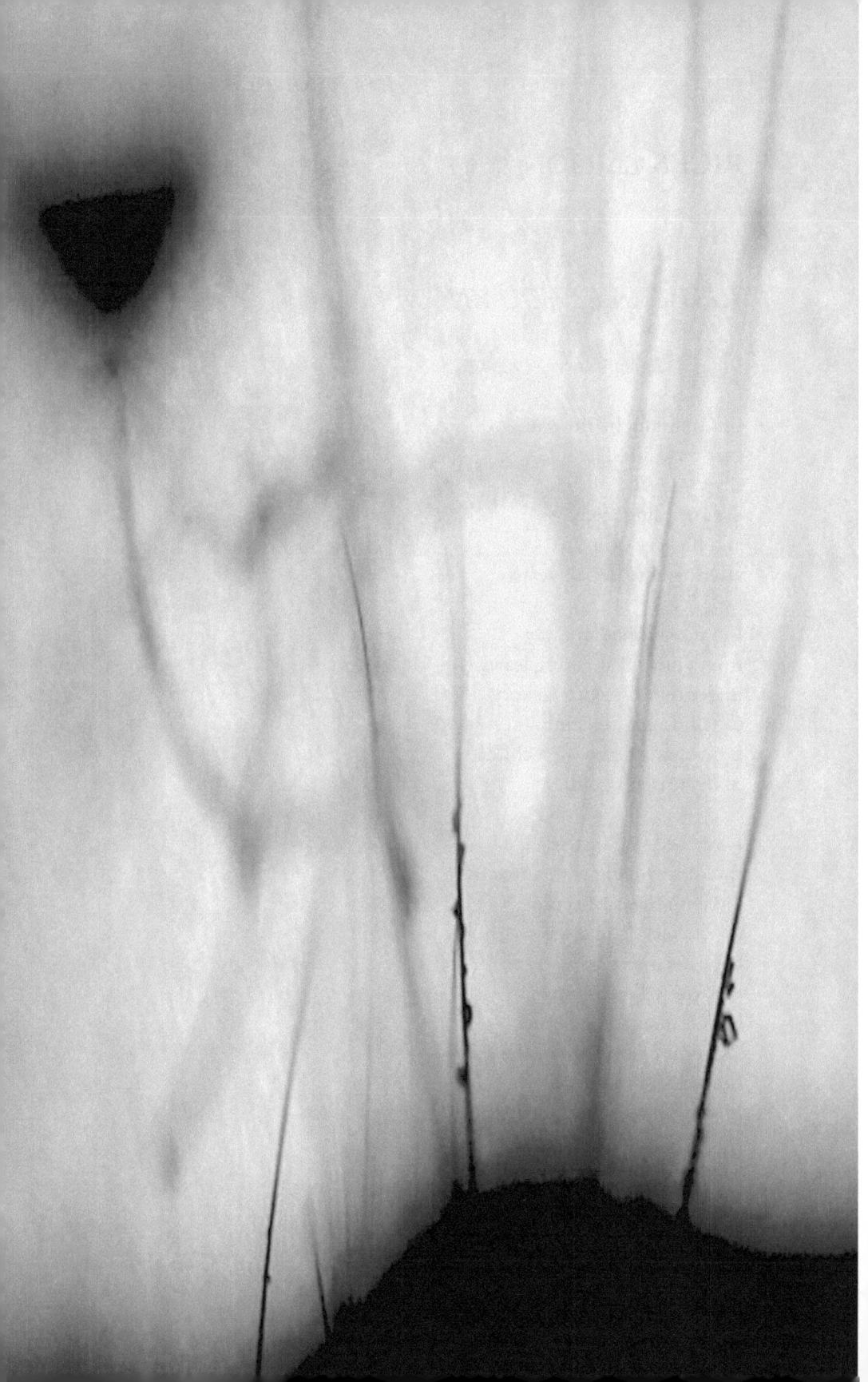

RICKS CARSON

JUST TO LET YOU KNOW

To Jane Carson, 1925-2013

I'm standing by the river
that unwinds, like one
silver measure of time,
over bending reeds
and flickery trout,
wearing at stones of years.

I'm not all that far away
from your spirit raking leaves
under that October hickory
so tall, I used to climb
into what seemed, to a child,
to be heaven's gold.

I watched you yesterday
smoothing icing with a frosting
knife on the cake cooling
on the rack. You always
bake me one when
you know I'm coming
back home. You look up.
No, don't worry about the cake—
I'll be there soon.
It won't have time to stale.

AND AFTER DINNER, A BOOK

Maybe it is two boys,
one slumped at each shoulder,
up since dawn, school all day,
soccer practice till dinnertime,
homework undone.
Maybe it is the clock's nine chimes,
or the wood stove's heat shivering the air.
Maybe it is the heroism of Reepicheep,
a bold mouse crestfallen when his tail
was cut off in battle, but his pride
restored when Aslan breathed on it,
like God did on clay figures in Eden.

This reading is like a prayer to
my father, who never read to me,
never breathed on my bruises and fears.
And so we drift in and out of
words, my sons' heads nodding,
my tongue sleepwalking
toward the page where the brave mouse
knows it is his time and, stout of heart,
strokes his canoe to the edge
of the known world and on through
the curling-back waves,
and *Narnia,* like old resentment,
slips through my fingers.

MY FATHER, IN HEAVEN, IS SORTING

After Li-Young Lee

I know my father.
He is not reading.
He's assembling discrete piles
of his ashes to make himself
who he used to be.
He liked how he was.
This is not a joke:
there is no irony in heaven.
He finds the wave in his hair,
his perfectly clipped nails,
commingled with ashes from his stinky pipe.
Arthritic fingers, now straight
and deft, never tire of putting
his mind back together, either.
Here's his motherless boyhood
on the farm, his tour of duty
in the Pacific, his wedding
to the most beautiful woman.
His orange groves, frozen
black as a burnt match, green up
and bend under lush fruit.
Angels have been busy, like
therapists: the divorce is
as if it never happened. The belt
he whipped me with,
the flakes of memories
of his three estranged children—
God himself has absorbed them.

From the kitchen my mother
calls out "Dinner's ready."
We wash our hands, find our places
around the pine table,
and together we say grace.

SHARON LASK MUNSON

GLIMPSE INTO A MARRIAGE

They drift to the porch after dinner,
the still of evening heavy with scent
from hollyhock and moonflowers.

They seek a flutter of cool
after a day dense with heat.

He, tie off, white shirt-sleeves rolled,
she, in a flowered housedress,
slide into warm metal chairs,
the day's Free Press between them.

She picks up the "Home" section,
tears out recipes, breaks their silence
to share aloud, *Dear Jane Lee.*

Next door's radio intrudes.
Amos and Andy spills out
from the Miller's open window.
Shrill sounds of a streetcar slice the hush.

He folds back the front page,
comments on President Truman,
offers opinions on Korea, the Rosenberg trial,
takes both sides of the problems
at Henry Ford's River Rouge plant.

Twilight fades. He fills his pipe
loosely packing his favorite Dunhill London.

She rises, steps inside to check on children sleeping.
When she returns streets lights are on,
stars emerge, the moon a slender arc.

They welcome night's darkness,
hear the trill of crickets,
watch fireflies flit beyond the hedgerow.

No one sees their hands laced, fingers braided,
or the kiss he plants on her palm.

GRACE

We are about
to sit down for dinner.

I light the blue candles
bought that very afternoon.

My husband's eyebrows rise.

That's new, he says.
Candlelight looks good on you, I respond.

We were newly retired.
It was time to shake things up.

*

I remember my parents when they retired.
Mother added a new carte du jour to their dinner.

We have more time, she told me.
You girls are on your own.

I realized she was adding
a touch of grace to their lives.

It began in their living room
with glasses of sweet red wine.

Next, Mother added
a small bowl of nuts.

Sometimes she and dad watched the evening news.
Often they quietly shared the day's events.

Mother added a salad course
to begin the dinner meal.

Growing up, I remember salad
being served with the meal.

But now Mother began a starter course.

She said it made the evening meal
more leisurely.

As always, they ended the meal
with the kettle whistling.

Tea and cake was a tradition.

Looking back, Mother planned
four courses for their retirement dinners:

cocktails, mixed greens
main course, tea and dessert.

*

All I added was candlelight.

I look across the table.
His gray hair appears blond again.

There's something about subdued light
that softens surroundings

produces a romantic setting.

He smiles at me in the mellow light.
I grin back.

NORITA DITTBERNER-JAX

PARK POINT, DULUTH

1.
The blast of the ore boat,
one long, two short and as the engineer
calls back, the counterweights move down
and the Lift Bridge goes up, a feat
of exquisite balance.

Masabi Miner glides into harbor
riding low, all 1000 feet, longer than my city block.
The cars on either side of the traffic gates
wait for the lion of commerce to pass.

2.
I am a tourist and not. This is
my daughter's city, her job
to be tough and tender,
the city struggling, hardscrabble
neighborhoods and the prosperous
four-square houses which stand
against the wind.

How she loves its streets, hills
rising up from Lake Superior
like loaves of bread,
a mythical landscape.

3.
I cross the road each morning
to walk the beach and greet
the dogs, walking smartly.
If I'm alone, I sing, "My Lord,
what a morning!"

4.
One morning at the beach I saw
a woman on crutches enter the water,
a guide at her side.
Then she gave over the crutches
and dove in.

5.
In my little house, I live alone
and not alone. My children come and go
as they did in childhood.
Leggy grandsons bound the steps
to the deck dangling car keys
and bringing me pizza.

The man upstairs rises before dawn
to water the planters downtown—
baskets of blossoms, colorful
as hats at a royal wedding.
He does the work of the flowers.

6.
Friends stay overnight and we see
each other's nighties. One stares off,
embracing the lake while the film
of her life unrolls. Another speaks,
two speak, the silence when they're gone.
I walk to the queue and watch
the waves push against the seawall,
and explode into air like our laughter.

7.
Toward evening at the beach
parents pack up, shake out blankets,
but their children—the toddler spooning the lake
into a hole in the sand, won't look up.

8.
On the deck I watch twilight settle in the trunks
of the trees, but the crown of the pine
still holds the light. The neighbor's dog is quiet,
part of the composition of evening.
Faint birdsong, not morning's call.

9.
City dweller, I love the horizontal line,
the sky, the lake, a seamless line of water,
not the wild horses of yesterday.
The beach is empty except for a figure
crouched in prayer at the edge of the water.

HIGH UP: SUNRISE

An old moon thinning in the west above trees,
copper for a moment,
bright and brief.

Eastward, the cathedral emerges from darkness,
behind an urban forest
and farther back, the cemetery.

The buildings downtown break the tree line,
piled like turrets of a kingdom,
and that long absence in the landscape
is the Mississippi River.

Nearer, streetlamps fade like moonlight,
a garbage truck lumbers in,
an engine starts, neighbors heading to work
and already the Amazon van is circling.

Looking up, the sky curves
at the horizon, holding us every
ordinary day.

RANDY MINNICH

LATE WINTER SOLILOQUY

Hard-eyed, hunched over the wheel.
What I should have said.
What I'll say next time. . .

Oh but look at the trees!
The earth gives birth to them.
They rise right out of the ground,

up and up to a million fingers
stretching for the sun. Their buds
are carefully wrapped right now,

but bulging. Cardinal song is flowing.
Sap will soon. Now, where was I?
Oh. Never mind.

SOMETHING LIES BEYOND DEMENTIA

You don't know where you are,
you don't know what to do.
All day your eyes dwell on nothing at all:
nowhere when I come, nowhere when I'm gone,
but leap into mine when we touch.

A river, I think, runs below what we know
and there our deeper selves swim.
When the world's winds no longer raise ripples,
though sunshine and moonlight fall flat on our pond,
we still surface, sometimes, with a swirl.

THEN YOU WALKED IN

Not You of my children.
Not You of my grief,
but You of rebirth,
You who plucked me from deep water.

You of the eyes I fall into naked,
of our nights as we slumber entwined,
our heads on your pillow, toes ten by ten,
awaken bedazzled by sunlight and us,
roll in our joy till we cuddle exhausted,
love as our kids can't imagine we can.

You of our days, of our children's children:
those laughing barbarians pour from the bus
through Nana's kitchen to rape the refridge,
flop down to watch forbidden TV,
pinch, nudge and giggle—
they mentor us back sixty years.

You of evenings no longer hollow:
reading, writing and sewing together,
two black cats and one white dog
in uneasy truce at our elbows and feet,
in this room full of living,
of love songs, not echoes.

You of renewal, of picking tulips
in autumn: we waltz
as we wrinkle and creak
toward tomorrow.

THE COLORS OF THE WORLD

I seem to seek the sunlight—always:
streaming golden through the clouds,
flashing indigo from bunting wings.
I must have been born of cork.

Oh, cork can feel despair:
post-partum grief—a child born incomplete;
rage as fanatics dismember the world.
But even underwater, cork sees sunshine
overhead, bobs irrepressibly up to find it.

I see rainbows through my tears.

Pete says he was born of lead.
For him, the sun sets sepia.
Skies may be blue, parasols pink—
he doesn't know. His inner eye is colorblind.
He sinks, and sinks, and sees no bottom.

He thinks he lacks the chemicals of joy,
some enzymatic trigger isn't sending
dopamine surging through his neurons.
A trickle, maybe. Not enough.

He shrugs. No one chooses lead.

So what are the colors of the world?
What are they, really?
I can only tell you what I see.

II
SOCIAL CONTEXTS

LAURENCE SNYDAL

THRIFT STORE

Salvation Army, St. Vincent de Paul,
Goodwill Industries. Emporia where
Discards, detritus, are scattered asprawl
Sheet metal shelving, where the very air
Breathes disillusion. But it cheers me up.
I find the duck puppet, bone-handled knives,
The brazen ape holding the candle cup.
Survivors, witnesses of other lives.

Shades of dissatisfied desire lie side
By side with memories of wasted weeks.
Here is a mute museum of things tried,
Later found wanting. Perhaps he who seeks
Novelty here or joy could better find
Them in the longer aisle, the deeper shelf,
The fuller line of merchandise, the kind
Of bargain bins, bizarre, inside himself.

Still on my mantel stand the brittle bits
I've salvaged from a multitude of pasts,
Backward glances to where my poor heart sits,
Stunned with the certainty that nothing lasts.

THE WHALE LINE

*"the upper end of the line is taken aft . . . resting crosswise upon the . . .
handle of every man's oar, so that it jogs against his wrist in rowing, and
also passing between the men. . . . Thus the whale-line holds the whole boat
in its complicated coil. . . . All men live enveloped in whale-lines."*
　　　　　—Melville, Moby Dick

These lines I write tonight lead me to think
I can escape the whale-line of my life,
My house, my garden, and the way I drink
The summer into fall. While my dear wife
Prepares for bed, I take my pad and pen
And scribble out my thoughts. These are not years
Of discontent but rather hours when
I right all wrongs and smother all my fears.

Melville laid his whale-line to jog the wrist
Of everybody in the boat. A rope
That could twist, twine and turn into a fist
That gathered all togethers into hope.
Melville understood this hope, this tightening
Web of word and world. He knew how the whale
In his broad breaching, brought us the frightening
Three words he then assigned to poor Ishmael.
"I alone survived."
　　　　　　　　So far as I know
No one survives alone or wants it so.

C.P. SURENDRAN

INVITATION

(For Sonu)

Put out with wine the heart's old, purple fire, and wait;
Watch an absence thrive white in the wild jasmine
Breaking out on vines. Come in April when the house is
On fire. Or in June when the lone boy up in the loft
Flings dawn, like crushed glass, on the windowpane.
Or in November, when leaves chilled yellow by the light
Of a dead star, wither and fall, scattering bug-eyed ants.
Come any time, really. The moon here is mortgaged
To silence. Now that nothing can be said or done
Perhaps you will consider staying on for coffee, sun.

SURPRISE

At dawn, I go for a run down a narrow road
Each foot nearly out of step with the other.
A rogue root,or a stone loosened from its hold,
Could trip my knees held in place by braces.

I return and lie across the arms of my sofa
—Mary and her son—a variation of the Pieta,
And open, as the sun sweats summer brown,
Graham Greene, whose god is always down.

At noon, I doze through old journeys in trains
Past towns I will not revisit, or remember;
Once there was a couple on the upper berth
Making love, the woman pulling the red chain

As she arrived, halting the night. At dusk,
I boil noodles in a pan, an ear to the shadow
Stealing up the stairs, pausing at the door, puzzled,
As if a thing that had been dead years ago

Still stirred, like wind dragging round the bend
Dry leaves yet muttering to each other of the end.

SELF PORTRAIT WITH BANDAGED EAR

There is not much you can say about suffering after what Auden sang
Of the Old Masters[*] and of the boy who flew to his last feather,
Before plunging, as high as he soared, down toward a green, green sun,
As the plowman tilled, the skull bleached, and the ship sailed on.

From a wall, built to keep the tide of mud and the potato eaters out
You stare at the suits and gowns, who wrapped your madness like a gift,
And brought you in, the wine from Arles reddening their soft, soft palms,
Marveling at your violet nights in South of France; the almond blossoming,

Iridescent crystals lighting up, like bulbs, the blue, blue deep.
There you walked through the stars melting in their holes; past the cypress
Stranded in flight, leaf from leaf, rooted to the secret that yet forbids
The tree to take leave of the trunk; past the cafe, sulfur-yellow, red,

Like the drawing-room of hell, an ear in hand, toward Brothel No. 1,
Looking for young Gabrielle, to share a shame, Vincent by name,
An effect of light, the substance of life. She screamed at what your gift
Revealed. How partake of blood, blood and flesh, universal supper,

And not doubt the sanity of all? To Saint Remy, you went, tick-tock,
And onward to Auvers; from south to cold north,
Carried your madness, the Mulberry Tree, unsold art, intact;
Flecked out from the fissures of burlap's blank, blank face,

Man and crow crowning infinite space, looking finally like themselves,
And not; wasted, but, for all that, free, free like ringed fire. Is it pride,
That shapeless thing broken in man and tree? And still they tried
Remembering it, unbound between defeat and defeat, in your portraits.

The beauty of breath, clear and steaming, like pug-marks in the snow.
You turned the brush inward, and stabbed your way inside out; not the
        coat,
Bandage, hat: but the wool, thread, and fur, the rasp, the rasp of a poor
        man's wear.
And your blue eyes wondered what you'd done, (the bullet in the gut

Scattering the birds, perhaps?), to rate what's on the wall $71.5 million?**
How well the scented evening dissipates into the night, like a jar collecting
And emptying yellow, yellow clouds. The one who nailed you on the wall
Will pick up the bill; of suffering, he must know a little though he owns

Half the sea in which Icarus drowned. The other half, singular to each,
Is where you trawl, captain of a battered ship passing from wreck to wreck,
Hauling in drowned, heroic light, and sailing close to the wind,
Alone and beaten, toward the Old Masters waiting on the beach.

* "Musée des Beaux Arts," a poem written by W. H. Auden on the fall of Icarus.

** Philip Niarchos, a Greek shipping tycoon, bought the painting at this price, and it was
in his private collection for a while, according to reports.

SARA BROWN WEITZMAN

RODIN'S "THE HAND OF GOD"

Erupting out of a great block of marble,
a huge hand—

not an old god's
but a smooth young hand,

the polished Carrara
fingers, delicate yet strong

as a pianist's—
holds another square of stone

out of which a small human figure
is emerging, left unfinished

to remind us
that nothing is complete

or needs to be.

ADAM

He's usually distracted
as though he's looking

for something over his shoulder
or just beyond his vision.

When he does talk
he speaks about slices

of his day but not the core
of what he feels is missing

from his life.
Yet sometimes he can tell

her specifically
what displeases him

about her
management of the place

the children
and what he wants

for dinner.
"Ribs," he says.

WHAT'S MISSING

My friend says lately he feels that something
important seems to be missing from his life.

He's begun to frequent secondhand stores
so often the clerks must wonder if he's in pursuit

of a lost Vermeer or an unsigned Rembrandt.
Now an old master himself in finding treasure

in yesterday's lapels, he rummages through the rubble
of other lives, lingering over a Depression glass bowl

his mother used to own or fondling a tweed jacket
like one his grandfather wore. He keeps the past

like a swatch to use to match what he thinks he's lost.
But nothing's quite old enough to match his memory

nor moldy enough to smell like the attic in his mind.
Nothing he buys ever fits the longing for whatever it is.

VAN GOGH'S ROOM

A second chair for Theo
or in case he ever had a guest
though this most unlikely.
His few garments neatly hung up.
The bed made. Nothing writhes
like a cypress, or swirls like stars
or splays beyond the frame
like a vase of irises. Sparse, calm,
nothing's out of order.

But this is only half of the room.
What he did not show us: an easel,
some drying canvases, his brushes
and old rags, and the despair
he couldn't find a drawer for.

ECOSPHERE

Developed by NASA, the Ecosphere is an enclosed
bioregenerative ecological system in a glass globe.

Dwarfed beside a great conch shell
with its eternal memory of the sea,

this glass globe seals in a complete world
like our own in exact proportions

of minute brine shrimp, snails, algae,
microbes, pebbles and sea water,

a delicate world in perfect balance
but tepid, colorless and so silent

without tides or birds or wind or fire
without rain or stars or seasons or flowers.

As though already ghosts, these tiny creatures move
hardly at all. Yet what a storm I might shake up

but for the danger of damaging one, even one.
Then how the weight of that death would reverberate.

DANIEL M. JAFFE

ENCHANTED

Moments ago, when you initially shoved through the bakery's glass revolving door, your pupils dilated as if reacting to an ophthamologist's squeeze of drops. You barely noticed the high glass case across the room filled with variously shaped treats; rather, you focused immediately on the face speaking the Mexican-accented "May I help you?" You were struck by the seeming disjunction between manly bass voice and womanly blue eye shadow over dark-complexioned lids ending in heavily mascaraed lashes, orange-rouged upper cheeks, pink-painted lips, wavy ruby-red-dyed hair tied into a bun above a forehead devoid of wrinkles. Neither clearly a "she" nor a "he," this salesperson had integrated both into a self-styled blend. Your thinking settled on "they," acknowledging the limitations of a language evolved from rigid notions from the past. They. They must be around thirty, you decided, ten years or so younger than yourself.

"Everything looks so beautiful," you blurted, ostensibly referring to the tiramisus, cannolis, sugar cookies, and so much more, but referring privately to this salesperson whose stocky torso was blocked by the high pastry case. Was the hidden chest square muscle or shapely softness? Slacks or skirt? Was the faintly drifting sweetness a woman's perfume or a man's aftershave cologne? Impossible to tell.

Although you'd intended to purchase just one pastry to enjoy before bed later in your hotel room, you found yourself ordering a second while asking numerous questions about this cherry-topped cheese cake slice and that, anything to prolong the interaction, to continue hearing the resonant masculine voice snaking into your ears and down. You watched as those long fingers tipped in red-painted nails set one pastry into the pink box beside the other, and you imagined those fingers tangling in your curly brown chest hairs.

Might their smiling eye crinkles be more than routine customer-service politenesses? Flirtatious invitations meant especially for you?

Now that it is time to pay, you fumble nervously with your wallet. You hand a credit card over the high glass counter such that your pale fingers brush against their brown ones eliciting a tingle you haven't felt since the early innocent years of dating two decades past.

Will they make chitchat while the machine hums its credit card processing? 'I haven't seen you in here before,' they might ask. 'Do you live in the neighborhood? Are you just passing through? Might I see you on the sidewalk tomorrow watching the marathon? Are you married/partnered/looking?'

"Sign here, please," is all they actually say in that resonant masculine voice as they—still displaying eye crinkles of smile—set the receipt down on the high glass counter, holding it in place for you with two red-nailed fingers curled in a caress shape that could perfectly cup your cheek. Did they pay attention to the name embossed on your credit card? Will they remember your name, your face, the earnest gaze in your brown eyes? 'Oh yes,' they might say the next time you stop in this bakery, whether tomorrow or on another visit a year from now. 'Oh yes, I remember you—you're the Sfogliatella/ricotta cheese pie. How could I ever forget those deep brown eyes and that curly brown hair with just a touch of gray at the temples?'

As you exchange thank-you's, as you debate whether or not to invite them for coffee at the end of their shift, the crinkly-eyed gaze and deeply resonant voice address an older woman who has just stepped into the bakery through the glass revolving entrance door behind you. "May I help you?"

You slide the pink box from the counter and leave, but not before glancing back. After you leave—another glance through the plate glass window. No, they are concentrating on the customer, not straining to see you outside on the sidewalk. You sigh, walk up Broadway toward your hotel.

You pass a pharmacy, a men's clothiers, a bookstore. You pass a diner, a Japanese restaurant, an empanada shop. You wait at red lights, you cross, you feel the weight of the pastries in your hands as you see before you their hovering face.

Your reaction surprises because for two decades, you've dated only men. You've never dated women, never wished to. Nor has it occurred to date anyone striking you as in-between genders, or both genders, or neither. For twenty years, you've enjoyed only masculine sharings in bed. Traditional manly sharings.

Yet now, it is precisely the blend of masculine and feminine that has set your heart . . . racing. Yes—racing. You can't deny the heat within, the heavy breathing, the acceleration of heartbeat. Certainly, you've attended your share of Pride parades and applauded the ranges of gender expression. But you've never seen anyone quite like this.

Who the hell are they? And why have you been thunderbolt struck?

You picture yourself in bed with various iterations of their body you have not yet fully seen, even clothed. And in each imagining, passion overwhelms as you touch and hold, feel and grip and squeeze. You tingle as those long graceful fingers stroke all over your body while your own stubby ones roam theirs—whichever the shape, hard or soft. You wish to press against that body, feel it press back. You wish to wrap that body with yours and feel enwrapped by it, regardless of the gender source of heat.

Yet what you desire most is to elicit an endless stream of eye crinkles marking joy inspired by you.

In your imagination, they return your passion, show you the tenderness and affection you've truly been seeking each time you've hooked up with this man and that, asserting to yourself that all you've really been desiring is sex. Telling yourself you're better off without the messiness of love. Saying this over and over in defensive excuse for never having found it.

Never having found love because of never having experienced the right kind of person? Have you, all these years, been boxing yourself into an assumption about the limited nature of possibility?

You can barely hold your hotel room keycard steady as you tap it against the locked front door, as you ride up in the elevator, as you tap the card against your room door keypad and enter. You set the pink box down on the dresser and set the pastries carefully in the mini-fridge below, touching paper wrappers that they touched mere moments before. Can you feel a lingering warmth?

The cold of the refrigerator brings you to your senses. Looking for love in all the wrong places all these years? Then which were the right places—Italian bakeries?

Don't be ridiculous. How could you possibly be experiencing such earth-shattering doubts based on a single three-minute encounter with a stranger? You're reacting like a teenager crushing on some heart-throb movie star, an image, a persona onto whom you're projecting longings. Onto someone who does not actually exist.

You're just lonely, you tell yourself, so of course you latch onto the first person offering a smile. Lonely after playing Mr. Professional for four days at a literary translation conference, informative as it's been.

And you're exhausted from attending lectures on underrepresented languages in translation, on methods of translating idiomatic expressions across not just languages, but cultures. Exhausted from participating in several Spanish-to-English translation workshops, offering feedback to younger translators on samples of their work. Exhausted from attending readings, from giving readings, from participating in committee meetings on the translation society's finances, and other meetings evaluating entries for this year's translation awards. Exhausted from spreading good cheer at group lunches and dinners.

In fact, you've been so exhausted day after day that you've had no energy to cruise the bars as you'd originally planned when booking this hotel in Chicago's Boystown rather than at the conference hotel downtown. But today, Saturday, the conference ended before lunch, so this afternoon, exhausted as you felt, you finally took to wandering "your" neighborhood and exploring.

Now's your time to rest so that tonight you can go on the prowl. You'll go bar hopping in the hopes of picking up some pleasant fellow, one whose conversation will be as interesting as his love-making will be hot. And cozily familiar.

After nine in the evening, out on Halsted Street, you scan the young crowd of men and women both, white and black and brown, sauntering along the sidewalk to wait in line at one dance club or another. As you glance from face to face, you catch yourself checking for blue eye shadow, ruby-red hair, dark complexion over a stocky body either muscular or curved. You listen to them all chatter and tease with a sassy "Girlfriend!" or campy "Say what?" accompanied by finger snaps. And you listen for the exact pitch of a certain resonant voice. Nada.

A thought occurs and you check the Internet on your phone . . . . Damn, of course that Italian bakery on Broadway is closed now. Will it be open tomorrow, Sunday? Not that you know if they will be on shift then. No, it will be closed because the Chicago marathon will be routed right down Broadway itself. And you'll be flying back to Seattle the following morning, Monday. So that's that. You should have made a move when you had the chance, but you didn't because you were unprepared to act on the unexpected. On impulse rather than planning. On sudden desire rather than reasoned calculation.

They will remain a mystery in your fantasies.

Maybe you'll encounter someone like them back home. Not that you ever have so far. But maybe you will. Now that you know what kind of person to look for. Maybe.

Realizing that in any bar tonight you would simply be hunting for them rather than being open to realistic company, you abandon the foolish fantasy and return to your hotel room where you drown your frustration in the Sfogliatella that they touched.

You save the other pastry for breakfast, a last taste of them. You shake your head—you must be on a treacly romantic sugar high.

A tossy-turny night. You're awakened around seven a.m. by festive whoops and hollers from the street four floors below your hotel room. The marathon. While sipping Keurig coffee in your room and savoring the ricotta cheese pie and thinking of that face, you flip on the TV to watch marathon coverage before heading down to watch for a bit in-person. You see a New Year's Chinese dragon dance alongside runners in Chinatown. You see a mariachi band on a sidewalk beside runners in a Mexican-American neighborhood where a woman holds a hand-written sign alongside some runners: "Carlos, hay tacos al fin"—Carlos, there are tacos at the end. Food as incentive, a motivation you understand.

You scan the TV crowd, just in case, but you-know-who is not there.

You're an idiot.

Quick shower and you head down to the street. You find an empty spot amid a thin crowd on the sidewalk, stand and applaud the runners in their red/blue/yellow tank tops and black shorts or orange/white/gray T-shirts and black leggings, each sporting a white number on a blue field across belly or chest, some hatless and others wearing white/red/black/green kerchiefs or caps.

"You're doing great!" reads a hand-painted poster held high by a dreadlock-headed woman across the street. "You got this!" some husky men shout at passing runners. "Looking awesome!" a blond-bearded guy yells. One community. Tall runners and short, thin and heavy.

This marathon is freedom, you think. This is striving. This is hope in action, belief in self. This is anything is possible. This is go for it and don't let anyone or anything stop you.

Then you see a tentative wave from across the street. A long-fingered wave in your direction. At first you're uncertain, but then: the waver's complexion is dark with blue eye shadow; ruby-red hair in a bun tops the head; pink-painted lips are smiling, thick beautiful lips that would fit so perfectly against your own. Blue T-shirt tight over thick body. Jeans.

You gasp, surprised even after all your hopeful imaginings.

Do they truly recognize you? They must encounter hundreds of customers a day, yet they remember you? And they're standing right here? Across the street from your hotel? What are the odds? Unless . . . might they have followed you yesterday after serving the old lady customer who entered the bakery just before you left? Might they have dashed out and run after you, wanting to hold sight of you for as long as possible even while lacking the nerve actually to approach? Might they have been equally thunderstruck yet equally shy and unaccustomed to acting on impulse? Might they have planted self purposely across the street from your hotel this morning in the hope of bumping casually into you?

Not allowing yourself another moment to think or question or doubt, you gauge the approaching runners, take advantage of a light lull in the flow, dash-weave your way across the street, and you make it to their side, breathing hard from the dash. From the excitement.

"So nice to see you again," you say, sucking air, inhaling the sweetness of either perfume or aftershave cologne.

"Encantade," they reply in that deep manly voice. 'Encantade.' Neither the Spanish masculine 'encantado' nor feminine 'encantada' for 'enchanted,' but a new form asserting with clarity a unique and confident sense of complete self. Encantade.

They lift a hand—not to be shaken, but to be kissed. You readily oblige, pressing your lips against the back of that graceful hand. You gaze at their square jaw and thick muscular upper arms, as well as the gentle, bra-supported curve of their bust. Singularly beautiful in integrated combination.

Wordless, you bend your elbow and protrude it slightly out. Without prompting, they slip hand through.

You both turn to watch the runners. To watch them together.

As the crowd cheers its support for the runners—"Way to go!" "We're proud of you!"—the two of you look at one another and publicly share a private smile. Your eyes linger on one another's. You feel something wonderful and new.

Yes, you think with an unrepressed giggle. Yes.

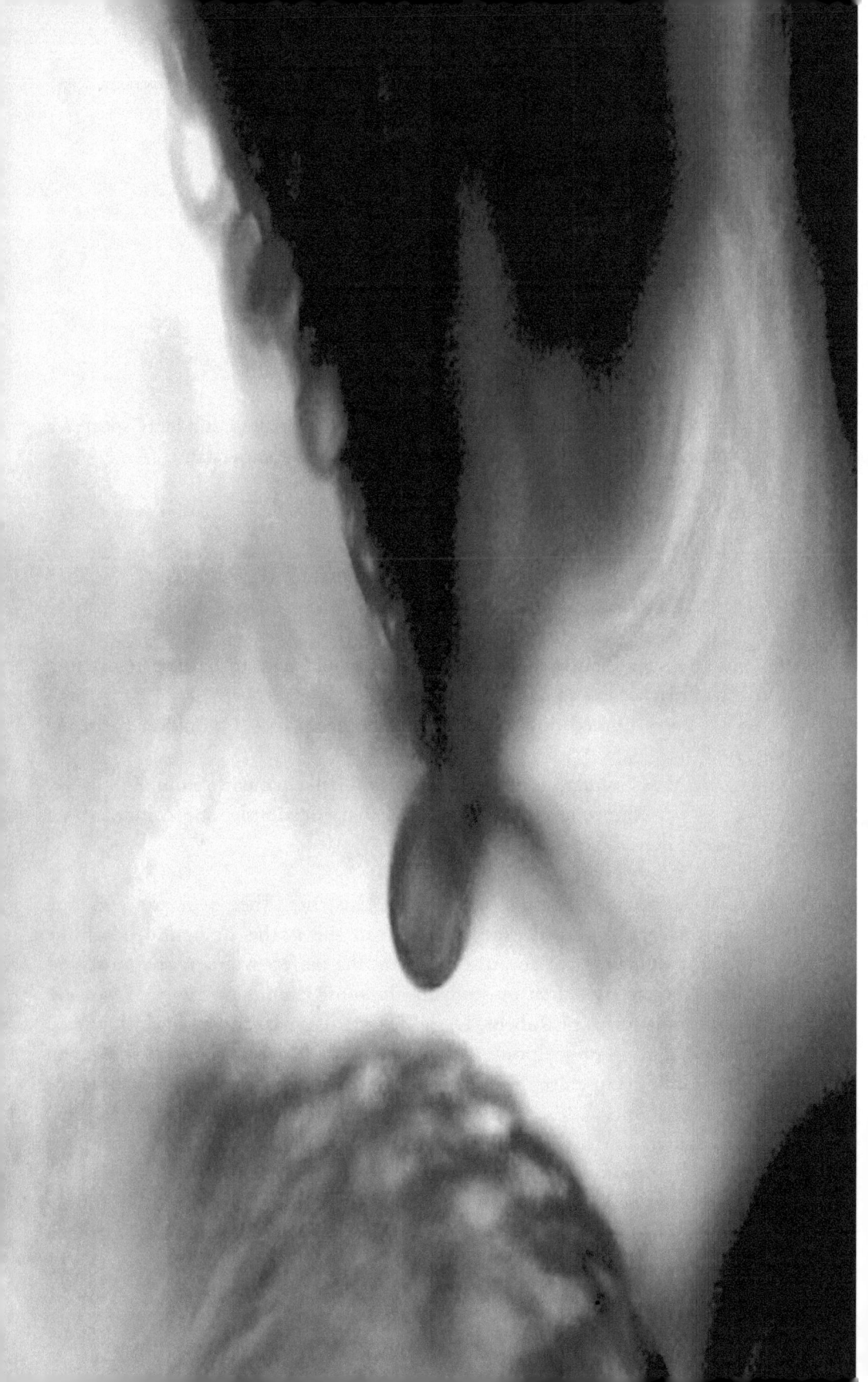

LARRY LEFKOWITZ

THE PERFECT WOMAN

Barry, who came to see Dr. Blau, a psychoanalyst, suddenly spotted a woman in his waiting room. "It's her. *Her! Do you understand? Her!"*

"Who?" asked Dr. Blau.

"Her! Her!"

"Miss Goldfarb?"

"I don't know her name. The Embodiment."

"Miss Goldfarb? Of what?"

"Of all!" exclaimed Barry.

Doctor Blau tried to calm him. "I would hate to have to resort to a straightjacket. It's so passé."

Barry calmed down. "It will not be necessary—I wouldn't harm my All."

"Miss Goldfarb is here in connection with a patient of mine."

"'In connection with'—I accept that. Obviously, she couldn't be a patient herself."

"Why do you say that?"

"Perfection doesn't need a psychiatrist. The two concepts are irreconcilably opposed. You see, Doctor, she is the Embodiment of the perfect woman. I am an artist. To paint the perfect woman, one must find her. I began my search by studying the most famous paintings of women. The ample forms of Rubens, Degas' leggy ballerinas, and so forth. I studied every painting or sculpture with 'Woman' in the title: Soustine's 'Woman and Child,' Lipschitz' 'Woman and Gazelles,' Fontanesi's 'Woman at the Spring,' Rembrandt's 'Woman Bathing in a Stream' and many more. Then, Doctor, and only then, did I begin to catalogue in my mind the perfect parts of the female form—the eyes of the girl drying herself in Renoir's 'Bather,' the breasts of Adele in Rodin's 'Torso of Adele,' the legs of the girl in Burne-Jones' 'The Depths of the Sea.' Are you familiar with any of these, Doctor?"

"Unfortunately not, my taste runs to"—he gestured toward a painting on the wall—"Lictenrobbe."

"A pity."

"And when you find the perfect woman, you will paint her?"

"Paint her—and possess her."

"And you believe Miss Goldfarb is your perfect woman."

I don't know," sighed Barry. "I thought so before, but now I am not sure. You see, it was her lips—not her lips—the lips of the girl in Renoir's 'Bather' that caught me. Your untimely intervention prevented me from knowing that—I didn't get past her lips. I mean, to Adele's breasts, or The Depth of the Sea's legs. There were her eyes and nose and other parts yet to be compared."

"So why did you cry out that she was the Embodiment?"

"Because I got a glimpse of her ankles."

"Her ankles were—unusual?"

"Doctor, her ankles were perfect. They reminded me of nothing so much as the ankles in—

"Spare me the references. My artistic knowledge is largely limited to the Lictenrobbe on my wall. The gift of a patient."

"Very well. *The* ankles. Is that sufficient?"

"And from Miss Goldfarb's ankles joined to her lips you built your perfect woman. Like a Picasso I once saw."

"Doctor, when you have been searching for *The* woman with all the attributes, Miss Goldfarb is the first to possess *two* attributes, and hopefully all of them. Until I saw her, I had reached the point of despair, of breakdown, of total collapse. That's why I came to you."

"You had concluded that the search was an impossible one."

Barry sighs, "I had gotten to the point where I had started to believe that it was what the great paintings of women *hid,* rather than what they revealed, that would provide the solution. That I had not found the perfect woman because I had been following false trails. If, to take one example, I could only see the face of the naked woman in Degas' 'The Tub,' I would find her living counterpart."

"And did you?"

"Doctor, the naked woman in 'The Tub' has her back to the viewer."

"So how could you possibly see her face?"

"I tried to look in *back* of the painting in the museum in order to see her face.

"Did you succeed?"

"I didn't get the chance. A guard hustled me out of there as soon as I got my hands on the frame. At the police station I tried to explain. They finally let me off on the condition that I agree to see a psychiatrist.

Doctor Blau nodded, "And so you came to me."

"Yes."

"And you still have the desire to get behind the paintings?"

"The desire left me the moment I saw Miss Goldfarb. I no longer wanted to get behind. My one desire was to get inside—of Miss Goldfarb. Not in a physical sense . . . in a spiritual one." He hesitates, "Or perhaps in a spiritual-physical one."

"Barry," said Dr. Blau, looking at his watch. "The time for this session is over."

"Very well," said Barry.

On Barry's next visit, Dr. Blau told him that he had pondered his case and believed he could help him. "In a child's fantasies, his mother's womb expands to contain the entire world. The photographs of your paintings you showed me reflect your still present child fantasies. I believe that you wish to undo your birth and return to the womb."

"Miss Goldfarb is not in any womb."

"Your paintings are somewhat mystical. Much modern art has an almost mystic quality. It often gives one the feeling of being enveloped. The artist feels at one with his work in a mystic union, not unlike the nursling on his mother's breast who feels one with his mother. Freud explained the Mona Lisa's smile as the blissful smile of the breast-fed infant. Perhaps I can use the Mona Lisa to bring you back to your mother instead of fixating on Miss Goldfarb. I want to show you some slides."

"A bit of projection, Doctor?"

"Droll, I suppose," replied Dr. Blau. "Are you relaxed?"

"The artist is ever on guard," Barry answered.

"Against what?"

"Against the world."

Dr. Blau snapped on the projector. The slide within projected a vaguely circular form.

"Ah, the breast," exclaimed Barry. "Most Rubensesque of forms!"

"Go on."

"Monet would have liked that one."

"Monet?"

"Yes," said Barry. "Monet, no less than Rubens, loved breasts. He didn't paint them as breasts—rather as haystacks."

"Haystacks?"

"Haystacks. Do you know, Doctor, that no less than eighteen views of haystacks appear among Monet's works. Haystacks in the morning, haystacks at noon, haystacks in autumn, haystacks in the snows of winter."

Dr. Blau nodded. "All breasts, in actuality."

"Yes. As were Van Gogh's sunflowers and Kandinsky's discs."

" Artists unconsciously emphasize the breasts because they cannot accept the womb" Dr. Blau said.

"This artist can."

Dr. Grade, eagerly, "Ah, really?"

"Really, provided it is perfect. Provided it can serve as . . . " Barry paused. "Perhaps I will paint you, a gift in lieu of paying you."

Barry began to walk around the room with his hands "framing" Dr. Blau from various places, as if preparing to paint him.

"You do that so painstakingly. Are there any rituals in your life which you feel subject to?"

"Excluding the ritual of all rituals which so long has guided my life."

"How's that?" asked Dr. Blau.

"The search for the perfect woman, remember?"

"Oh, I do. Yes, aside from that."

"When I paint, there are certain colors I apply to my paintings before others."

"Always?"

"Always. A ritual is not a ritual unless ritualistically followed. Red must always be applied first."

"Why?"

"It would be insulted to be applied second to any other color. It would pale to pink. Red is a blatant color and demands its rights, the foremost being *primoapplicato*".

"Eh?"

"First application," explained Barry.

"You really believe that colors have feelings?"

"What artist does not?" Vincent looked at the painting hanging on the wall. "Except maybe Lictenrobbe. Kandinsky even found a relationship between music and colors. He wrote a play called 'The Yellow Sound.'"

"You said that you follow ritualistically a definite order of applying colors. I would be interested in learning the sequence."

Vincent folded his arms. "It is an artistic secret and shall remain one. Something between me and them."

"Them?"

"The colors. In revealing that I apply red first I have already revealed too much. Yet concerning red, I *will* tell you something."

"Yes?"

"Red is an awful color for the fluid of life."

"Blood?"

"Precisely," said Barry. "I would infinitely prefer blue—an aquamarine blue, like the ocean from which the fluid of life originally came."

"The expanding, all-embracing ocean," explained Dr. Blau. "The womb to which you wish to return."

Dr. Blau snapped on a slide of the Mona Lisa. "I was speaking of the all-embracing ocean. Does it not attract you? Do you not wish to return to the womb of your ontogenetic origin and the great sea of your distant phylogenetic past?"

Barry stared at the slide. "Yes—to return to it as I once sprung from it. This is all I ask."

"All?" said Dr. Blau. "Surely not all?"

"All," repeated Barry as if hypnotized.

"What about your *other* All—the Embodiment."

Barry, amazed, "Why I forgot all about her—the first time in years she has completely left my awareness."

"And Miss Goldfarb?"

"Why she has left me, too."

"Completely?" persisted Dr. Blau.

"Utterly," Barry declared.

"This *is* promising."

"The moment you mentioned the all-embracing ocean I had a vision of my mother embracing me. And when I saw the slide of the Mona Lisa, her smile seemed to envelope me and I felt suddenly as if I were once again a babe at my mother's breast. And then I was no longer on her breast but one with her, in a deeper sense. And I felt—not consciously, not until you spoke of them, did I realize that I felt—the Embodiment and Miss Goldfarb both slipping away together, hand-in-hand, as it were . . . "

"The Perfect woman is dead," concluded Dr. Blau. "Drowned in the all-embracing ocean—the attraction of the returning womb. All power to the great amniotic sea!"

"I feel exhilarated," exclaimed Barry. "Completely refreshed, as if a wave of nothingness has drenched me. . . . At this moment, nothing else matters and nothing can be an obstacle in my path. . . . I can overcome anything. . . . I can paint everything . . . and nothing. . . . I feel like crying. . . . I feel like laughing. You have done it, Doctor. Why I feel I can even apply red *last*. Forgive me for ever having doubted you!"

Dr. Blau, put his hand on Barry's shoulder, "I forgive you. The Profession forgives you."

"Embrace me!" shouted Barry

They embraced.

BRIAN MICHAEL BARBEITO

BREATH

I go through from inside to the outside deck via the automatic doors of an impossibly large ship. Just beyond handsome beige wooden slats that meet white painted wrought iron dividers topped with a teak rail are nothing but waves, the waves of the salt sea. I sit down and watch the horizon line. Some birds appear, birds that are tropical and that follow the ship. I wonder then where and when they rest, and it puzzles me. I sit in a chair with faded orange cushions. A woman comes out and her dress is long and is a print, decorative and unapologetic.

The wind makes it to dance.

I wish I had a camera, she says, *because I would get you to take a picture of me. My dress is part of the wind and I look like a bird. Can I sit next to you? I don't want to bother you.*

Sure.

The woman says she is from the Carolinas now, but lived most of her life in New York City. *I am no Southern Belle.* Her intonation denotes that she is not below such, but rather more expansive, even cosmopolitan.

She remains on my left. A man approaches from the right but I don't see him. She does. She says to him, *You are one fine man. I have had my eye on you. And what a head of hair. Every time I lay my eyes on you I can't take them off. Other men just don't compare.*

I look over, turning my head right to a forty five degree angle. He is a bit shy. He has flyers in his hand and is smoking a cigarette. *I handed out these flyers advertising a party and I put the wrong information and now I have to go around and hand out the new ones. A pain. But I'll get it done.*

He takes a long drag of smoke into his lungs and exhales. The woman and I look at him and then glance out to the sea. *By the way,* he says to me, pointing to a table messy with wine glasses and beer bottles, an industrial strength ashtray with half its metal lid missing, *I don't know you but wanted to*

mention that you handled yourself really well in the midst of that fiasco last night.
My husband and I were watching the whole thing. Bravo. Admirable.

I have no idea what he is talking about because he has mistaken me for someone else, which is a pattern, which is something that happens often.

Thanks but it wasn't me. I wasn't even near here.

He is surprised. I breathe in smoke. The woman breathes in smoke. He breathes in smoke again. We are all thinking.

Say, I say, *What was it all about anyway? Sounds intense.*

Abortion.

Abortion?

Ya. There is a group of women here who think the new anti abortion laws are great. I could hardly believe it from anyone, but from women makes it worse in my mind. I was so angry.

He is political. The non-Southern Belle with the beautiful dress nevertheless says something but I can't make it out for a gust of wind, wind somehow like a breath exhaled by the sea skies. I am generally apolitical, though I have a few ideas here and there that lean left. I let them talk.

He listens to her and is upset about something and then voices his disagreement. They continue on though and are friendly but there is still some problem. Yet, they seem to find common ground on other things, more than not. Their voices fade out. I am thinking. I wonder what will happen if someone mistakes me for a person other than one that had a gift of oratory in debate, or attended an information technology training weekend, or someone who worked construction in the north of towns for a company that I, in reality, had never even heard name of. I wonder some more, about other similar things that have also happened, like the man who identified me as the person who *Did not deserve one bit what Lisa and them did to you . . . no way, not you, who's a good guy and they are wicked evil and I am sorry you had to go through that.*

I don't know any Lisa or group like that.

But so far the reviews of the persons that are not me but look like me are good reviews.

I wonder what would happen if some authorities approach and say simply, *Can you come with us please,* and though it is a question on paper, is not a question in real life but a statement, and I have been mistaken for someone who did something, well, bad, untoward.

Two men come out and sit beside me on the right. One is of German descent. He told me this before. He chews on his cigar. *I am a fisherman, from California*, he says, as if simply continuing a days' old conversation.

There are many rules where I come from about fishing, I offer. *If you get caught out of season they can impound your car, your boat, basically anything.*

That's right. Where I go it is the same. Your Canada country population can fit into my California by the way. And, he puts his hand in front of him to help his point, and makes a gesture of some sort, *there are rules for a reason, and they should be obeyed. It's to protect the poor fishies.*

I laugh inwardly at hearing this big and otherwise tough guy, chewing on the thickest cigar I have ever seen, say, "fishies," instead of "fish."

Beside him I see another man. His face and affect, clothing and something about his general aura all remind me of an old friend who committed suicide. Joseph Campbell said that once you reach over thirty everyone you meet will remind you of someone else you already met. True enough. And then what about fifty? What happens then? Maybe unless you are an extrovert, you don't want to meet anyone else. This man looks like the suicide had he lived another decade or two. The man wears a collar shirt, a golf shirt or something close to one. Non-descript haircut, average height and weight if there are such things. I sense he is not an asshole though, but rather an okay guy. The suicide was also kind, especially as the world goes. Golf shirt is thoughtful but thinks about worldly things. He is talking to someone on his right about points, aero-plan, miles, and he keeps glancing at his phone. This mediocrity consumes many people, perhaps the majority.

I breathe deeply, drawing the tropical air as if right to my stomach. Then I take a drag of nicotine and chemicals in smoke and bring them just as deeply in. I don't really want to talk to any of these people, one way or the other, but there is nowhere else to go to smoke. Its hard maintaining, to coin a phrase, "lonership," upon a ship. Someone apparently caused a fire on a balcony and there is no smoking any longer on such personal outdoor spaces. Everyone pays for the sins of one. Plus it's gotten late, and alcohol is a strange thing,—it loosens the mind otherwise inhibited and lubricates the lips. People say things they otherwise would not. I don't know that I want to see or hear or know what waits dormant in most peoples' minds and behind their lips.

The ship continues at eighteen to twenty knots, but it feels much faster than that in my guts and blood and bones. Maybe I am too sensitive, empathic towards the immediate and not so immediate environment. Luckily, a song sounds, and it's Fleetwood Mac. It's somehow soothing, a calm against the cacophony. Almost everywhere I go, they play Fleetwood Mac, because there is something universal about it. I listen. I listen then to Stevie Nicks as she sings *Dreams,*

Oh, thunder only happens when it's raining
Players only love you when they're playing

The wind picks up. A storm is beginning but they don't close the area. The man with the exemplary hair excuses himself and goes inside. I am back with the bird-dress lady, who is kind and articulate, animated and eccentric and quite beautiful, statuesque. She speaks of many things seemingly at once. America. The Black experience. Diasporas. Education. Employment. Travel. Relationships. Even diet and nutrition. And hens, 'Hens,' which I sought clarification on, and was her designation for women that, as she put it, . . . *talk gossip, talk cheap talk, talk nothing but shit and lies about others, people that spread darkness and not light, not realizing that their darkness is going to come back and visit them double-fold in time . . .*

It begins raining hard.

That warm tropical rain.

The wind pushes it into the deck area.

We stand up together. She is tall by any metric. But I am taller. She asks me if she can hold my arm to go inside, and it is windy, for the breath of nature has become much more pronounced.

I guide her inside at her request.

Where is the women's washroom, she asks.

I don't know. I know the men's is here. But I have never gone to the women's washroom. She walks with me to the stairs and I ask her if she will be okay to find one.

Yes.

I ascend the steps and she disappears down a hallway. I would normally offer to help her a bit more, but I have begun worrying about many things, half formed fears, mistaken identities and the faulty perception of people, even of good people. I am thinking of storms, of politics and division, of life and no life, of health problems and health care, of alcohol, tobacco, and vessels that travel in the night through strong tropical storms.

At the top of the steps I am not out of breath, yet I pause and take a deep breath anyhow.

Then I begin to make my way to my room, walking alone under one green electrical sign after another that illumined the way. I can feel the ship rocking back and forth more than usual, a ship perhaps five or seven stories high and housing more than three thousand people.

The night storm has gathered so much strength by then that I can hear the winds whistling even from the inner corridors of the boat.

They sound like spirits calling out diatribes, rhetoric, pleas, strange joys plus metaphysical pains and warnings, all songs and long wild unabridged strange poems in the middle of a living dream. It is all mixed together in my brain and spirit, and I think of the sea and its vast expanse, of the Atlantic, the Caribbean, of how it rains, the sometimes pregnant sky birthing endlessly through time and cycle its own waters, and how the wind often takes these and places them everywhere, blows them with a breath, and they land sometimes in drips and drops like tears across and down windows, mostly never seen or noted, but having existed nevertheless.

There are spirits simply everywhere, and I think to myself then that many of the so-called dead are more alive than the living.

MEERA JACOB ELAMATHA

HONOR AMONG WOMEN

Fifteen-year-old Sheila frowned at the scene unfolding on the TV screen in irritation. Surrounded by relative luxury in her family's cosy front room, she started to curse the impulse that had made her pause in between channel-surfing, on this channel. She liked to watch old Malayalam movies from the 1980s and 1990s, when the world appeared more innocent and real. She may be a daughter of the latest century, but her soul was an old one. However, over the past half hour, she was slowly coming to the realization that maybe her soul was not all that old.

It was an old movie, starring her favorite actor Mohanlal, along with a pretty actress which she thought was the famous Parvathi. God only knew the name of the film, and now, she was just so disgusted with the plot-twist that she simply turned off the TV and scowled into the distance. Her mother walked into the room and ruffled her hair, which she tried unsuccessfully to avoid. It also made her grumpier.

"What's with the long face, molu?"

Sheila the teenager just rolled her eyes, quite sure her mother would never get it. As though reading her mind, her mother simply chuckled and tweaked her nose.

"I'm here if you need help." The older woman walked off to the kitchen, her aim a steaming cup of chai. She took a deep breath; she could smell the thunder in the air. It was the perfect weather for chai.

Left to her own devices, Sheila mournfully contemplated the darkening skies outside. She got up and walked out on the veranda and sat down on the top step leading outside, and stared at the sky. The thunder clouds were so dark, they looked blue. A cold wind began to blow, and Sheila wrapped her arms around her body and hunched in on herself.

It was so wrong! Her conscience made its presence known. *Stupid movie.*

"Here you go." Her mother walked up and handed her a steaming cup.

Inhaling the familiar aroma, Sheila felt a bit consoled. That was when it began to rain. At first in drizzles, then with a vengeance. She looked at her mother who was sitting on the wicker chair, her eyes closed in bliss as she enjoyed her tea. Her mother loved the rain, and she loved to watch her mother enjoying the rain.

"If I get raped, will you and Chachan make me marry him?" The question was out without conscious thought.

"Hmm . . . what?" Sheila could see her mother wrench her mind from somewhere far off and give her a strange look. She waited patiently while her mother looked at her like she had sprouted a third eye and webbed feet.

"Of course not!" she replied at last. "What an idea!"

Something in Sheila calmed and she settled back against the wall behind her and took a sip of her tea. Her mother still watched her curiously. The rain blocked out the world, cocooning mother and daughter in an invisible veil of comfort.

"In that movie I was watching, the hero's sister got raped by the son of an important businessman." Sheila said after a while. "He then insisted that the guy marry her, in order to preserve her honor."

She turned and looked at her mother, "Why would he do that?"

For a long time, her mother did not say anything. She simply stared out at the rain, coming down in torrents and debated how to answer her child. With an insight borne of motherhood, she knew her answer would be a turning point for Sheila, the point where she would bloom and spread her wings, an adult in spirit, if not quite in body. She had been waiting for this moment since her birth, but she still felt so inadequately prepared, to help her daughter's metamorphosis, so to speak. But she had to try.

Sheila was still waiting patiently, uncharacteristically so for a flesh-and-blood teenager.

"For a long time, people associated a woman's honor with her virginity." Her mother began, a bit hesitantly. "You know all about patriarchal society, how women are oppressed etc. etc."

Sheila nodded to show that she was following.

"Women were seen as weak creatures who should always be protected under a man—her father, her husband, or her son. She was never free because she was always vulnerable. Her virginity was her gift to her husband; it denoted her loyalty and love. Therefore, if a woman was found not to be a virgin at the time of her marriage, she was said to have no honor because she had given what rightfully belonged to her husband to another man. This being the case, when a woman was raped, it was considered justifiable recompense for the man to marry her, thereby preserving her honor, because her virginity was now in the hands of her husband."

"But she was raped! She did not gift him anything, it was taken from her!" exclaimed Sheila quite worked up. "And, isn't honor a part of a person's behavior? So shouldn't the man, with his lecherous behavior, be the one without honor?"

"I know dear," her mother sighed. "But remember, this was when society was completely patriarchal, and objectified women. They never thought from the woman's side, what she suffered, what she would have to endure for the rest of her lifetime with no hope of anything better because divorce was unheard of and considered the height of dishonor."

The jolt of thunder rumbled through Sheila and the dark closed around her as she thought of the countless women who would have had to follow society's dictates and marry their attackers and be victimized for life. The very thought of all those men strutting around, stuffed full of *honor* made her want to gag.

"People don't think like that now, though." said her mother "Well, not many anyway," she amended her words. "Things have changed a lot for women over the centuries. Not least because there were always pioneering women, *and men*, who pointed out the injustices dealt out by society and paved a better path for future generations."

"So, it's all good now?" asked Sheila in a doubtful voice.

"Of course not," her mother laughed. "There are still injustices, against women, against children, and against men. Every generation requires a few pioneers who are willing to sacrifice themselves and forge new paths and new ideals. It is a never-ending battle, on both sides."

The rain seemed to gain in intensity and the wind was lashing it well into the veranda. Lightning seemed to tear the sky asunder, and thunder roared. But Sheila reveled in this display of elemental fury. After all, wasn't nature always depicted as female? And man had never quite managed to tame or conquer her, and he never would. She was just that powerful, just that unstoppable.

Looking at the glitter of pride and determination in Sheila's eyes, her mother felt a small proud smile unfurl on her lips as well. The names and faces of countless female warriors flashed through her mind, some wreathed in the shadows of history while others held quite close in the confines of her heart. Fighters all, in myriad ways. The flaming torch now had a brand-new bearer, and nature was celebrating her coronation.

Written in response to the comments made by Indian Supreme Court Chief Justice Bobde, in March 2021 when hearing a case against a young man who was accused of raping a minor girl. CJI Bobde told the man, "If you want to marry, we can help you. If not, you lose your job and go to jail. You seduced the girl, raped her. . . . We are not forcing you to marry. Let us know if you will. Otherwise, you will say we are forcing you to marry her."

Malayalam words used in the text:
>   *molu*: affectionate form of addressing a girl child
>   *Chachan*: father

GAYE D. HOLMAN

THE ELUSIVENESS OF WHOLENESS

Is wholeness a state of mind? A way of life? An unobtainable dream? The more thought I give to the question of wholeness, the more I doubt if it can exist. Oxford defines wholeness as a condition of harmonious whole and a state of being unbroken and undamaged. That's a big ask.

Is it possible for a person to truly experience wholeness? Certainly, there are enough workshops, retreats, articles, and conversations about it to be obvious that this is a desired condition. But in this imperfect world, can any of us be completely harmonious, unbroken, or undamaged? Probably not, my cynical self says. I think it's more likely that if a person claims to be whole, in reality they are not. And those who know they fall agonizingly short of the definition, may be closer to wholeness than anyone knows.

I spent my professional life working in the criminal justice system, getting to know men and women who have fallen so short of wholeness that they are banished from society. I have written about their shared agonies, comforted them as they cried in private over the harm they have done to others. I've been cussed by victims and their families as I put words to my perceptions that we are moving our justice system away from wholeness, making the world a meaner place for all of us.

These days I'm continually reminded of a high-profile crime that occurred in my city thirty-six years ago. Three young people, heavily into drugs, were responsible for the grizzly stabbing death of a young man from a fairly prominent family. Urged on by his sociopathic wife who wanted his insurance money, two friends fell under her spell, stabbed the husband to death, and dumped his body into the lake of a well-known golf course in town, making the headlines even larger. The murderous trio received life sentences with the possibility of parole after twenty-five years.

I became well-acquainted with the two women involved. One became my clerk in my prison education job. I worked beside Rita for years, and kept in touch with her after I left. Through letters, she frequently shared her anguish about her past actions as well as her desire to be free. "Born again" into a life of religion, Rita yearned to live rest of her life in service to the victim's memory.

She has accomplished much in her years in prison, and remains free of any disciplinary problems. She chose jobs that she felt would benefit others—recording books in braille, training dogs for the disabled, and serving the chapel programs. She approached the parole board on the fourth, and last, time armed with a notebook filled with certificates of achievement, a master's diploma in Christian counseling, and dozens of letters from the community supporting her release.

But in spite of all her achievements and support, Rita does not think her life has real meaning. Only a breath of free air, the ability to help her aging mother, and the chance to talk to others about her life's shortcomings in honor of her victim will allow her wholeness, she says.

)()(❋)()(

Thirty-six years ago, another family was decimated. Their oldest son was killed, and they walked through his blood on the stairway of his home. The pain, the anger, the hopelessness of the future without him dealt them a paralyzing blow. Their anguish was indescribable. I understand they did not fully recover. They could not find their way. The parents eventually divorced. Their loss took over their lives.

They spent the next thirty-five years making sure their son's death was avenged. They contacted media outlets, traveled across the state to make their appeals, and did everything within their power to make sure paroles or pardons were not granted to any of the three. Recognizing that Rita alone had demonstrated rehabilitation, they said they did not care. They worked to see that the required objective criteria for parole was set aside. They wanted all three to remain in prison the rest of their days. Nothing less would satisfy them.

When Rita became the last of the trio to receive a serve-out on the life sentence, meaning she can never be released from prison, they celebrated in the media, and breathed a sigh of relief. "Now we can have peace," the brother was quoted. The family hoped that by permanently removing the three people who reminded them of the worst day of their lives, that they would find wholeness again.

Of course, the family was wrong in thinking their lives would finally become free of the anguishing memories these now aging people brought to their minds. Criminal justice reform groups took up Rita's cause. Articles in her support appeared in the paper. A website keeps her plight constantly in the public's attention. Perhaps the family will cringe if they spot a "Free Rita" T-shirt as they walk down the street. Will the hoped-for peace remain with them?

✕✕✽✕✕

It is a tale of tragedy. A tale of people searching for wholeness that may never come. Who is the closest to wholeness? The one who works consciously each day to make amends for the horrors she has brought onto others but feels she will never be whole? Or the good, but still-grieving family who thinks they may again find wholeness with the cost of three lives in payment for their son?

I end where we began. Is wholeness possible? If so, do we know when we have it? Is it possible that people who feel they have finally achieved wholeness, have not? And for those who feel wholeness is impossible for them, is it possible they are closer to wholeness than anyone knows?

* Her name has been changed for the purpose of publication.

CHARLES BROCKETT & HEATHER TOSTESON

ANTHONY

When does it become acceptable to become your environment?

Every time we read the transcript of our interview with Anthony, we pause, amazed at the level of growth and maturation he was able to achieve for himself during the twenty-five years he served in some of Georgia's worst prisons. There is a seeking intelligence here that allowed him to survive a traumatic childhood and equally traumatic adulthood and come out whole. Angry—and whole. Entering prison at seventeen, he made a vow to himself, "You a man when you walk across this. When you walk across this in twenty-five years, you still going to be a man." He did more than that. He came out a moral, humane adult. *How* he built that inner structure is the heart of his story. A tall, handsome man in his early fifties, we first met him when he spoke at a meeting of A.B.L.E., a social change group advocating criminal justice reform.

Early Influences

Anthony's early life was brutal and traumatic. One of fourteen children, he was orphaned at seven when his mother was beaten to death by her boyfriend. Three months earlier one of Anthony's brothers, who had been arrested with two of his other brothers, died when his jail cell was set on fire and he was severely burned. Forbidden to see his brother because he was a child, Anthony remembers his mother and brothers emerging from the hospital room crying. His family believed that the police had set his brother's cell on fire. "And that's when I really started looking at life in this aggressive, fuck-it type mode," he said.

The question of where his anger originated is probably less important than all the many ways it was stoked by his subsequent experiences. After his mother's death, Anthony and his siblings were separated and sent to various foster settings. The one Anthony talked about most was the group home where he stayed the longest. It was his third or fourth placement. He admired the women who started the home: *But when you have that many troubled kids in one place and you don't have counseling, you can imagine what it turn into. I didn't want to be someone who got beat up every week. So I became aggressive.*

He described how they were punished: *They had a long hallway, and if you got in trouble, they would put kids at each side of the hallway with belts and you would have to undress and you would have to run from this end to that end and they would whip you, and that's where my ability to fight came from. I went through that one time. I went and the first boy who hit me, I stopped and beat his ass. And then I ended up having to fight all the kids in the dormitory because the dormitory parents said, "Git him" and so I had to fight all of them. I was about nine.*

Speaking with us, Anthony could clearly see that his aggressiveness had strong environmental origins, but back then he didn't. *At that point in my life, I'm rebellious, angry, mad——but I've lost the reason why I'm mad. I don't remember how my brother died, not on a conscious level. I don't remember how my mother died. On a conscious level it's not there, but on an unconscious level it is. The various abuses, the molestations in the foster homes, they're in the back of my mind. But when I try and analyze my anger, they're not there. It wasn't until I actually was in prison that I understood.*

He was clear that anger is preferable to fear: *Kids should not grow up enraged or in fear. They should definitely not grow up in fear. I would prefer they grow up enraged.* He saw how his aggression evolved and his sympathies narrowed: *I can actually see the transition from being a defender of people. I used to be the type of kid who if I saw you bullying this guy, I'd say, "Nah, fight me." Because I was good at fighting. And I can see the transition from that to "Man, forget it. If he don't fight for himself let him get beat up." I can remember how it progressed.*

The impact of labeling was not abstract to him. At ten or eleven, Anthony punched the father in his foster home and ran away after the man had grabbed him by his penis. When found by the police two days later, he was put in juvenile detention: *The judge labeled me as incorrigible. I'm like ten or eleven years old. So incorrigible meant to me that I had been violated. I didn't know that it meant that I was bad. Because again no one explained anything to me.*

Anthony liked the juvenile detention center. It felt cleaner and more orderly than the foster homes he had been sent to, but by this time, Anthony's lack of trust was profound and affected his perception of all the social institutions that he came into contact with: *Going back to my mind state at the time: I hate the police because my family said it was the police set my brother's cell on fire, so I've always hated them. I don't trust social workers because in my mind it was all about business. And I don't like secret organizations. . . . I hate them because if you spend time in the foster system you spend a lot of time in the court system because the court has dispensation to allow these people to put you here or there. It was always these secret deals that decided your life. They come out of the room and they shake hands and then they send you somewhere and you get abused and what kind of deal was that? And then they'll find out about the abuse and they'll move you to another place and then another deal will be swung and then the people make you feel like they doing you a favor by having you there. You know, "I didn't have to take you." "Nobody wanted you." dadada. And you going, "And you swore on that deal for me!" So you stop trusting that these people have your best interests at heart.*

Delinquency

Anthony's fighting got him kicked out of several more foster placements, and his schooling suffered. He had never done well in school, although he seemed to do well in sports and in drumming. His illiteracy went unnoticed because in each new school he was placed by age rather than accomplishment. Anthony now realizes that he is smart: *I know that now because I can read and learn anything. I never been to mechanics school, but I bought a book and rebuilt a car. I never studied computers but when people have computer issues, they call me and I say, "Let me read up on it and I'll get back with you." I can grasp things like that. But in school I just never could.*

Sixteen was a pivotal year for Anthony. He dropped out of school, joined Job Corps, served his first adult sentence, next a juvenile sentence, then was arrested on the rape charge that would, by the age of seventeen, send him to prison for twenty-five years.

Job Corps, in his description, was both a wonderful reprieve from some of the strains of his life in Atlanta and a fertile training ground for advanced criminal behavior. He had joined to study electrical wiring and plumbing, and to avoid prosecution for a burglary charge. He liked the mountain setting in Franklin, North Carolina and Job Corps felt similar to foster care, although the young men in it came from up and down the Atlantic coast and were older and more aggressive. His Atlanta peers were cowed. Anthony was not. In the style he had perfected from his foster care experience, he asked who was the baddest dude around and promptly picked a fight—which he won. This established his standing among his peers but had the unexpected, to Anthony, consequence of expulsion from the program. He talked his way back in by agreeing to avoid other altercations because he liked the quiet and cleanliness of the mountains.

But his basic values and lifestyle remained unquestioned. He was not alone. The occasional visits to Atlanta were orgies of delinquency: *Imagine this. A hundred kids out of the mountains, brought to Atlanta and let off the bus with a "Meet us back in six hours." People ended up with life sentences. We were able to come to the city, do whatever we want, get out on the bus and be out of sight for months. For the criminal mind it was a perfect opportunity, so we would come with plans—we're going to rob this, break into this, and that's how we came down to Atlanta.*

On one of these trips, Anthony was arrested for a "snatch burglary." Sent to adult jail, he responded exactly as he had in foster care and Job Corp. "Now I'm in the big boy game. I'm sixteen. I look like a girl, so now its time to man up. So I go in fighting." Anthony immediately attacked the jail inmate in charge of his cell and was put in the hole, a closet sized room with no windows, a hole in the floor for a toilet, a mattress for a bed. He contemplated suicide but there were no means available. His court-appointed lawyer didn't ask his age and he was tried as an adult and was given a year, six and a half months of which he served in jail.

When he came out, he tried to go back to a foster home, but they told him he was too old: *So I'm sixteen, homeless and I have a felony. No skills. Can't read and write. Don't know where my family at. I started stealing everything I could. Petty crime. Breaking into stores. Breaking into people's houses. Got a job helping rebuild this guy's house. I would live in the house while we doing the job.*

He was arrested for one of these burglaries, but this time was sent to juvenile. While there, watching the news one night he heard an announcement that a woman named Annie May had been beaten to death. She was his sister. His girlfriend was able to enlist the help of the chaplain, and Anthony was allowed out for the funeral. This allowed him to meet the rest of his family, most of whom he hadn't seen since he was seven. This reunion simply deepened his involvement in crime: *Two of my brothers had just gotten out of prison that week. One of them had did ten years, the other had did fifteen, and we all got out at the same time. Their mentality no better than mine. The three of us together, we can make stuff happen. You know, I want to be part of the family.*

I said sure, whatever, I'm down. So I became sort of the enforcer for the family.

Then Anthony started dating a fifteen-year-old girl, and was caught in bed with her by her irate mother, a police officer. At first the charge was sexual assault, which was then raised to rape. Anthony claims their relationship was consensual and that if in the early 1980s they had had rape kits, there would have been no signs of force. At first he didn't understand the seriousness of the charge: *At the time, I didn't see it as a big deal. The rape was only one crime. They could have sent me to prison for any number of things that I did. I didn't know sexual assault was a major life-changing situation. All that mean is I got me some. But by the time I went to court it was rape. Twenty-five years in prison.*

When it came time to go to trial, just before they began to choose the jury, the judge called a recess and called Anthony into his chambers: *He said, "Look man, you ain't but seventeen. If you go to trial now, they will give you life. Look, go ahead and plead guilty. I'll give you a twenty-year sentence. You'll do maybe five in and fifteen on probation. Now, if you tell anyone we had this conversation I'm going to deny it to my grave." I say, "I understand."*

So we go out there. I pled guilty. He gave me twenty-five year. I'm like, good God almighty, that's not what he said. Remember, I got probation on another robbery, which was another five years. By the time I finished with the court system, I had 165 years total. And I'm mad to death. Can't read. Can't write. But I'm mad.

Incarceration & Survival

In Jackson, the diagnostic prison, Anthony behaved as he did in foster care and jail. He immediately attacked his white cellmate for calling him a nigger, then, as soon as he emerged from three weeks in the hole, he attacked his former cellmate's brother: "It made sense to me. I figure if my brother was there, I would have done the same thing. So I figure, let's get it out of the way."

He was promptly sent to Mount Vernon State Prison, which he described as an old school penitentiary. "They give you the same old speech, 'You think you're bad, we've seen worse. You're not bad. We break you here, we break you there.' Dadada." But more than the hard labor, Anthony's concern was self-protection. He ran into one of his previous co-defendants, someone even smaller than he. Anthony revealed at this point that at seventeen he was only 5'5", with a voice that was still changing, revising all our mental images of his behavior. "But super aggressive," he repeated. He used this aggression to protect his friend from sexual assault—which again sent him to the hole.

But the hole was not the worst place for Anthony, any more than high max and solitary would be later. It allowed him some respite from the need to be so constantly primed to fight. He had been so malnourished that he actually gained weight on the day-old ball of mashed oatmeal, okra, and poke salad he was fed once a day. When released, he immediately got into another fight, went back in the hole and again returned larger and stronger. "It was my trend."

Anthony did not restrict his aggression to fellow prisoners. He described why he attacked one officer: *He was new. Making comments you shouldn't make in prison. Referring to us as a group as "bitches," "criminals," "you ain't shit, if you get out of line, I'm going to—". . . daddadadah. So I'm sitting around looking at the old vets, they just sucking this up. And in my mind, that is slave mentality. And I say, "You all scared of this dude?" Officer is like, "You have something to say?" So I busted him in the mouth.*

When Anthony talked about his fights, he slipped easily back into his mindset at the time: *My situation in my mind was permanent, and I had to remove this threat.* As he spoke with us he viewed his behavior with some detachment and humor, but he also gave the impression that he still felt his choices, given the circumstances, were appropriate. His choices were no longer driven completely by force, however: *You have to establish your rules if you are going to survive in that environment. And my rules are: I don't snitch. I'm not afraid of anybody. I don't tolerate disrespect from anybody—it doesn't matter if you're an inmate, guard, or warden. And I don't steal people's stuff. I did my whole sentence like that. I tried to make sure that everybody knew that.*

 After attacking the officer, Anthony was sent to Reidsville, the most notorious of Georgia's prisons. Reidsville was a very different environment and he had to reconsider his approach: *These dudes are killers and I know they are killers. I'm meeting people who been in prison twenty-five years already, two guys who have been there thirty-five years. I'm meeting guys who killed four people and six people. I'm meeting people who killed their family. I'm thinking, "Oh, this is serious. All I got is a rape. Now I have to step my game up." But I don't want to catch another sentence in prison. I don't want a murder charge in prison. But I got to strike fear in these guys in some kind of way or I got to establish a level of respect. And I did both.*

Anthony established respect by keeping his word: *If I told you I was going to be there in five minutes I was there in four minutes and fifty-eight seconds. And that goes a long way in prison. If I told you I was going to do you, you know you're going to get done.*

The other way Anthony established respect was to offer to fight the biggest man in prison, Big Bubba, who was six-feet six-inches and weighed 280 pounds. Anthony explained his reasoning to his opponent: *"If you beat my ass, everybody expect it. If I win, nobody will beat my ass as long as I'm in prison. Let's fight." We fought and he beat my ass. Last fight I ever fought. This was the respect thing.*

Another important collateral benefit of the fight was that he started being mentored by a fellow prisoner, Iceman, who was skilled in karate, and served as a trainer for the prison CERT teams. Anthony learned martial arts, jujitsu, karate, and boxing. "I already had heart," he said. "Now I had skill."

Anthony wanted respect from the administration as well. He had earned their fear. By this time he had a history of five assaults on officers: "My rule with the officers was the same as with everybody. You don't treat me with respect, I'm coming to get you." When an officer called him "inmate," he reacted: "Wait a minute. My name isn't inmate. I can never allow anyone to call me that." He ended up fighting two officers, then an entire CERT team: "So, they take me in the elevator and try to beat me but there were so many of them in that little space, they couldn't really hurt me." He was taken to the fourth floor, but protected from the officers who wanted payback by a very old prisoner whom he had helped early in his stay at the prison, who announced, "'You can fight me, but I'm not going allow you to go in and jump on that kid.' So, he saved me," Anthony observed. "I started learning from this. If you do good things for people, they tend to come back. They don't come back right away, but—"

High Max & Self Actualization

SAFETY: Anthony was put on high max for five years for assaulting the officers: "High max, you spend twenty-three hours in your cell, come out for one hour. But it was cool because now I'm focusing on me." It may indeed be that Anthony was able to develop a measure of insight because when he was in high max he didn't have to focus on physical threats in his immediate environment. He would say that when he came off high max the first time (he went twice, each time for five years), "I was ready in the sense that I knew prison wasn't going to break me."

Anthony also began to be more introspective now that he felt that his safety was more secure: *When you go through prison you go through stages. I didn't know it until I was there. First you have the disbelief—twenty-five years! Then you got the anger. Then you get to the self-pity—Nobody care about me, nobody send me any money. Nobody even know I'm here. You go through that depression thing. And then you say, "Fuck it, I'm going to do me. So what is it I need to do? I'm going to get my body in better shape and I'm going to learn how to read and write."*

LITERACY: Anthony wanted to learn to read and write because without these skills he was not able to act in his own defense in the penal system. For example, when he entered prison, he had a 165-year sentence. A white inmate he met at Jackson, one he had defended from rape (not because he liked him but because he disliked the men ganging up on him), had read about his trial and sentencing and told him to write the Sentencing Review Panel to ask that his sentence be reviewed because the sentence seemed disproportionate for a first adult felony conviction. Anthony didn't feel he could admit that he couldn't read or write, so responded noncommittally. Picking up on the reason for his hesitance, the inmate wrote to the review panel for him. The appeal was successful and Anthony's sentence was reduced to twenty-five years.

On high max, Anthony learned to read by following the advice of a fellow inmate: *He say, "Read something you like. Read a fuck book. There's going to be a lot of oohs and aahs, but I guarantee you'll like it and finish the whole book." And he's right, I finished the whole book! But it made sense. It still makes sense: Read something you like.*

LEARNING: Anthony experienced an intellectual awakening that would be startling anywhere: *So I started reading these books. Then I bought me a dictionary and began reading about different words. Then I started watching the news and really listening to what they were saying and when they said a word I didn't know, I'd look it up. And then we started like little debates about politics and social situations. I'm still mediator. I'm still somebody you don't fuck with. But now I'm becoming more intellectual. Then I find that my favorite subject in the whole world is Greek mythology. Yeah, trip me out! The very first Greek book I read was The Iliad. Then I had to read The Odyssey. Then I had to read Dante. And then Lucretius. Then I got into Kant, a German philosopher. Then Nostradamus. Then I started getting into math. I would study fractions for three months, then algebra for three months, then geometry or trigonometry for four months.*

COMMUNITY: This intellectual drive became, improbably, a shared experience. *We started a class where we were teaching other guys. There were forty of us on high max and out of that only two had their GED. We made a neighborhood challenge. "We got to be here, so lets do something with it. We going to make sure everybody can get their GED." So at nine o'clock we're going to turn all the televisions off (televisions don't go off until 11) and we're all going to study. Whoever is good at whatever subject, you teach that subject. And the rest of you going to shut up and learn something. My theme was math, so I taught math on Monday. Another guy was good in history, and he taught history. We did that for months. Then it was about time for some of us to start coming off of high max, so we said, look we got to take that test. But we agreed we were all going to take it at the same time. So we called the schoolteacher over and everyone passed except for one person.*

Character, Criminality, Environment

Anthony began to wonder what it was that led some people to prison and others not. *I started looking at my environment—this guy's locked up for child molestation, this guy's locked up for double murder, this guy killed his whole family, I'm locked up for rape. And whenever we got to debating, I would say, "Look, we all came from different environments, but we all ended up right here. How the fuck is that possible?"*

"What do you mean? We all got caught."

"Yeah, but we different. You went to school, you went to college. You had a mama and daddy." It never made sense to me how all these people with different personalities and different situations ended up right here. So it had to be some common thread. And then it was, I'm just like these dudes. I'm aggressive. I'm selfish. So I saw those things as what brought us to this fucked up place. So, yeah, I saw them as character flaws.

This line of inquiry brought Anthony into conversation with the warden and the prison psychiatrist. One day Anthony stopped the warden as he passed the solitary cell in which Anthony was confined and said, "My mind isn't right in the sense that I can't understand: What makes me different from Ted Bundy? What makes me different from Charles Manson?"

"I don't know, you need to talk to a psychiatrist," the warden answered.

"Can you arrange it?" Anthony asked.

"I'll see what I can do." No psychiatrist appeared, so Anthony persisted, in his usual tactful fashion, the next time he saw the warden. "Hey Warden, I try to respect you as a man. But if you can't honor your word, you're a bitch."

"Who you calling a bitch?"

"Your actions are bitch-like. Because as a man, if I tell you I'm going to do something, it's done."

The psychiatrist soon appeared. He told Anthony he couldn't put him on the caseload because he wasn't officially classified as mental health. Anthony told him that was a matter of opinion but that he just had some questions and needed answers: *Every month you all come by our cells and ask us these simple questions: "Do you know what today's date is? Do you know who is the president of the United States? Are you OK?" And everybody here passed that test. But man, guys over here are throwing feces on each other. That can't be normal behavior.*

The psychiatrist said, "In this environment it is."

"See, that's one of my questions," Anthony went on. *When does it become acceptable to become your environment? I've been raised around criminals my whole life and for some reason I don't really fit. I've never done drugs, I don't drink, I don't abuse women. But I'm a criminal. How did that happen?*

So the psychiatrist started to give Anthony books to read about socially deviant behavior, showed him how psychological profiles of criminals were done. Anthony read but nothing felt like it fit his situation. Not until he read *The Odyssey* for the third time. The excitement he had felt at the time was still vibrant in his voice as he described that moment of insight: *It was when Odysseus had got so arrogant he stood up on a mountain and said, "I, Odysseus, conquered Troy." It made perfect sense to me then. Because I had made my whole life about me. My mom died when I was seven. I hadn't thought about her since I was eight. My brother died when I was six and I hadn't thought about him. That's when I started thinking, "I got to start bringing other things into my life. I've got to start being more empathetic toward other people's situations." It was already there. I think it is for everybody. But it can be forced out by hardship or circumstances, and I allowed it to be forced out.*

Anthony described why he felt the psychiatrist himself was only unintentionally helpful: *He was helpful without knowing he was helpful. His ignorance was helpful. Like I asked him, "How would you know if you was insane?" He said, "You wouldn't." I said, "Exactly." But he didn't understand. So I said, "So if you were insane, you would think you were sane and everybody else is crazy." He said, "Yeah." So I said, "So I'm not insane because I don't think the rest of you all is insane. I just think you all live life in a way that's totally foreign to me. So I don't think you're crazy. But I'm talking to a guy next door who is totally crazy because he think we all crazy except for him."*

ANGER MANAGEMENT: Anthony was required to take both anger management and substance abuse classes, although he never used drugs. He defined his own issue not as anger management but as anger abuse. Anger management was the closest he could come. But he objected when the instructor told him they needed to get away from "learned emotions, like anger and rage." Anthony disputed him, saying, "No, if anger was an emotion it would have to be innate. The behavior expressing anger would have to be learned." The instructor kicked him out of class, but later, taking a refresher training with the psychologist who developed the course, the instructor brought up Anthony's objection and the psychologist told him that Anthony was right. Anger was innate, its expressions learned. So, the instructor apologized to Anthony and gave him his certificate. Anthony accepted both, but told the instructor: "Man, if you only talk to people you agree with, you're not going to learn anything. You got to have that outside agitator, you know."

The instructor, impressed by the whole interchange, told him he was going to be OK. Anthony objected: "Right. I have twenty-five years in prison, I have nowhere to live, no education, no money and no family. How am I going to be all right?"

"You have logic," the instructor told him. "You're going to figure it out."

"And that's how I did my last ten years, " Anthony said.

FAITH: Anthony spent much of his remaining time in prison focusing on his spiritual life. He was drawn to Islam for three reasons: "Number one they were all black men and I needed to see that black men can do something other than what I had done. And in Islam you have to study, it's a requirement, and you are going to be tested on your knowledge and there is code of conduct and a code of ethics and I thought I needed all three of those."

But what he felt was the greatest contribution of his interest in Islam was that it exposed him to other religions as well: *You have to study so I started studying about Christianity and Judaism and Hinduism and Buddhism as well as Islam, and I came up with the conclusion that the Bible is one chapter in that big book, the Koran is another chapter in that big book, so that helps me expand as far as accepting other people.*

MENTORING: Anthony also started mentoring younger inmates about how to survive in prison: *I tell them, It's simple, man. This is prison. You're going to be here a while. Here's what you do. Don't snitch. Don't borrow money from anybody you don't think you can beat in a head-up fight. And never ever compromise your principles. Principles are like rubber bands, the more you stretch them, the weaker they get. So never ever, not one compromise. The best way to establish a solid core is to establish a solid body, so I would teach them how to work out and then I'd tell them, "A body is designed to carry something bigger, so now let's work on your brain."*

Purpose: Anthony had some advice for Corrections about how better to prepare people for reentry while in prison, especially the importance of positive expectations. Corrections, he said, like the military, breaks people down but, unlike the military, fails to build them back up: *It does a great job at destroying you but don't replace it with anything. If you come out just thinking "I got to survive," that's when you get back into what you were doing before. I had a great expectation when I came out: I'm going to succeed without causing other people detriment. People said how? I told them I don't know, but it won't be from sucking from people who don't have anything to give.*

Anthony pointed out that prison encourages negative emotions by depriving people of purpose: *The only emotion you really need in prison is anger and rage. That's all you need. You have to be ruthless and you have to stay mad at something. That again is a failing of the prison system: There's nothing to feel good about.*

Purpose gives us a sense of time and of future: *Once you give a person a purpose that regulates their time. You have no sense of time in prison. You have no sense of tomorrow or next year. If you have no sense of tomorrow, you have no expectations, if you have no expectations, you have no plans, you don't have a future. And that's how you spend every waking moment in prison. And then you come to society and that is the same mentality you deal with. When you see people out here robbing and killing, they have no sense of time, they have no plans. Society creates that when you totally disenfranchise people.*

Now a homeowner, Anthony pointed to HUD as an organization that helped shape and promote purpose. *Some organizations understand this. Like HUD, the housing thing, they understand this. I don't know if it was on a conscious level or if it was just happenstance, but once you establish a foundation with a person, HUD mandates certain things for a person. You have to be in a house for five years, so that's time. You have to maintain a house, so that's a purpose. So, I'm asking, did they luck up on this philosophy or did they read Kant?*

Reentry

Anthony had been out of prison for six years when we talked to him. He was in a stable relationship, had stable housing and a steady job. On a personal basis he helped other people who were reentering and also worked with A.B.L.E. to help reduce structural barriers to reentry by such actions as Banning the Box. He was proud of what he had accomplished and was determined not to return to prison.

He still faced challenges controlling the expression of his emotions, especially if he felt he was being treated unfairly, but those expressions almost never involved physical violence although they often involved active, furious defiance. "I've been in prison twenty-five years. It was hard at first for me to maintain a job. I still had attitude. I was still defensive and argumentative."

Anthony obtained a union job at FedEx by applying online. A woman in Pennsylvania interviewed him. He immediately told her he had a history, but she asked him how old he was when it happened (sixteen) and how old he was now (fifty) and told him she would take a chance on him if he had a clean drug screen and a clean driver's license. He knew he wouldn't have gotten the job if he had applied directly in Georgia. He sometimes felt exasperated because others didn't work as hard as he and his co-worker Carlos, both ex-offenders with strong work ethics. But Carlos reminded him, when he was tempted to quit, "Bro it's not even about you. What about the next dude getting out of prison looking for a job and they use you as an excuse for why they won't hire him?"

Anthony identified two significant systemic barriers to his reentry: being listed on the sex offender registry and, more troubling, probation itself.

SEX OFFENDER REGISTRY: One of the difficulties with the constraints of the sex offender registry and sex offender probation is that they treat everyone as if they were an active predatory pederast, so the level of surveillance is formidable. This is especially difficult if the actual act was having consensual sex with a girl a year your junior. Even though a judge had informed Anthony that the extensive state probation surveillance conditions for sex offenders didn't apply to him because his conviction predated them by fifteen years, he was registered on the federal sex offender registry because it was retroactive by thirty years.

There is a psychological impact to being on the registry that exceeds direct surveillance, which Anthony expressed poignantly. In his mind, listing on the sex registry effectively barred him from having children: *The best I can tell you is I never molested a child in my life. I hate having this sex offense because when I first got out of prison, all they talked about was stay away from churches, stay away from daycare and they said it so much and they bring so much authority behind it—like I'll send you back to prison for life—that I started to think, "Maybe I am a child molester." And I started avoiding kids.*

And then I thought, "This isn't even life." If you take away the political, the economic aspect of how we're living, life basically comes down to growing up, having kids, or if you can't have kids, watching other kids grow up. And that's the sense of time and purpose. I love watching kids, I love hearing them giggle. We live in a townhouse in a cul de sac. Across from us is a subdivision. You can hear kids playing, laughing. I leave the windows up so I can hear. But I think, I can't even indulge in that cause I'm registered as a sex offender and they have me so scared.

It lasts forever. Forever. I don't have kids. Shandra, my wife, she knows I would make a great father. But I can't. I don't want my child up under that "Did he touch you?" That's one of the real barriers for me.

PROBATION: But even more challenging to Anthony was his relationship to probation—one that he believed, with some objective confirmation, was designed to push him back into prison. He felt that their actions and attitudes were, like prison itself, exclusively focused on breaking him down, proving that he was innately criminal. He was determined to prove them wrong. This struggle started as soon as he was released:

When I first got out of prison I had forty-eight hours to report to probation. Remember, I don't have a car. I don't have any money. But I got to get there. So I get there. He says, "How things going?"

I say, "They're OK. But I don't have any place to stay. I've been gone for twenty-five years. I don't have any money. I don't have a job."

So this probation officer, this protector of the public interest, says to me, "I don't give a fuck. You can live up under a bridge for all I care, but just give me the address of the bridge you live up under."

Anthony was determined to prove his officer wrong: *The next time he saw me, I had a car. The next time he saw me, I had a job. The next time he saw me, I had two cars. And the next time he saw me, I had two cars, two jobs, and a house. So each time he saw me, it was like I didn't give a fuck either. So he started telling his supervisor, "Anthony is too arrogant."*

At the beginning they had me so scared. I would walk down the street and people would come up to me and say, "You just got out, didn't you?" "How you know?" It was my whole persona. I go into a store and I'm afraid to touch anything, even if I want to read it. I said, "Fuck, they making me into what they want me to be."

So I went into there one day and—again I don't recommend this to everybody—the probation officer begin every meeting the same way, "Now you know we can send you back to prison, right?" Every month. Every month. So one day, I just said, "Fuck you. Do what you're going to do." He said, "Huh?"

"Man I work two jobs, I bought two cars and I bought a house. I'm engaged to be married. Nigger, I'm doing better than you. What the fuck am I trying to do running around trying to live up to your expectations for me for?"

So he called his supervisor. This is how they decide to break you. They come in, they got their hands on their gun. "Who is it?" Now I have seven probation officers, with guns, standing around me. "We could send you back to prison."

I say, "Man, like I told him, fuck you all. Do what you going to do." The head probation officer, they call him chief, he say, "What's your judge name? I'm going to call him." I say, "That mother-fucker dead. He fucked up my life and died. I don't give a fuck about him. I don't give a fuck about you. You not going to make me what you want me to be. I ain't going to be no homeless, begging bum scared out of his wits because you niggers" (because there won't nobody but black men around me) "want some power. Now I'm going to live my life or you can send me back to prison."

They sent me home.

Anthony had gained the enmity of his probation officer. So when sometime later he had to leave his apartment on short notice on a Friday evening, even though he informed his officer he was leaving and would call him Monday to give him a new address, the officer first thing Monday morning had a warrant sworn out for his arrest. (The rule is you must inform your officer of a change of residence before moving.) Anthony spent $4,800 to hire a lawyer to represent him at a probation revocation hearing "because I don't have any rights in a probation revocation hearing." But Anthony was not without support.

The probation officer said, "He quit his job and we don't want him to. We want to revoke two years." The judge say, "OK."

They say, "We hear rumors he's using drugs, he's staying out all night partying."

But if you have a lawyer they have to let him speak. My lawyer said, "Your honor, my client works two jobs." (I work at the Kroger warehouse 1 a.m. to 12 p.m. the next day, then go home, shower, eat something and go to a part-time job at FedEx for two and a half hours, then I go home, shower, eat again and go to sleep and get ready for the night. I did this every night for seven-eight months.)

My lawyer say, "Your honor, my client has never used drugs. You can test him now."

The supervisors from both my jobs came to court. My ex-girl came to court. The first person that gave me a job came to court. The judge was so mad, he finally gave me a turn to speak.

I said, "Your honor, the probation department is not trying to help anybody reenter or acclimate to society. Their job is to take my manhood, take my self-esteem, take my pride and stomp on it and make me desperate enough to go back to prison." Then I started to tell him about the things they were saying and doing.

The judge was so mad, he said, "From now on Mr.L__ you never have to report to them again. If they want to see you, they have to come to you. And if you're not there, they have to call and make an appointment with you."

Anthony's challenges with probation continued and put a heavy toll on his relationship with his partner. *Before we even got into a relationship, Shandra and I went out and I said, "Listen, I'm a good person. And I'm a good man. But there are going to be outside pressures on our relationship. The question is going to be if you can handle them. You're going to say yeah, yeah right now. But I explain to you, precious, they going to come from the police, they going to come from the probation officers because they know that one of the main ingredients to keep people from reoffending are strong community ties, personal relationships, and a job. They can't just go into the jobs anymore and say, 'I'm just coming in to see about Anthony. He's under probation care.' And then they'd fire you. They can't do that anymore, so they go after the relationship."*

My probation officer right now calls Shandra almost every week and asks her, "Are you OK? How is Mr.L __?" And Shandra says, "Why that woman keep calling me?" And I tell her, "Her job is to create outside pressure on the relationship to the point you want to break up with me."

Now Shandra beginning to understand it. One night, about one o'clock, we both asleep and the police come and bang on the door—boom boom boom— and we got three floors. So on this particular night we're on the third floor. I go downstairs. There are about nine police cars there. With their lights on. They hiding behind walls and the bushes with their hands on the guns. "You Anthony?"

"Yes."

"Just checking to see you're home."

"What the fuck?" There are nine cars out there. "Why you all doing this?"

They just walk off.

The next day, we went to the police station and made a complaint and they ain't been back but that's the kind of outside pressures I told her were going to come because I know how this system works. It is not designed to help me stay in society.

Anthony when he started his interview emphasized that what he really wanted to achieve through his story was to have "the emotional content of reentry to be exposed." The reasons for some of these actions will surely be differently interpreted by probation—some are from their point of view simply procedural requirements they have no control over. With the new Department of Community Supervision, which has a more rehabilitative stance, the abusive nature of the interactions has probably toned down considerably. But these procedural requirements do have relational costs that work strongly against effective reentry—ones that Anthony has described vividly—and that have practical costs for us as a society. As stringently as Anthony asked himself in prison whether criminality was innate or learned, we have to ask ourselves if *recidivism* is innate or learned—and, if so, who is doing the teaching?

We are richer for having in our midst someone with Anthony's resistance, which is also resilience, intelligence, insight, passion for self-improvement, and a defiant and noble commitment against all the predictions, all the odds, to living a richly productive life *without causing detriment to others*. Anthony's anger remains a powerful challenge of him and those around him, especially those tasked with monitoring his reentry. But what would we as a society have lost if he had ever agreed to take himself at society's estimation as stupid, worthless, unwanted, and innately bad?

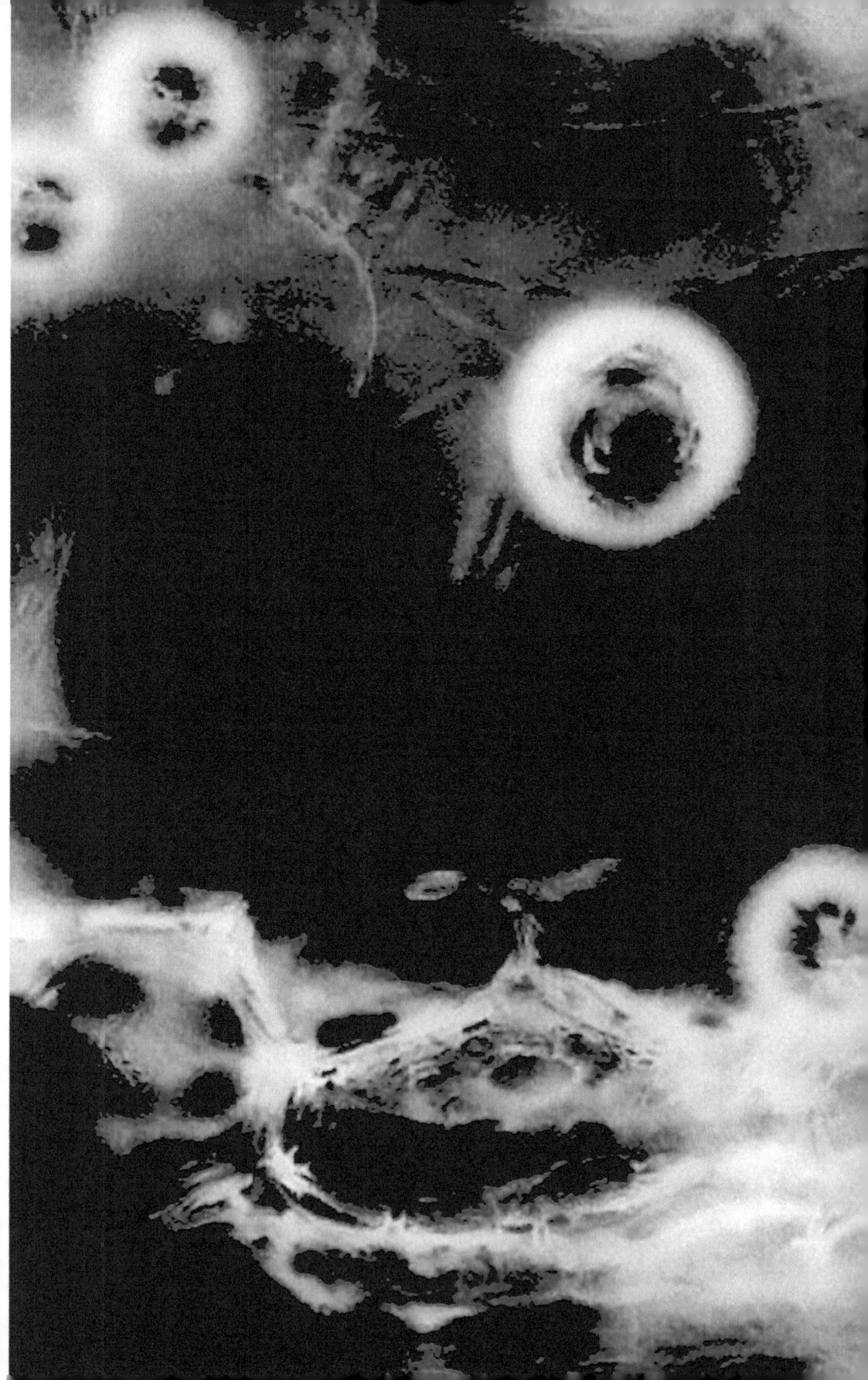

NANCY WERKING POLING

INTRUSION

Partner, that's what Pastor Alice calls the lady who lives with her. As if they're cowgirls or work together on *Law and Order*. Clarisse is the partner's name. She has a job teaching English lit at the college.

"What a waste," Dallas Hines said about Clarisse. Only to the old timers, though. She's real pretty, Clarisse is, blonde, with a stately posture. If he were fifty years younger, Dallas says, he'd bed her and change her mind about liking women. That's what he claims.

Thelma tries to imagine what two women do in bed, as there's no Tab A to insert into Slot A. It occurs to her that she never gave any consideration to whatever kind of knicky-knacky Pastor Bill and his wife, Marsha, engaged in. Homosexuals are different, though. Whatever they do, it's unnatural, disgusting.

Dr. Hessinger, head of the college biology department, chaired the search committee. A strange looking bird, he is. Around his bald spot a circle of long hair is pulled back in a ponytail with a curl at the end. He testified to Pastor Alice's skills as a preacher, counselor, and administrator.

Word of the church hiring a lesbian pastor has spread in the community. There's been so much curiosity that local TV channels gathered outside the church on Pastor Alice's first Sunday. When Thelma watched the evening news on TV, she saw that the only people interviewed were those who think Pastor Alice is the cat's meow. Nobody asked Thelma. She would have told them that she knows a thing or two about sin, and homosexuality is a sin and she prays every day that Pastor Alice will repent and sin no more. That's what Jesus would say. Like he told the woman at the well: "Go and sin no more."

There have also been "Letters to the Editor" in the local newspaper denouncing the church for going against God's laws. A lot of Adam and Eve, not Adam and Steve remarks. The whole business is an embarrassment.

Willard Hapwell, who works for an advertising firm, designed a logo:

"We All Belong," in the middle of a pink triangle. He explained it during Minute for Mission one Sunday. It means that race, ethnicity, and sexual orientation do not disqualify anyone from being an active part of the fellowship. The logo has been made into pins, stickers, and a banner that hangs to the right of the chancel.

Somebody handed Thelma a pin. She doesn't wear it.

)(O)(❋)(O)(

In their bi-weekly physical therapy sessions Allen doesn't treat her like the old lady she is but like a—like a special person. He makes her think she can accomplish any goal they set together. Lift those weights, stretch that hip. His smile lightens her heart. Yet he stands before her one Sunday, greeting her in that sweet way he has, and introduces the man standing beside him.

As his partner!

Meanwhile, Pastor Alice has organized a monthly intergenerational dinner and made a point of welcoming older members, even arranged for their transportation. Several times Allen and his partner, Vince, have sat across the table from Thelma. Together the two men are hilarious, and she finds herself laughing more than she's laughed in years. They also ask her questions. As a young woman did she work outside the home? They're especially interested in her years teaching junior high English. She must have been tough to survive in that kind of setting, they've told her, and she knows they're right. She was tough.

This evening Vince is in charge of the program. His elbows on the podium, he leans forward in intimate conversation. He's not amusing like he usually is but tells what it was like to be a gay adolescent boy. "In the locker room I figured that no one would know I was gay if I told crude jokes about fags. Do you have any idea what that does to a thirteen, fourteen-year-old kid? I was the brunt of my own jokes, and I hated that part of me."

As he continues, as he speaks of his gratitude for the acceptance shown him by this congregation, Thelma's eyes water. She thinks back to her years of teaching and remembers boys taunting each other. Was there a Vince among them? Should she have made more of an effort to understand and intervene?

)(O)(❋)(O)(

"O Father and Mother of us all," Pastor Alice prays. Thelma doesn't close her eyes. A habit carried over from the old church building, where the congregation worshiped before the move to the suburbs. She used to look up at the stained-glass windows and absorb the peaceful scenes illustrating the twenty-third Psalm: the meandering sapphire blue stream, sheep grazing in the pasture with its variegated hues of green. Over the years, whatever was going on in her mind—heartache over the still birth of her only child, worries about whether Alton was really on a business trip, the hysterectomy—so much of the past haunted her.

Here the windows are squares, of clear glass. An old oak tree stands outside the window she always sits nearest. She studies it every Sunday during prayer. The scar, oblong and blackened, from where a major limb once broke off. A heavy branch running parallel to the ground, extending outward like a bench. She's seen children play on it after services, sometimes straddling it like they're riding a horse, sometimes walking it like a balance beam. She imagines the tree once surrounded by its brothers and sisters and cousins. All of them gone now, some chopped down for firewood or to make way for suburbs, others maybe struck by lightning or eaten by termites. How did it happen that this tree alone survived? Maybe it thought, with all the others gone, *At least I'm surrounded by a lovely meadow*; later, *At least the builder left me standing.* Then, *At least they left me standing when they built the church.* The tree has had to adapt.

"Amen."

In front of Thelma a woman she doesn't know, who's about her age, places her arm around another older woman, gives her shoulder a squeeze. They turn to each other and smile.

There's something between these two, a bond. Have they had to love each other in secret? For years, decades? Others like them have been cut down or struck by lightning's violence. They and their love survive.

Thelma opens her hymnal. She used to be a soprano, but now her voice wavers on any note above B-flat. She joins the congregation in singing "How Lovely is Thy Dwelling Place."

The song ends. There's the rustle of bulletins, the bumping of hymnals returning to the racks.

Suddenly the sanctuary is eerily silent. Thelma looks to the front and blinks in bewilderment. Everyone else is staring too.

At the foot of the steps leading up to the pulpit, an unknown man faces Pastor Alice. Boldly, solemnly. His navy-blue suit, white shirt, and striped tie indicate he isn't one of the mentally ill men who on occasion wander in from the street. In his right hand he clutches a Bible against his heart. His left arm holds a little girl, no more than three years old. Her arm circles his neck while she studies his face. Unlike the few children her age scattered throughout the sanctuary, who wear summer casual attire of shorts and t-shirts, this girl has on a pink organdy dress with puffy sleeves and black patent-leather shoes. Matching organdy bows adorn the ends of her light brown pigtails.

There's something menacing about the man, the way he scowls, his thick black beard, his piercing blue eyes not unlike those of Jesus on the cardboard fans they had at the old church. But this man is no Gentle Savior.

In the pew in front of Thelma the women she noticed minutes earlier move closer together. In front of the women Allen protectively puts his arm around Vince. The young mother next to Thelma quickly swoops up her little girl, places her on her lap, encircles her with both arms. The new organist looks as if she's watching a horror movie, her eyes wide open, her jaw gaping.

Pastor Alice rises from her red-cushioned seat. Later she'll admit she has no plan. Should she shake the man's hand and welcome him or kick him in the groin?

As Pastor Alice steps across the dais toward the intruder—for that's clearly what he is—he shifts the little girl to his other side. He continues to face Pastor Alice.

With his left hand he raises the Bible above his head. "You are an abomination unto the Lord!"

Pastor Alice trips over her robe as she descends the three steps, forcing her to grab hold of the nearby newel post. Standing no more than three feet from him, she brings into focus what a big man he is. Well over six feet tall, he has to weigh at least two hundred and fifty pounds.

His response to her approach is to lower the Bible slightly, extend it behind him as if he intends to use it as a weapon.

He turns to face the congregation, his voice as intimidating as his size. "How can you call yourselves God's people?" he thunders. "You have turned from righteousness. Leviticus 18:22: 'Thou shalt not lie with mankind, as with womankind: it is an abomination.' Also in Leviticus: 'If a man lie with mankind as he lieth with a woman, both of them have committed an abomination; they shall surely be put to death; their blood shall be upon them.'"

By now the ushers, two men and two women, have come up the side aisles to the front of the sanctuary. Having never considered the value of burly ushers, the church has instead appointed elderly men who want to stay involved and women competent at bookkeeping. Nonetheless, the four, all in their seventies, gingerly approach the visitor from either side. Pastor Alice shakes her head a gentle no.

"Let him say his piece," she says.

"The Apostle Paul, he himself speaks of the sin of homosexuality in Romans 1:26 and 7: 'For this cause God gave them up unto vile affections: for even their women did change the natural use into that which is against nature.'"

Thelma's dumbfounded. Who is this man? Does he think he speaks for God, thundering up there with his Moses voice, his size that dwarfs Pastor Alice, his confidence that he has the right to decide who's going to hell?

The intruder places the little girl on the floor and again raises the Bible high, this time with both hands. "'And likewise also the men, leaving the natural use of the woman, burned in their lust one toward another.'"

The little girl, her eyes downcast, steps away from him a few paces. Out of nowhere Marie Rivers reaches out and draws her close. She offers the girl the activity bag handed out to young children at the beginning of services. All the while Marie allows her hand to rest on the child's shoulder.

What kind of father is this man, Thelma wonders, bringing such humiliation upon one so guiltless? Suffer the little children to come unto me. Suffer the little children. Suffer the. . .

"Read your Bible, people. It is the word of God. To ignore God's word is to choose the everlasting pit, the fires of hell." Here he employs his most dramatic tone of voice yet: "The wages of sin is death!"

Thelma, who considers herself an expert on sin, looks at the two women in front of her, at Allen and Vince. At Pastor Alice—why, an aura surrounds her. A protecting light. There's no hint of anger or fear on Pastor Alice's face. That woman, Thelma realizes, that woman has been called by God. Thelma gazes up at the banner: "We All Belong."

Without considering her actions, she bolts from her seat, stands straight, thrusts her shoulders back, plants her feet firmly. She reaches for the hand of one of the women in front of her, who stands and reaches to her right for her partner's hand. Who stands and reaches in front of her for the hand of Allen. Who stands and reaches for Vince's hand. Who stands. . .

Thelma begins to sing. "Blest be the tie that binds/Our hearts in Christian love." Others pick up the strain. Hands joined, all of the worshipers move to form a large circle surrounding the man and girl.

Thelma's eyes fill with tears. She looks around to see others take tissues from pockets, wipe their cheeks. We all belong. We all belong. That includes her. She belongs to this group of people who stand here, hands joined, singing and crying. And they belong to her. Her whole body feels indignation melting, the shards scraping at her core for years floating into the ether, giving way to a softening. There is no place in her heart for anger or condemnation.

Not even condemnation of the man who now stands in the middle of the circle. He takes hold of the little girl's hand again. His tone softens. "God told Jonah, 'Arise, go to Nineveh, that great city, and cry against it; for their wickedness is come up before me.' But Jonah did not. . ."

He seems suddenly to realize that he's surrounded. He looks from side to side, confused.

"Our fears, our hopes, our aims, are one," the congregation sings in robust voice, "our comforts and our cares."

The man breaks through the circle, pulling the little girl behind him.

Everyone turns to watch him leave. On the back of his jacket someone managed to place a sticker: "We All Belong," within a pink triangle.

This story was inspired by an actual intrusion at Downtown United Presbyterian Church, Rochester, NY, in the mid-1990s.

EISHA A. MASON

VIGIL FOR CHARLEENA LYLES

The Underground Museum is a portal into dimensions of Blackness.
A community treasure, sandwiched between a repair shop
and carpet store, it's also known as the *underground temple.*

Stepping over the threshold, enter this vortex where material
and spiritual dimensions intersect. At each turn, pass from
one gallery to the next, journey deeper into sacred chambers
of the temple. A metal door swings open to the rambling courtyard,
protected from the hustling city beyond these walls.
The air is warm. Daylight fades. Leaves stir in the gentle evening breeze.

We have come to honor Charleena Lyles—
a mother, just one hundred pounds, standing five-foot-three,
shot dead in her kitchen by Seattle police,
"Grasping a knife in her hand," they said.
Her children witnesses, they fired seven times—
two in the gut, two in the back, one each in the chest, arm and hip.
Savage bullets penetrated her belly, killed her fetus, fourteen weeks old.

Families, activists, artists, elders gather. A stillness permeates
this crowd. Every chair occupied, those standing make room
for ever more people filing in. Children snuggle, embraced
by their parents. Others sit cross-legged at their feet. All of us
gathered at this holy place. Speak her name—Charleena Lyles.

We are here to weep, so we will not break,
to grieve in the strong bonds of Black family.
We have come to pray for healing and strength.
We have come for comfort and counsel.

Surrendering to inner sight, worlds that lie in between,
the outdoor stage transforms into an altar.
Our walk to the fire pit morphs into a processional.
to the inner sanctum of an ancient African temple.
As dusk slips into a welcoming night
like the glow of fireflies on a summer's eve,
we light our candles from our neighbor's flame,
illuminating the darkness with our light.

The children begin the roll call. From their young,
no-longer-innocent mouths,
"Mike Brown. Freddie Grey. Ezell Ford."
The presence of ancestors growing strong and palpable
at the sound of these voices and the calling of names.
"Malcolm. Martin. Harriet. Ida B." They emerge
out of the darkness, encompassing our circle,
bathing us in the aura of eternal love. We are held
in the bosom of these ancestors.

The fire pit morphs into the granite sarcophagus,
the Kings Chamber of the Great Pyramid.
Hush! Behold the body of Charleena Lyles
lies beautiful in the royal coffin before us.
Her spirit rises—awake, aware. Though they say
she struggled with mental health,
radiant peace emanates from her calm countenance.
Welcome the spirit of Charleena Lyles.

Taking form in the shadows—Sheneque Proctor, Mary Turner,
Latasha Harlins, Tanisha Anderson, Sandra Bland.
Black women who found no safety in this harsh world,
no protection from the violence that stalked them.
No justice for their deaths, erased from America's memory.
But tonight, we lift them high with songs of love.

Our prayers for Charleena rise in the night.
We seek out her star in the Milky Way.
As we listen for ancestral guidance,
peace covers us in a heavenly cloak.

The ceremony concludes—flames extinguished.
Hugs and soft words as we depart.
Together we shall press on for justice
with generations of ancestors at our side.
They guide us forward, ever forward toward
Freedom's bright and glorious day.

HOW TO WALK ON HOT COALS

Is it easier to rage
than feel the pain—
the kind you think
you won't survive?

Better to rage
than fall prey to grief—
the earth cracked open
beneath you?

Will attacking the foe
save you from Fear—
your breath caught
short in your throat?

Does it comfort your heart
to spit out your disdain,
protect you from questions
you'd rather not ponder?

It's never enough.
Relief does not last.
Your fire is burning too
hot.

Pause. Time to stop.
Hold yourself close.
Sooner or later, you must
tend to your wound.

Let the tears come.
Let loss settle in.
Let despair fall to the floor.
Make space for the ghosts
hidden in shadows.
Let Grace
minister to your soul.

Let Peace overtake you
though you fight all the way.
Let Love rise from the
well deep within.

Flow in the vast current
of Love that you are.
Remember courage is
what you are made of.

Complete your journey down
to the Heart's Underworld
Return to the surface
bearing Light.

Only when you sit calmly
in the fire of Life
can you walk on hot coals
and not burn.

LINDA QUINLAN

BABYSITTING DANNY

Danny and I met for the last time
at a Fifth Street bar
two doors down from his mother's old haunt,
where I ran numbers for her
to the bookie joint across the street.

My hand reaches for him,
then retreats.
He is a tear waiting to fall on my cheek.

I taught him to steal at Woolworths.
He emptied his small pockets
and delivered his haul
to older girls he wanted to please,
balloons, eye liner, and candy lips
that bled into our mouths.

His mother was forty-three
when she was found dead,
empty pill bottles beside her,
no last words
in an apartment above Katz Bagels.

I wanted to steal something for him,
to give him his mother's laugh,
the way she held a martini
and a cigarette.

I paid for his beer
and offered nothing more.
He lagged behind me.
My car door opened and shut.

Six months later he's dead.
Beer bottles on his floor.
California sun on my face
when I get the call.

A gun in his hand.
No suicide note.
A lone picture of his mother
on his nightstand.

FATHER TOM

(A priest at St. Rose)

Forty-five years after Faz's suicide
Tommy finds me on Facebook.
His sister perched behind familiar eyes.
A distinct cooing of someone long gone.

He was twelve and I fourteen
when I taught him to French kiss.
I had totally forgotten
what he remembered as divine.

He asked for pictures of his sister
and I had many,
Teased brown hair, black nylons
and a look of toughness we all flaunted.
In one she's standing beside Diane,
who carries a switchblade in her pocket.

We didn't talk about the mental hospital
or how we all schemed to break her out,
give her back her daughter
stolen from her arms
and move to New York City.

Her daughter is over fifty-five now,
brought up in some suburb.
I hope she is loved,
has a fuck you swagger
and devours Italian food.

Neither of us cries.
Until I'm alone in the car
and the oldies station plays
"Tommy, can you hear me?"

I was a pinball wizard at Revere Beach.
Faz cheered me on
and insisted we hang by the Himalaya
raising our voices
toward the waves.

Before the time
when nothing would bring her joy.

JOHNNY TOWNSEND

REPARATIONS, ONE FAMILY AT A TIME

There's been much discussion of reparations over the years and, while several countries have made progress in repairing some of the harm committed against historically oppressed populations, the U.S. government has remained resistant. But as we continue to fight for justice on a larger scale, we can start considering reparations on a personal level. Whether we're white or not, let's ensure our wills leave most of our wealth and property to historically marginalized people.

Most of us have neighbors or coworkers who are black, Latin, Asian, indigenous, or who belong to another marginalized community or ethnicity. They don't need to be our closest relations for us to include them in our will. God knows many of us have biological family members we're not particularly close to, either.

When my partner died in 2005, he didn't leave a will. Since we weren't legally married, his estranged sister inherited the house, the car, the pension, the money in the bank—everything.

When I began another committed relationship a few years later and bought my first home, I immediately consulted an attorney to draw up a will leaving the house to my new partner. But I also included a secondary beneficiary. If my husband were to precede me in death, the property would go to a friend.

At the very least, we can all ensure that our second beneficiary be someone from a marginalized community.

Studies have revealed that a large part of the wealth gap comes from inherited wealth. A family that's been in a position to pass down even a small amount of wealth, property, or opportunity over generations will have a family member alive today who's been able to attain a strong education and a good job, who probably owns a home rather than rents.

I'd never have earned my first college degree without my family's support, and the down payment on my home was gifted me by my father.

I see a great many people in my position—white, educated, well-traveled, with "good" jobs—who look down on those struggling. "If I can do it, why can't they?" Oblivious to the ways our struggles, real as they are, were lessened by our privilege. I'm still living paycheck to paycheck, after all, and that's with a tremendous head start in life.

Unfortunately, with corporations gaining more control over our lives, even those of us with privilege often have a lower standard of living than our parents. Everyone is struggling these days. And if we have children, we want to ensure they're taken care of first after we're gone. So not everyone will be in a position to pass on wealth to non-family members.

But some of us can. Perhaps we're single. We're childless by choice or circumstance. Perhaps we have children who have done well for themselves and don't need all our money and property. Whatever the situation, some of us *are* in a position to make reparations on a personal level.

We should certainly keep pushing for tuition-free college and vocational training, universal healthcare, subsidized childcare, fare-free public transit, and other policies that help level the playing field and make life more livable for all people.

Most of us already have "causes" we'd like to leave money to, whether that be PBS or Greenpeace or the American Indian College Fund. We want to support organizations that demand the wealthy and corporations pay their fair share of taxes to benefit all of society. There's a lot of competition for every penny we might leave behind.

But let's consider adding the option of transferring some of our wealth to people in our lives from a historically marginalized community.

And let's talk to a neighbor or an attorney today.

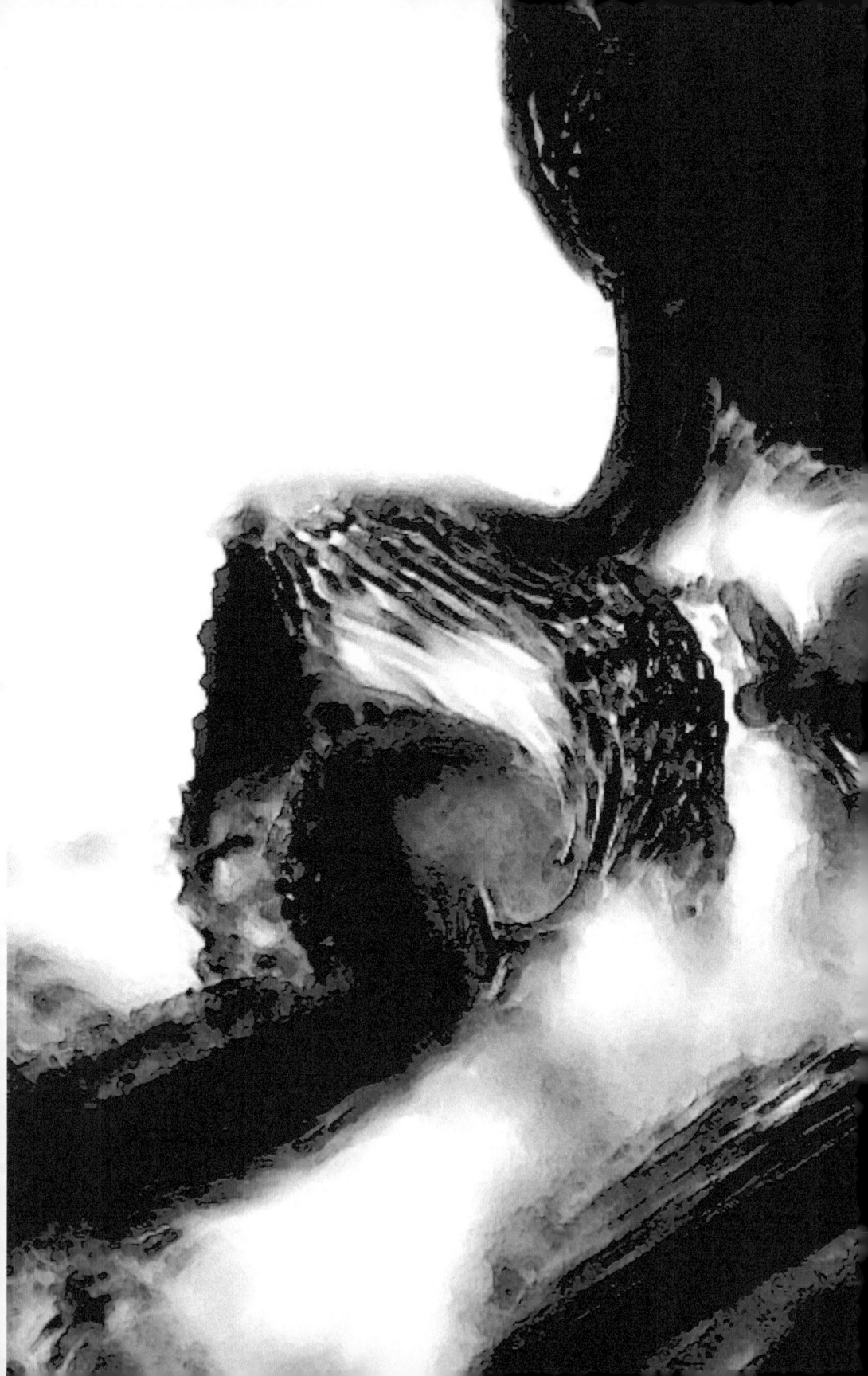

III
MYSTERY OF THE MOMENT

TED MILLAR

GPS NEVER WORKS (IN MY DREAMS)

I had that dream again last night.
I'm in a car, a bus, a plane.
Eventually I'm on foot trying
to reach some undisclosed location
that never seems attainable
but nevertheless feels important.
Sometimes I encounter familiar
landmarks that in any other ordinary
sojourn would be reassuring,
but instead serve to disorient
and prolong my frustration.
Family, friends, even celebrities
make occasional appearances
as fellow travelers, never navigational
assistants. Like my childhood
optometrist driving with me through
the Pacific Northwest when I went
around knocking doors looking for
"our house." Then I was alone
for a little while until I ditched
the car in a pond into which I rolled
backwards when the brakes failed.

It never occurs to me to open GPS
on my phone, as any rational
contemporary human being today
with a smart device would do.
I'm just a pinball bouncing
through the game until my alarm
wakes me with "Can't Find My way Home."

I wonder what Freud might have had to say
about all this, or Carl Jung. Hell,
even Doctor LeNorby, the therapist
I saw on and off for ten years who looked
like what we think of when we imagine
cool high school science teachers.
He'd probably cock his head to the right,
glance past me at the clock
when I'm looking away, and announce,

"Time's up."

ONE KIND FAVOR I ASK OF YOU

The last to be buried here was in 1912.
According to her headstone, "Zitkala Humphrey"
was seventy-six, a "beloved daughter, wife, and mother."
She's here with both sides of a family
that stretched back to colonization
and predeceased her by at least a decade.

Further down the hill
looks like a Halloween display:
misaligned markers,
                    characters once
proclaimed in limestone   reduced
          to aphasia,   ringed in onion grass and sumac.

Willard Turner was either "aged eleven years"
or "owed eleven ears."
Might Agnes McElroy still
be among the living, as fetching
at 110 as the day she married
"Norman" beside her?

If I lift the stone lying at my feet,
I'm bound to uncover a cavalcade
of politic worms, earwigs, millipedes
in quiet congress doing whatever
it is subterranean arthropods do.
Unless someone beats me to it

in the next forty years, I could bring a fresh
face to this place. My wife will not concede,
though, having already announced her intent
to be with her grandparents and eventually
her father. We really should be together.
That would entail being first in my family

to eschew the ancestral ground,
which will no doubt piss off my parents.
I could ask my kids to scatter my ashes
over the Hudson River, thereby
almost guaranteeing nothing by which
to remember me by but a couple hundred poems

in binders, journals, some pictures.
Have you heard the urban legend
about Walt Disney cryogenically frozen
in an abandoned movie studio
with John Wayne? Interesting prospect.
I often wonder what this woeful world

will be like the day those anachronisms
thaw and toddle down Hollywood Boulevard
attempting to order coffee at Starbucks
or chat up aspiring actors/singers/models
whose significant relationships are now
solely digital. Gazing out at the world

that left them cold, I don't foresee myself
doing anything so desperate. Wherever
you lay me, kind people, is fine, so long
as you come by every so often to read
me a little verse, and, as Blind Lemon Jefferson
sang, see that my grave is kept clean.

FIVE MILLION YEARS

That's the present scientific consensus
about how long we've got before
our sun calls it quits.
Most likely our own innovation
will have swallowed us long before then.

Still, I wouldn't mind being there,
knowing I'm the last one standing,
having endured all the slings and arrows
mortality threw at us, our entire
evolution through woes and wars,

joys and jests from cradle to grave,
culminating in ignominious me.
With no one to judge, I could sit
along the bank as the supernova
binges on celestial leftovers

free from frustration over those
who avert their eyes, shake their heads,
and wander off in willful ignorance.
If there is a place the myths
all promise we'll meet again,

please don't put out the light
til I arrive.
Fill me in on everything I've missed,
and I'll do my best
to keep the dream alive.

MARY KAY RUMMEL

WELCOMING NIGHT

I'm learning to let the dark
into my house, my body—my soul,
to let trees show me night is a scouring
strong enough to smooth rock.

I'm learning to let the night in,
the way it engulfs those cottonwoods
on the hill across the pond.

Sometimes darkness comes inside hungry,
pulling a leash that's tied to an oak.
I try to welcome it's growl and roar.

On midsummer evenings dark crawls
up trunks to crowns—
there's a letting go, a slow reversal.

The crowns of old trees hold
the yellow moon while around me
roots quiver—silence is their talk.

Tonight I watch fireflies weave
across a black scrim of leaves—
the blink of my time in air.

At night I look for what's solid.

EIGHTY AUTUMN MOONS

1

Geese cross the eye
the moment when leaving
finds its wings.

In silt   in shadow
you will speak with pine boughs softer
than any syllables.

Seed heads of golden rod
soft as rabbit fur but underneath
stiff as bone.

A bloom of dust
passing through time
to write your name.

Clouds set down their crows
beside water, waiting, as if
there's something more to do.

At dusk the Great Blue Heron
claims a pond rimmed and burning
embers of maple leaves.

2

All those small or immense things
that burned so brightly in your heart
turn to drops—motes of darkness
falling slowly, covering the ground.

You write what you can.
The vision is always present,
But you are not. Try to find
your shadow among the shadows.

Slow the dying cricket nocturne;
hear voices sing back to you.
Egret angels in golden grass—
what you have come for.

Eighty Autumn moons
and have you said enough?
Listen to what pine and cedar say
when no wind stirs.

SUZANNA C. DE BACA

EVERYTHING IS A SHADOW

Everything is a shadow around me on the path.
I see you everywhere, hiding in the dim light of dusk,
in the fog of dawn. You are the space beneath the hedge,
the line cast by the tall tree, the mask of the moon.

I know a story about fear. I thought it was you,
a primitive witch, unformed and untamed, who reflected
ugliness and greed and loathing and shame, who whispered
that my needs were better unexpressed, unmet and denied,
who plunged me headlong into the depths of the forest,
who told me to hide my face from the world.

I know a story about collective shadows, the blind spots
outside of the light of consciousness, the contaminants
that infect our hearts, that cause us to descend into madness
and rage, spew our hatred like bile. Because when we cannot
see the darkness, we become it.

But as I go inward, a small flicker ignites,
and what has been concealed is enlightened.
Once illuminated, I see that you are not the danger,
not the trap, not simply the darkness. You are the warning,
the searchlight, the cool haven, the harbor.

You were hidden for so long. But life can turn quickly.
I see you now, emerging in the dim light of dusk,
in the fog of dawn, in the space beneath the hedge,
the line cast by the tall tree, in the umbra of the moon.
I thought you were a shadow but you are a shelter.
You say come sit by me, in me, and I will comfort you.
Come out of the darkness and I will give you rest.
For everything is shadow. Everything is shade.

EVERYTHING IS A GRAVE

I thought the grave was a hole
in the ground, but you are everywhere:
The splattered robin's egg on the sidewalk,
so intensely blue, the doe shot in the timber,
silent like a fallen soldier, the remains
of the raccoon, stewing in the meadow.

Here you are: Bees in your hexagon hive,
frozen in place like mummies, the fireplace
grate filled with ash, the road filled with bones.

I thought the grave was supposed to be
a place of rest, the ending of all that is.
But when you died, in late January
the snow was so high and bright,
the earth so cold that they had to cut it
with a special tool. We shivered and sang
over your casket, the vapor of our breath rising
creating a translucent cloud. All I remember
is the frigid air and the sound of the dirt
we threw down on your casket.

There is no comfort in a metal vault.
At least a pine box decays. But when I walk
the fields and find the bones, when I hear
the squirrels excavating tiny craters
by the walnut tree, when I spread ashes
from a tin box around the yard,
when I see the little spider, suspended
forever spinning, hung on her own thread,
I see we are not finished. The light catches
the web. Even undone, it is a masterpiece.

The flesh turns into earth, the ash turns
to dust. A new bee takes flight.
The seeds take hold in the ground.
Everything is a grave.

MORTUARY BEE

Mortuary Bee,
you spend your short life moving from job to job,
serving the hive, keeping it immaculate, keeping order.

You begin
by cleaning the very hive cell in which you were born,
tending, and scrubbing away all traces of your birth.

You move
to nursing the young. You check the larvae, and feed
them royal jelly from the hypopharyngeal gland in your head.
You attend to the drones and lovingly care for the Queen,
feeding her, cleaning her, and removing her waste.
You carefully spread her pheromones throughout the hive,
signaling that she is healthy.

You become
a fixer, repairing cells of the honeycomb, arranging beeswax.
You create wax scales from glands on your abdomen,
chewing small pieces and molding them into hexagonal cells.
As you fly, as you age, these wax glands start to atrophy.

You move.
Now mature, you forage. Flying in search of resources
for the hive, you look for pollen, nectar, propolis, and water.
Such danger stepping into the wild, the world. You are afraid,
but you push yourself. You ascend. You glide. And oh,
what unfolds before you: the coneflower, the dahlias, the flox
and roses. Such sweet smells and dizzying colors. The sounds
of songbirds and frogs and crickets and dogs. You are giddy

at the brilliance, at the beauty. What a marvel, this universe
outside the hive, this cosmos that sustains you.

You may be called to help in a variety of roles: Pollen packing,
propolizing, fanning, carrying water, guarding the entrance.
You do not question. You serve as needed.

And in the end,
you tend to the dead. You remove the bodies
of your fallen comrades from the floor of the hive,
sweep away deceased larvae. Sometimes there is a plague,
a wave of death, hundreds of bees dying from foraging
on poisoned flowers, or from a freeze. It is devastating,
this time of grief. The buzz ceases in sadness.
The hive is silent. But you do not stop working.

In winter,
you drag the bodies out to the entrance of the hive
and pitch them over the side. Then you fly down
and drag the carcasses away from the hive.

In summer,
stronger from the abundant pollen, you drag the corpse
through the hive entrance, then fly with the body hanging
below you for a distance. You drop the dead to the ground.

Then, in your fourth week of life,
your fourth week of unceasing labor,you will sense
your end of days. Soon you will remove yourself
from the hive. You do not want to be a burden.
If you die in the hive, someone will have to drag you away.

So you fly.

You fly far from the home you have known,
the friends you have served, the sound of the hive,
the familiar buzz, grows faint.

You soar
past the flowers and the over the grasses,
lower and lower, your body weakening,
your wings barely moving. As you close your eyes
you see your life, from larvae to nurse, attendant
to fixer, gatherer to undertaker.

Frail now,
your vision blurs.
All you can see is a pulsating cube, so majestic,
an amber heart beating. In its light, you see coneflowers
and dahlias and hear the robin's song. The rich fragrance
of the fields fills your senses, all in a lattice haze.
Everything is a shining star with six golden, glowing sides.

You fall.
You fall, and in your last breath
the hexagon envelops you, swaddling you
in the softest cloud, catching you, enshrouding you
gently in lavender
and honey.

HEATHER TOSTESON

MARY SALAAM

A young man in a grocery store stopped and watched Mary Salaam and then asked, "M'am, are you saved? Because I see a halo over your head."

It isn't the only time she has had someone say something similar. Another man said to her, "I don't mean to be fresh, but you just light up."

Sister Mary is seventy-one. She still works as a charge nurse at a nursing home. She teaches Arabic at the Atlanta Masjid and regularly attends meetings of interfaith groups in Atlanta, such as the Children of Abraham and the Interfaith Sisters. She is small, elegant, and wears a wonderful collection of hats and head scarves, which she wraps tightly around her head, their ends tied into a rose above her ear, so it looks like she is wearing an elegant cloche from the Roaring Twenties. She is very down to earth, as careful with her speech as she is with her dress.

There is, as these strangers observed, something about her that lights up a room. I found her spiritual journey one of the most interesting of all that I heard during this project. What struck me was its continuity, although in her life Sister Mary has moved from being a non-professed Baptist, to Methodist, to Pentecostal evangelist, to Muslim.

In a follow-up interview, I asked, "Mary, when you changed religions, did God change for you?" Not at all, she told me. Her personal relationship with God remained unchanged—intimate, all-absorbing.

Having your own personal relationship with God is like being Muslim now. I'm very conscious of how I do my prayer—because I'm conscious of how I want to be with God. That is what I want to do. This doesn't make me more Muslim. There are things I want to do because they are pleasing with me and pleasing with God. I know God does not need me, but I need Him. It's for me that I'm doing it. If I miss any prayer, it bothers me. If I oversleep, I still do it because I need it.

From the very beginning, Mary has had a strong, guiding need for congruence between her inner experience of faith and the outer expression of it. As a child in rural south Georgia, she went to a Baptist church with her mother.

They would have you sit in the front row—called it a mourning bench. But I never had a desire to sit up there. They'd always take communion— but they would pass me by because I was a child. When I learned what it was about, I realized I was more observant than they were. After church, people would do other things outside of church that didn't go with what was being said in the church. It didn't coincide. I didn't understand it. They did something different on the outside. So I didn't join.

This keen observation of the congruence, or incongruence, of speech and action—and clarity of response to that incongruity—can be heard throughout Mary's life. It didn't make her give up on religion; it made her keep questioning and seeking.

As a child, when they had revivals and said, "All Christians raise your hands," Mary never would. "I didn't understand. But I always said, I was going to be able to raise my hand one day." But she would be sure she understood exactly what she was doing first.

Mary's need for congruence between intention and action, inner *understanding* and public faith, has always been intriguingly balanced by an even stronger intuitive and visionary capacity. The dance between these two capacities has determined her spiritual path, giving her the abilities to immerse herself deeply and also to separate out and find more congruent faith forms when needed.

When she moved to Atlanta at nine or ten, she started attending a Methodist church with a neighbor. She went to tea on Sunday evening and Sunday school in the mornings. But she didn't join. One Sunday, she was singing *This little light of mine, I'm going to let it shine*, and found herself standing silent before the preacher.

"What are you going to do? Join the church?" he asked.

"I guess so," she said.

"Now, I understand it was the Spirit of God moved me. I didn't. None of my family is Methodist."

But Mary became an ardent Methodist. She sang in the choir, taught Sunday school. "I would do everything they had," she said with a smile.

Mary married just before she turned fifteen. "I had gotten pregnant. I lived up the street from a minister. His wife was my teacher. He said it was the best thing I could do," she explained. She continued to be heavily involved in the church, over the years taking her six children, five girls and a boy, there with her all the time.

Then tragedy struck. In her account of this time, we hear several themes that run through Mary's life. The role of visions. Her stoicism and generosity of spirit, even in times of heartache. How her faith provided her with a touchstone, a compass, giving her the strength to question religious authority when it was used punitively.

What took me out of the church—one of my girls got killed. Five years old. Hit by a car. In the eulogy, the minister, he made the comment, "If her mother had been there, this might not have happened."

This man doesn't even know the whole story. Before my daughter was hit and was killed, she had gotten hit before. We were coming home from church and crossing the street and she pulled away from me and got her shoulder hurt.

Charlene—we called her Bit—she was an angel. Everyone loved her. She went clean all the time. If she got dirt on her dress, she'd take it off. Never went barefeet. She wanted to do grown-up things. She would tell me what she was never going to do. Go to school.

She would iron and wash. I heard her one morning out on the porch screaming. "Mama! Mama! That woman was coming out for me. Tell me who was that lady? All white. Hat. Shoes."

"Where did she go?" I asked and she pointed at the cemetery.

I was separated from my husband at the time. Two older girls would spend time with their grandmother. Bit didn't usually go. But this time she wanted to go. So I called her sisters back and they got her. On a Friday.

Later I fixed something to eat. We had no phone there—I used the telephone of my neighbor. So when I heard my neighbor call me by my full name, I knew something had happened.

I had a dream after she had her screaming. I dreamed my sister was moving, her silverware was falling out and I picked it up and there was always more that was falling. I found a grave with a silver ax—and I started throwing silverware at it.

At the time, the hospital was in walking distance. So I started walking. But they had moved the hospital. A man stopped and reminded me of the change and took me to the new hospital, up on a hill, like my sister's house in the dream.

The man who hit her was so sad. I told him I understood, she'd done the same with me. Jerked away from her sisters, just like she did with me.

Mary stopped going to church after the funeral. But her daughters were going to a Pentecostal Holiness Church and asked her to go with them.

She did, but she had no desire to join. Until one night, she had a powerful experience.

I felt someone gripped my shoulder. Next thing I knew, I was on the floor. I saw this scroll. I could read off the scroll. It said, you can't do this and you can't do that. I have never felt the same anymore.

Mary felt a strong imperative to make her life congruent. She told the man she was going out with that she couldn't continue seeing him unless they married. Her boyfriend and she broke up, then he started going to church and they married.

"After this experience," she explained, "I couldn't do anything that wasn't lawful. I worked in the church. I had a sunbeam church. I sang in the choir. I became an evangelist for three years. My husband went in the army."

During this time, Mary's visionary capacity became a powerful discerning tool for her. It started with the dream she had that foretold her daughter's death. "The Lord blessed me to see things. I could tell people things. This wasn't fortune-telling. This was the work of the Spirit. About things that were going to happen."

She would dream when her children lost things and they began to say, "You lose something, you go ask Momma." But her dreams and visions showed her other, more difficult things as well.

Mary started fasting, and her mind became very clear. She would read but not watch television or listen to the radio. In a vision, she saw her husband committing adultery. When he came home on furlough, they went together to the church on Thursday. "We prayed at the altar. I went back to my seat, and he turned and came to me on his knees, and I said, 'Don't tell me. I already know.'"

"'How?' he asked."

"I saw it as it happened," she told him.

She also heard an inner voice that urged her to go and talk with her mother-in-law about God. Her mother-in-law was angry with her for coming. She was returning to her hometown because she had cancer. "She jumped on me. I said I didn't know what God had for her, *I* didn't."

Mary prayed for her mother-in-law. "She was going okay for awhile, but then I realized she was going to die because I had a dream where her husband was coming out of a church—and he never went to church."

Mary's own mother trusted Mary's visions and asked her daughter to visit a friend, Mr. Coleman. But Mary answered, "If I ever feel led to go, I'll go. But I can't go just because you're asking me."

Mary, describing these visionary experiences, retains a sense of detachment. She experienced them, and continues to experience them, as gifts, not powers. But one day, after having cautioned her mother, she was led to go and see Mr. Coleman. He was with his wife and daughters. He had not spoken for months. Mary had them read the 23rd psalm. Then she prayed with him for about fifteen minutes. "And he said, 'Who is that sitting across my bed?' When he said that, he talked for years. I told him just not to drink—and he didn't drink for years and was well and then got to drinking again and got sick."

Mary's visions and their calls to action weren't always successful. She felt a presence with her in church one day, but when she tried to turn around, she couldn't. "Then I heard this voice that told me to stop to this house I had to pass by on my way home." Five men, all lapsed, lived there. When Mary talked to them about God and revivals, they brushed her off. But three of them died and one had a stroke. A friend of theirs, seeing this set of calamities and seeing Mary coming in to visit with the stroke victim, started to go to church himself.

"What mattered," she said, "was that they didn't believe me." I could see this still bothered her. Not that they might choose to act on their own, and reject her suggestions, but that they questioned the sincerity of her vision. She was *led* to talk to them.

Mary, even when her visions were disquieting, did not question their source or their authority. She left the Pentecostal church because of two visions—one by a woman who lived in LaGrange, Georgia, who told her, "If you don't leave the church, you're going to die." She meant a spiritual death, Mary informed me.

Then Mary herself had a dream in which she heard, "Come out from among and be you separated." She kept on going to church, but one time when she was in the pulpit evangelizing, she heard an inner voice that said, *I just can't come to church anymore.* She told me, "Then I remembered my dream, and I realized I hadn't done this." She hadn't come out from among.

Her mother, concerned, came to see her: "I hadn't back slid. I just couldn't come anymore. I told her when I understood it, I'd explain it to her."

Mary went to different churches, with her mother or with friends. She watched people: "They did some strange things, shouting, 'Jesus! Jesus!' and I thought, I *did* that."

"But," Mary went on, "I still knew I needed to be somewhere. So I prayed. I asked almighty God to give me a sign, so I would *know* this was for me. I knew there was something I needed to know."

Mary went to different churches, but she began to question what she had been taught: "I'd listen to all these ministers on the radio. I'd read in the Bible. God the same today as He was yesterday. But all these preachers had different messages."

If preachers could have different interpretations, did that mean Mary could have her own? Her questions centered on the Trinity.

And then I began to think about their telling me Jesus and God the same. And I'd read the Bible back to front and front to back. I thought about it. Jesus on the cross, "My God, my God, why has thou forsaken me?" <u>Who was he was talking to?</u> And he said, "I came to do the will of He who sent me." And I'm questioning that. When you're <u>in</u> something, you don't really question. Jesus said to Peter, "None is worthy to be worshiped except God." I couldn't accept Jesus was God anymore.

Mary continued to go to church, although she never returned to the Deliverance Bible Center. She kept going because God hadn't given her a sign. The sign came in an interesting way.

Mary was a nurse, had decided to be one at ten when she helped her mother care for her ailing grandmother and great-grandmother. In the summer, she made a large fan from a broomstick and newspaper and would stand between their beds fanning them. It was at this moment she said, "I want to be a nurse."

Now, in mid-life, waiting for a sign, Mary came to do private nursing duty with a Caucasian woman who had gangrene of the intestine. Her name was Mrs. Sanford and she was very sick. She was a patient at the hospital where Mary worked. She had tubes everywhere. A Foley catheter. The prognosis was grave. One Sunday when Mary was with her, the television was on and Oral Roberts was preaching. Suddenly Mary felt led and asked, "Mrs. Sanford, do you believe God can heal your body?" When Oral Roberts prayed, Mary set one hand on Mrs. Sanford's body and the other on the television set. She let the prayers and the energy run through her.

The next morning, the doctor came in and looked at Mrs. Sanford and said, "You have made a remarkable change." He talked to her daughter and said Mrs. Sanford could be discharged but would need a private nurse. Mrs. Sanford wanted Mary, so Mary added a day shift from 7-3 to her night work from 11-7.

One morning, as she was dozing beside Mrs. Sanford, Mrs. Sanford woke up and said, "Mary, you don't know who you are." She continued:

There's something about you people I can't explain. When I was a child, I loved to go to the little colored church. I could wear what I wanted.

But there's something about your people because you don't know who you are. I want you to find some old old preacher who can explain to you. Don't you know that a Black man carried Jesus's cross? You need to find an old old preacher that can explain the Bible to you because you don't know who you are.

"She said it three times," Mary concluded. "I'd been praying for God to give me a sign." This visionary charge from Mrs. Sanford for Mary to find Black identity and religious coherence opened Mary to the events that followed.

Shortly after, a man came by her house selling fish and a newspaper about Mohammed. He just left the newspaper with her after telling her about a temple he wanted her and her family to visit and about the Nation of Islam. He told her he'd provide transportation and left her his number. Two or three weeks later, Mary heard a voice ask her, "Why don't you check this place this brother is telling you about?" So she went with two of her children.

A man was talking—in a green suit. Subir Mohammad. A green suit and dark shades. He was talking about the Nation and everything. He brought on the speaker, Luther Weems X. When the brother got to introduce himself, he said, "Brothers and sisters, tonight we're going to talk about you don't know who you are." I turned to my daughter and said, "This is my sign." And he talked about things that had been puzzling me for a long time.

Mary continued to go to the temple. Along with her two daughters, she wrote letters to receive her X and after the third try received it. But Mary had reservations: "One thing I couldn't digest. They said man was God and I couldn't believe that. But I couldn't leave. I remembered my grandmother telling me to have patience and things would become clear."

They became clear for her after the death of Elijah Muhammad and the reformation of the Nation of Islam that took place with the succession of his son Warrith Deen Mohammed, who urged a transition toward a more inclusive and universal Sunni Islam.

He had different ideas from his father. It was a time when Black people didn't like themselves—they was always straightening their hair. Elijah encouraged us to do for ourself. But Warrith D. Mohammed—he came and gave a lecture. He talked about Almighty God being Creator of heaven and earth. He had a better perspective on spiritual life. Elijah Muhammad had said the White man was the devil, but W. D. Mohammed said <u>anyone</u> could be a devil. It was a mindset. And he broke with all that about the Black man being God. I couldn't accept *that part. And deep down in their souls, I don't think they bought it themselves. Now we look at people as being <u>human</u>—one race, one humanity. Because there is one God.*

Her conversion to a more universal Islam has meant that Mary has studied the Koran in English and Arabic. She has also kept her personal relationship with God. Her continuous experience with Christianity and Islam has made Sister Mary very tolerant and committed to interfaith work: "That's why I have no trouble with interfaith. It's just like an apple. You've got green apples. You've got red apples. You've got yellow ones. You've got some red and green. And we all eat them—and what do we get to? The core."

Mary's belief in Islam is an elastic one:

I have a <u>personal</u> relationship with my Creator. When you ask me what I am, I hesitate. I don't want to be labeled. Muslim means one who submits his will to do the will of God. There is a difference between a Muslim and a believer. You need to <u>become</u> a believer. Every child is <u>born</u> Muslim, submitted to the will of God. That's why they're called angels. That's why Nicodemus said, "You must be born again." You don't go back into the womb—just back to that first state when you were born.

Like many people who found their final home in another faith tradition, Mary sees being Muslim as an integration. She hasn't abandoned the Bible. Muslims, too, are people of the Book. Being Muslim allows her intellectual unity—she can believe in one God, one humanity. The clear focus on practice allows the congruence of belief and action that has been so important to her since she was a child and helped her tipsy mother and aunts across the wobbly plank bridge at the creek on Saturday nights, vowing that she wasn't going to have such a gap between her Sunday and Saturday behaviors. "I never drinked. I never smoked. Because when they drinked, they'd say the next day, 'Did I do that?'"

Mary likes the clarity of Islam: "There are five principles. One God. Fast. Pray. Give to charity. Make Hajj if you're able. Believe in the Books. The Angels. The Hereafter. It's just a way of life. 24/7."

She likes the mindfulness that Islam invites her to: "The teaching of Islam have you to look within yourself—and to have a peace of mind. To learn what your purpose is here. What you were *created* for. It brings you into humanness. You have to be conscious of what you say and do. You're constantly learning and changing. It's a *job*."

Islam, which she first encountered as a way of affirming racial identity, has provide her with a powerful way of organizing beyond it:

There is no race thing in Islam. We're <u>one</u> people. In the Koran it says

we were made different tribes and nations <u>so we could know each other</u>.
Why else you go on vacation? Things in this world are different so we can
enjoy it. Life is beautiful. Jesus said, "I come so you could have life more
abundantly." Most Christians don't practice what they believe in.

Mary feels that it is the intensity and personal intimacy of her own
relationship with God that leaves her open to other faith journeys: "Almighty
God knows your heart. He knows why you're taking the path you're taking.
Like the experiences brought me out of the church. I don't know your
experiences, so how could I know what is right for you? You have to answer
to your Creator."

Her respect for the sanctity—and inscrutability—of individual journeys
extends to her own family. Mary's children have not become Muslim
although they believe in its teachings and especially its practices. "They're
God-conscious children," Mary says. Mary's daughter, who joined Nation
of Islam with her but is now married to a Methodist, reads the Koran on
her own. She has refused to become a member of his church, but staunchly
defended her husband's right to become a deacon. "It just don't make sense,"
she told the pastor and church sisters who were pressuring her to convert.
"He's a good father and sings in the choir. You're stunting his growth."

The pastor told her, "Either you have to change, or we have to change
the policy."

Mary's daughter, true to her mother's example, said, "You'll have to
change the policy."

When I called Mary back after our interview, I asked her whether she
still had visions. She said not as often. She didn't need them now. But there
is something radiant and visionary about her life and actions. You can feel it
when she describes the pleasure she takes in teaching Arabic for beginners at
the Atlanta Masjid:

I cherish it. I do instruction to beginners. I conduct my class the way
God leads me to go. One brother said, "Coming to Sister Mary's class
is so rewarding." Sometimes he'd be spaced out. But I'd say things that
touched his heart. I just love it. I just love doing right.

She closes our conversation this way:

When we all sit down to think about it, it's all about love and care and
wanting to do good for each other, no matter who you are and where you
come from and whatever label you're carrying. When you come home
with me, I know you're over racism.

A woman who lives her visions—their mystery and their concreteness as
one and the same—and helps others do so too.

SARAH ROSENBLATT

EPHEMERAL MATTERS

I thought of the delightful edge sleep had over me,
and that amazing book before I drifted off
into dreams laced with symbolism
that I put aside in our cold house
as I venture to the kitchen to make oatmeal.

Some things are durable
others give way as soon as I touch them—
the mustache of a long-ago one-night stand,
the dramatic changes of the sky at twilight.

The weather collides with our butterfly glands
the muscles in our legs, our hearty eyebrows,
as we bear witness to the complexity of being

mammals, animals
with stomachs, lungs
and so few ways to the heart
of this matter.

My dog and husband snore on the couch.
Years push through rounded windows.
There are sounds of birds, chimes,
and beneath it all,

my dog's pink belly holds everything in place.

RESILIENCE

It's great when I wake up and
feel real enough to touch and be touched
and have no fear of being too delicate for
the oncoming day.
There's nothing wrong with being swept into it.

But what about yesteryear when I was
open to the elements?
(A free agent exploring
every which way of the environment?)

Falling headfirst
in red rover red rover,

all the hurts that brought me to this point,
ruffled by the windchill
but with nothing standing in my way.

TO HAVE LOVED

What I want to say about my dad was that he lived in the moment,
genuinely, without hashtags,
that he taught us to like walruses,
soak in the ever-present present.
To wallow and delight in it
to let it be with us.
There was no crying for that moment back there
because we were in this one fully,
drinking ice cold lemonade,
being real and altogether ourselves
with someone
who knew our ways
and our doubly-important points
about many things
now obsolete.

AGAINST ALL ODDS

The wind is relentless and remorseless,
its quarrel with humankind
hitting us at gut level.
The moon holds up against the elements,
the sounds of chimes,
the sleepiness in the house.

I want to sleep away winter
but I also want to live
each moment to its fullest.
After all the mistreatment my ancestors experienced,
I am alive, full figured,
the nightlight guiding me
to the bathroom.
Brushing my hair
affirms
I have survived.

DEIDRA GREENLEAF ALLAN

NOMAD

To be totally alone in this world chasing the moon
in your custom van down a desert highway

To drive your metal envelope through the night
serenaded by bouncing dishes   the tidal slosh

of toilet water   chattering forks and knives
steering toward a future

freed from obligation   as you've freed yourself
from the need to possess   to enact a purpose

Is it shameful to be so untethered   windblown
as a tumbleweed?

Motel signs call from the side of the road
neon lights buzzing like giant red mosquitoes

They long for your company   for an exchange
of money   words   the handing over of a key

as if there were some secret to be unlocked
some unknown worth knowing

that can't already be found in the dizzying arms
of this star-studded night

FARMHOUSE, MOUNTAIN LAKE PARK

for the Haynes family

Light slides over your face and strikes your hair, flare
of red, then green, and you, busy with chores, oblivious
to this moment.

But I am swept away,
along with these paneled walls and fly-specked windows,
hay barn shuttered in perpetual gloom,
sagging porch beside the tracks that squeal a lonesome
train song all night long.

How can I explain—
this feeling that we're all flowing together, I don't know where,
the dead, the living, this house, this yard. Swept along
as if we were nothing—as if we were a river of light.

This is what I'm about to tell you, but a curtain moves,
you look up,
and it's gone.

AFTER A LECTURE ON THE NUMINOUS, MONTPELIER, VERMONT

Walking home across the village green, I think, this is the kind of night
it could happen—a full-moon night that's bathed the entire town

in an unearthly ultraviolet glow. The maples seem to sense it,
they're waving their arms at the yellow frame houses around the square,

and the houses are leaning in, as if impatient to see this thing
I've been waiting for. Sometimes, it's so near I can feel it,

like someone's breath on the back of my neck or a stranger following
too close on the sidewalk. And then there's the snow that's begun to fall

—little blurs of light, as if stars were softening into something attainable. I
slow my pace, stare up through the feathery bombardment of white

into the great black bell of night. The trees suddenly stop their rustling and
the moon hides itself inside a fold of cloud. It's then I hear it.

WHAT SHE HEARD THE ROOM SAY

In the morning, amid radiator clicks and refrigerator hum, she hears them—not voices exactly, but something being said by tables, lamps, chairs—something penetrating the room like the barely discernible throb of a pulsar. Suddenly she feels the molecules of her arms and face dispersing like a just-opened air freshener. She imagines a cha-cha line of particles—a dancing throng of bosons and fermions and no one to say what's her, what's not. She stares at the objects around the room. They don't look back. Nothing happens. Yet she knows in a moment of great conviction the arbitrariness of boundaries and the song that everything sings. Outside, the rising chatter of morning presses against the window and invites her to rejoin the partitioned world and its specious divisions of matter. But she, or what appears to be her, does not move, though she knows now she's actually nothing but motion—immeasurable iotas afloat in a soup of undifferentiated energy making music with the lamps and chairs.

WOKEN

Cusp of morning,
a few birds

launch their eager arguments
at the dark.

Beyond my window a 747
drones across the sky

laying a vaporous stripe
across the night's dense asphalt.

What was it woke me
—birds, plane,

the heat of remembered fires
raked hot again in dream,

or the hiss and whistled sigh
of life embering—my life?

I toss in the tangled arms
of a new day

feeling it stir, pull me
with its fresh enticements.

Hope, that ravishing drug,
works through my veins,

speeds my pulse
even as this body fails

and words fall away.
Outside, other sounds:

paper waking stoop
with its urgent slap

and, somewhere in the distance,
a persistent music.

RICHARD SCHIFFMAN

MELTING TIME

All day long as the snow melted, as it sloughed off ledges
calving like glaciers, as it dripped and ran and runnelled
as sodden clumps thumped to pavement, as rafts of it it crashed
and splattered, as icicles cracked off eaves and runoff flowed
down gutters, as it streaked brick walls and soaked the crotches
of oaks, as it slid like christened ships from the limbs of pines,
as it glissaded from high slate roofs, as it collapsed like a lung,
as it leaked from sooty banks at curbside, as it gurgled and purled
and puddled, as sparrows drank and bathed in it, as it rose thin
as mist, as it billowed off to join forces with the nearest cloud,
I thought— the world never stops pouring into itself.
It gives and it takes with the very same hand.

EDEN IN THE A.M.

In a time of no wind, in a spell of stasis after stars.
In the almost-morning morning, in the dawn before
the solar dawning, the pause before the prelude,
the hush that wombs the day, just stay, stay put
before the roving eye can see, before the ear can hear
the no-news news. Be here, exactly where you are,
and where you aren't, in the unsown garden,
in the sheer unknowing, in the windless blowing,
in the fenceless land, in the I before the I began.
Abide, don't hide, but neither spin the wheel of fate.
There is still time. No time at all. Don't bum-rush
Eden's gate. The snake will wait.

LOUIS FABER

CARRYING

I carry my past
in monk's bag
that rests on my shoulder.

In it you will find
my history, or bits
of it, names I have
been given, given up,
memories of childhood,
pictures of my parents
who I never knew,
aged in my mind from
the photos in yearbooks.

I still have room
in my bag, perhaps
more room than time.

NOT SPEAKING

it was a Saturday night, she had
nothing to do and it was a safe place
for a single woman who hated bars.
She had been there before, danced a bit,
had a soft drink, and the men,
almost all in uniform showing
their branch of service, were polite.
He went there that night out of boredom,
his wife in their home several states away,
just for a dance, a bit of female companionship.
He was older than most of the men there,
stocky, sturdy he called himself, and he
saw her, also large framed, not fat,
sturdy he would have described here, older
than most of the girls in poodle skirts.
How they ended up doing so much more
then just dancing isn't clear in the picture
of their meeting I have created, but
nine months later I arrived, and she
placed me for adoption for our mutual good.
I did find her, years later, him as well, but
the dead don't talk much except in dreams.

QUANTUM ROMANCE

The inexorable flow of time
cannot be slowed by men.
That is the view of the poets
and of lovers when they are young.
But time does not flow, cannot.
It is an infinite series
of discrete moments
compressed so tightly
their boundaries defy observation.
There is only this moment,
and this, and this.
To say time flows is romantic,
just as to say I am a real
solid person, is romantic.
There is no romance in
an orderly collection of atoms,
of molecules strung together
just so, an atomic tapestry
that seems to paint a picture
that unravels on close inspection.
As our fingers touch,
in that instant and each
that follow it, we
attain a new quantum state
never to be precisely repeated,
and it is this state I
can only refer to as love.

CHRIS ELLERY

EVERY BEAUTIFUL NAME

And when you take your next breath as we enter the fifth world
There will be no X, no guidebook with words you can carry.
                    —Joy Harjo, "A Map to the Next World"

When I browse the names on the Virtual Wall, I'm surprised how many
begin with Q. I expected a galaxy of As and Bs—Aadland to Byus might
take an hour to read. Even the Zs are prolific.

There is only one X, though: 1LT Augusto Maria Xavier. A page to himself.
Lonely as a castaway. Rare as a mark on a treasure map. As if a fragment of
All can be less than the whole.

If you click on his name, you learn that Augusto flew an A-4C SKYHAWK
and died while providing close air support.

"His body was never recovered."

I won't try to explain my penchant for names.

Sometimes I get out the old phone book and read a column at random with
bardic reverence like the glossary of the Mahabharat or a Homeric catalogue
of captains, ancestors, ghosts.

I like it best when the people are real—by which I mean they really lived
one time or are living now. Or someday will.

I scan the death notices and birth announcements in my local newspaper,
sounding the names as a blessing.

Perusing those online sites of best baby names, I like to imagine new born
Olivia or Liam.

I can't help but imagine little Emma or Ava, Oliver or Noah when they get to the age that I am now.

A life should repay a mother's labor at least. So I imagine Augusto Maria Xavier meeting me for coffee in the Dairy Queen. He would be 80 this year.

Would he talk about Nam? Would I tell him my lottery number and explain why I didn't enlist?

Would I ask him about his middle name? "Why not Mario or Marius? Were you named for the Virgin? Or the Roman god of war?"

Augusto never answers me.

I live a long way from Vietnam, where his body came apart, but if what I read somewhere is true, some of his atoms are in me now.

My youngest child's second child is due in a month. She will get some of his atoms, too.

Her name is Eleanor Grace, which I like very much.

I helped to choose her mother's name, Elizabeth, and the names of another daughter and my son, Sarah and Benjamin. Well, the names came to my wife, like gung-ho volunteers, but I approved.

I still like these classic Old Testament names, although more and more the book itself repulses and terrifies, with all its news of exile, chosenness, judgment, genocide, apocalypse.

Well, all the old epics are written in blood, and some is good news.

The Mahabharat has hundreds of proper names. Long lists of allies and enemies. Arjuna himself has 14 different names, including one that means "scorcher of foes."

According to one list of *least popular* names I found online, the rarest of given names is Pax, which isn't surprising.

It makes me wonder how much the names we give our children help to determine who they turn out to be.

Sometimes it seems like people live into their names, as if David or Peter or Dawn or Lolita could itself be a kind of destiny.

I wish I could name some baby boy or girl Pax (it's a unisex name) and see what happens.

People call God by a lot of different names. We can't seem to help it, though it might be better if we refrained.

Shiva, Jehovah, Wakonda, Zeus, Allah, the Tao. A thousand and one epithets. But I guess the Ineffable is still the Ineffable. Absolute is Absolute.

All the difference must be somehow somewhere in us who do the naming and use the names.

Allah has 99 names. The one I like best is *al Waahid*.

I looked for this name on the Virtual Wall. While I was looking I decided for no reason at all to count the Ws, but I couldn't pass Walker without losing count.

So many Walkers!

There are 70 panels East and 70 West, tens of thousands of names, arranged by date of casualty, but *Waahid*, my favorite of the 99 names for Allah, is nowhere engraved in the granite.

Can you find Pax?

I know the answer. The question is for you. Everyone should read all those names at least once a year. The President and every member of Congress should have to read them all aloud like an oath before taking office.

And there are plenty of other names from plenty of other wars. They should read them, too—all our own soldiers, of course, but also allies, civilians, and even the "hostiles"—hosts of them killed in a host of wars.

There should be a Vietnam War Memorial that includes all the names together, U.S. troops, U.S. allies, the Vietnamese, both South and North, Chinese, Cambodians, Laotians—more than three and a half million in all.

Augusto is the very first name on panel 6E, right next to John R. Cowan and directly above Kenneth A. Bodell. I hope they enjoy one another's company.

Their atoms are mixing—if what I read somewhere is true.

Most people can grieve for a fallen comrade, a parent, a child, or even a pet. But what about the enemy?

Grief is nothing less or more than a sense of diminishment in homage of life.

Tat Tvam Asi, it says in the Upanishads.

This means "You are that."

Atman is Brahman.

Which means you and I are in essence one with God or Ultimate Reality (whatever name you prefer) and so with each other.

Which means we are one as well with Augusto and Kenneth and John, and one with all they killed in Vietnam, with all who died in every war.

And so also with Olivia and Liam, Ella and Lizzy.

Can you believe this?

I don't know if I can.

But I guess if God ever needs another name, any of these will do fine.

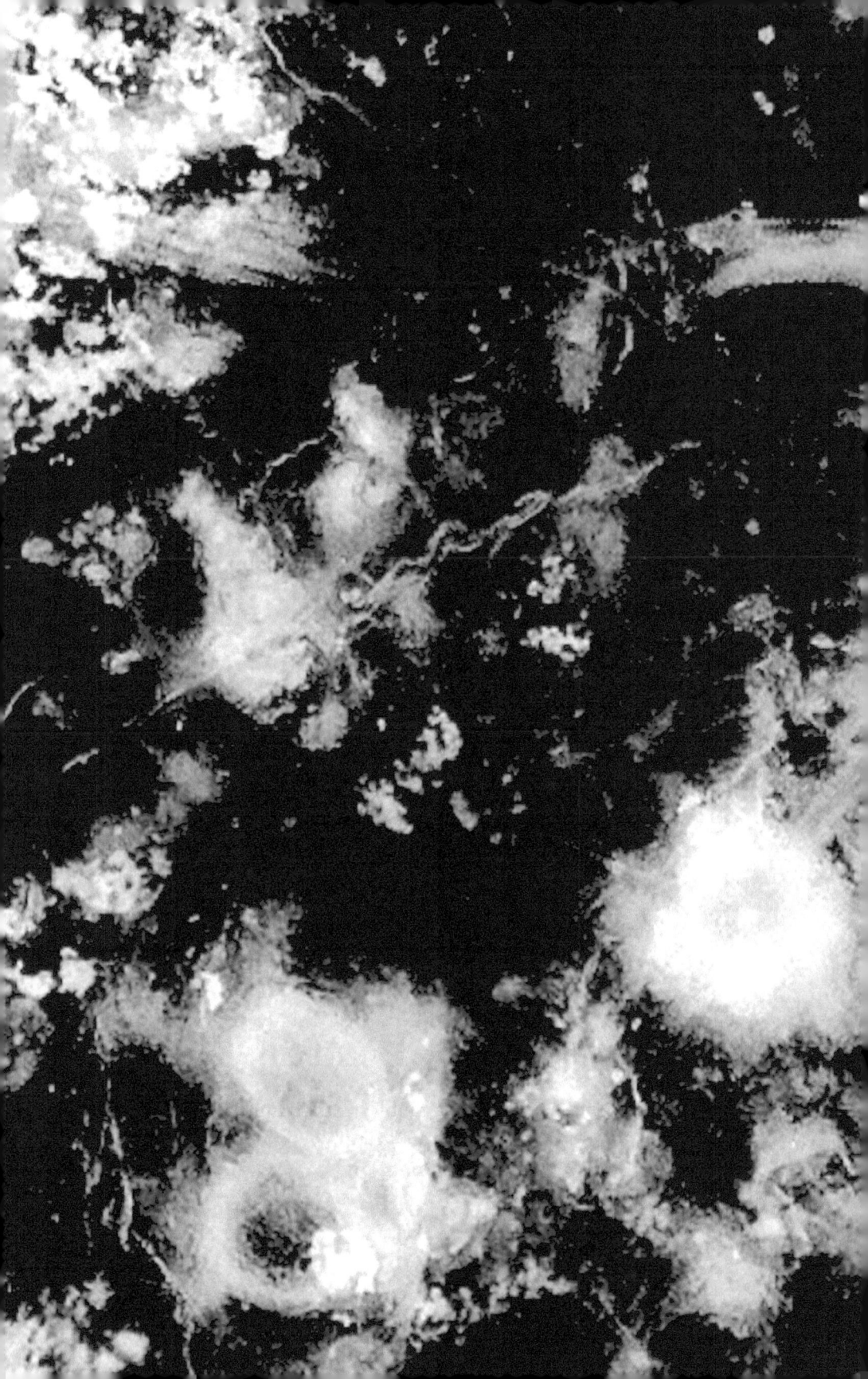

ACKNOWLEDGMENTS

Laura Apol previously published "The Gift of *Yes*" and "Light, Water, Bones" in *Nothing but the Blood* (Michigan State University Press, 2018) and "Hanna on the Monkeybars" in *Crossing the Ladder of Sun* (Michigan State University Press, 2004).

"Anthony" by Charles Brockett and Heather Tosteson is excerpted from their book *Sharing the Burden of Repair: Reentry after Mass Incarceration* (Wising Up Press, 2020).

Suzanna C. de Baca's "Mortuary Bee" was previously published on *Substack*.

"Mary Salaam" by Heather Tosteson is excerpted from her book *God Speaks My Language, Can You?* (Wising Up Press, 2008).

Gabrielle LeMay previously published "Night Train" in *Passager* (2022); "Night Peepers" in *Poetry East* (2022); and "Prom Night" in *Miramar* (2018).

Eisha A. Mason's "Vigil for Charleena Lyles" and "How to Walk on Hot Coals" were originally published in *Red Door* (World Stage Press, 2023).

Ted Millar's "One Kind Favor I Ask of You" was originally published in *GFT Press* (2016).

Randy Minnich previously published "The Colors of the World" in *The Potter's Wheel* (2019).

Johnny Townsend originally published "One Family at a Time" in *Seattle Times* (March 11, 2023).

Sarah Brown Weitzman previously published "Ecosphere" in *The Baltimore Review* (2013); "Rodin's 'The Hand of God'" in *Art Times* (2014); "Adam" in *Dash* (2013); and "Van Gogh's Room" in *Theodate* (2013).

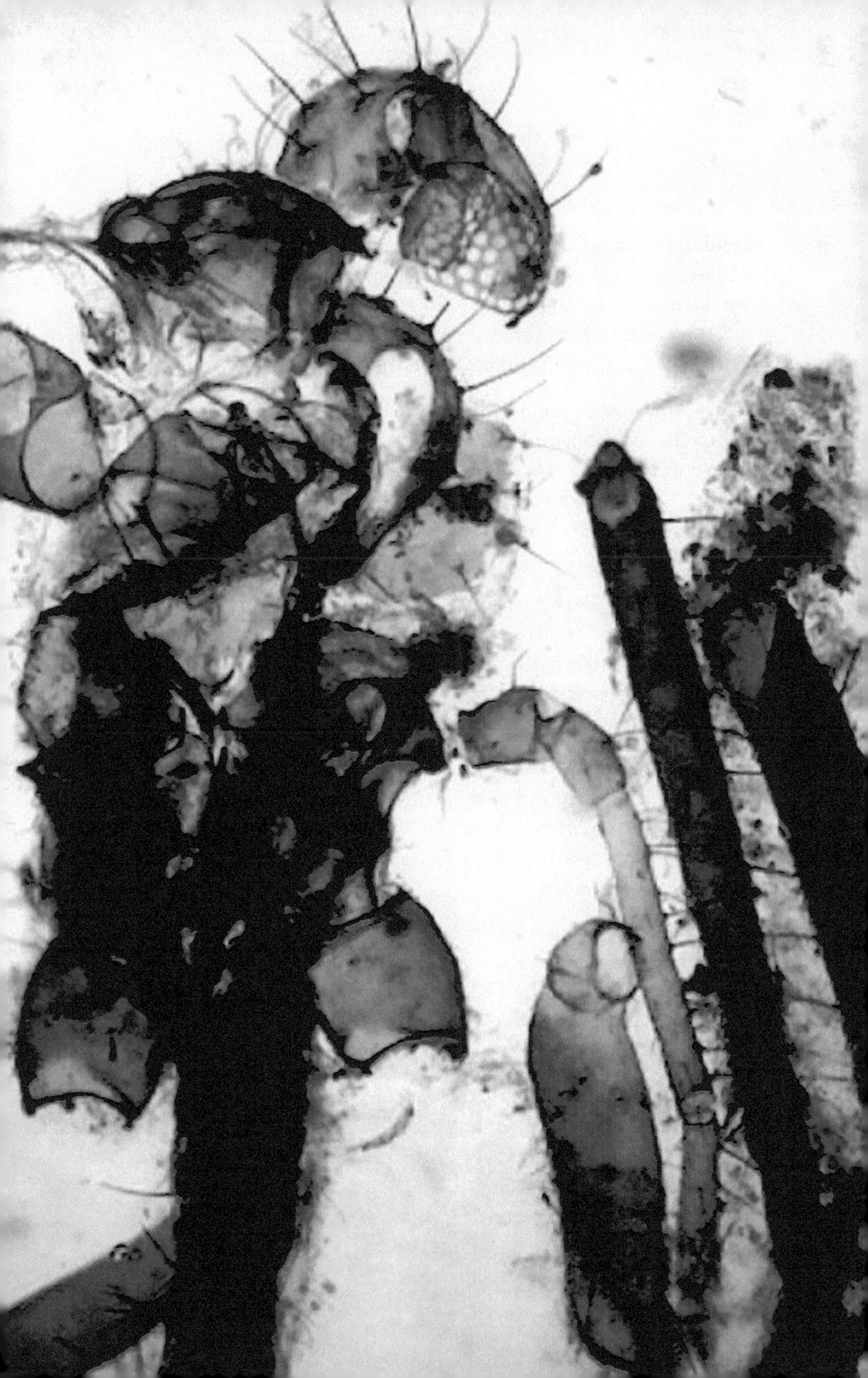

Contributors

Deidra Greenleaf Allan has been published in *American Poetry Review*, *Haibun Today*, *Puerto del Sol*, *West Branch*, *Umbrella*, and *Wind Magazine*, among other print and online journals. She was selected by Robert Hass in 2001 as Montgomery County (PA) Poet Laureate. She's received a Leeway Emerging Artist Award and been a Pew Fellowship finalist in poetry.

Laura Apol is the author of several collections of poetry, including *Nothing but the Blood* (winner of the 2019 Oklahoma Book Award and silver medal winner of the Independent Publisher Award) and *A Fine Yellow Dust* (winner of the 2022 Midwest Book Award). The 2019-2021 Lansing, Michigan poet laureate, Laura conducts creative writing workshops internationally, nationally, and locally.

Brian Michael Barbeito is a Canadian poet, writer, and photographer. Work appears at various venues such as *The Notre Dame Review* and *Fiction International*. Brian is the author of *Chalk Lines*, a book of prose poems, published by Fowl Pox Press. He is currently at work on the visual and written narrative *Mosaics, Journeys through Landscapes Urban and Rural*.

Patricia Cannon has been a registered nurse at UCSF since 2001. She has worked in cardiac critical care, neuro intensive care, hemeoncology, school nursing, and currently, in research. Her passion is her faith, photography, and the written word in all its forms. Her poetry has appeared in several magazines and books.

Ricks Carson's poems have appeared in a number of magazines, anthologies, and online. Among them are *The South Carolina Review*, *Kansas Quarterly*, *Chattahoochee Review*, *The Cortland Review*, *Atticus Review*, *Main Street Rag*, *Stone, River, Sky: An Anthology of Georgia Poems* (Negative Capability Press), and *Oysterboy Review*. He is a member of Atlanta's Side Door Poets group.

Beth Christensen is a psychotherapist in New Orleans. She has published short fiction and creative nonfiction in *Thema; The Avalon Review; Children, Churches, and Daddies;* and the *Adult Children* and *The Power of the Pause* anthologies from Wising Up Press.

Marian Mathews Clark grew up in a small Oregon town, similar to the setting of her novel *These Doors*. In 2019 she and co-writer Patricia Stevens were finalists in the O'jai Film Festival for their script *Timber*, also set in Oregon. A graduate of the Iowa Writers' Workshop, Marian lives in Iowa but still holds Oregon in her heart.

Suzanna C. de Baca has published her poetry in the Iowa Writers' Collaborative Dispatches from the Heartland, *Etched Onyx Magazine, Written Tales, Impermanent Earth,* and *Voices de la Luna.* She is a native Iowan, proud Latina, publisher, author, and artist who lives in Huxley, Iowa, population 4244.

Deidra Suwanee Dees, Mvskoke/Scottish American, grew up picking cotton on ancestral Mvskoke land in rural Alabama. A Cornell and Harvard graduate, she is author of *Vision Lines: Native American Decolonizing Literature.* She serves as director/tribal archivist at the Poarch Band of Creek Indians. Dr. Dees teaches Native American Studies at the University of South Alabama. *Heleswv heres, mvto.*

Norita Dittberner-Jax has published six collections of poetry. Her fifth book of poetry, *Crossing the Waters* (2017), won the Midwest Book Award in poetry. Her new and selected collection, *World Enough and Time,* will be published by Nodin Press in August, 2023. Norita is one of the poetry editors for Red Bird Chapbooks.

Meera Jacob Elamatha is a professor of English literature at Garden City University, Bangalore, India. She loves books, children, and cats, not necessarily in that order. Late night thunderstorms often inspire her to give life to the myriad stories clamoring to be heard in her mind. She regularly posts articles, short stories and poetry on her blog, *Amal Khubaya Speaks.*

Chris Ellery is author of five poetry collections, including *The Big Mosque of Mercy, Elder Tree*, and, most recently, *Canticles of the Body*. A member of the Texas Institute of Letters, he has received the X.J. Kennedy Award for Creative Nonfiction, the Dora and Alexander Raynes Prize for Poetry, the Betsy Colquitt Award, and the Texas Poetry Award.

Louis Faber has had work in *Flora Fiction, Constellations, Alchemy Spoon* (U.K.), *Arena Magazine* (Australia), *Dreich, Atlanta Review, The Poet* (U.K.), *Parcham* (India), *Glimpse, Defenestration, New Feathers Anthology, Tomorrow* and Tomorrow, North of Oxford, Rattle, Pearl, Midstream, European Judaism, The South Carolina Review and Worcester Review, among many others, and has been nominated for a Pushcart Prize.

Yessenia Gutierrez has published her poetry on Amazon. She started writing at age nine and since has written more than twenty books, some of which have not yet been published. But she plans to publish them soon! Besides writing, Yessenia loves to read. Her favorite poet is Robert Frost. She is a very lovely and strong person.

Thea Heard is a fiction writer who remembers, and still experiences, what it is like to be pulled equally strongly in opposite directions.

Lisa Hockstein is a graduate of the Naslund-Mann Graduate School of Writing at Spalding University. She has published fiction in *Rosebud* and collaborative poetry in *Good River Review*. She is currently working on a historical novel. New York is her home.

Gaye D. Holman is a retired sociology professor who also taught in Louisville-area prisons where she coordinated her school's prison program. Her book, *Decades Behind Bars: A Twenty-Year Conversation with Men in America's Prisons* (McFarland), is a result of her work with long-term incarcerated men. Her prison writings have been featured in *LEO Weekly* and *Motif: Seeking Its Own Level* (Motes Books).

Daniel M. Jaffe is an award-winning author. His short story collection, *Foreign Affairs: Male Tales of Lust & Love*, was chosen by *Kirkus Reviews* as One of the Best Indie Books of 2020. His novel, *The Grand Sex Tour Murders*, was selected by *Out in Print: Queer Book Reviews*, as one of their Ten Favorite Books of 2022.

Cyndy Krey makes her home in St. Paul, Minnesota. She recently retired from the IT department at St. Catherine University after thirty years of service where she received honorable mention for the Denny Creative Writing prize several times over the years. She belongs to three writers groups and has studied haiku and other poetic forms extensively.

Larry Lefkowitz's stories, poetry, and humor have appeared in many publications in the United States, Israel, and Britain, including *Thema, A Cappella Zoo, Third Wednesday Magazine, Yellow Medicine Review, The Vocabula Review, Runes, The Literary Review, Midstream, Crimespree*. His book of stories and novella *The Varieties of Jewish Experience* was recently published by Fomite Press.

Gabrielle LeMay is a former New-York-based medical writer and horse trainer/riding instructor. For many years, she split her time between Manhattan and the wilds of the upstate countryside. Her poems have appeared in numerous publications, including *Pandora's Barn,* winner of the 2004 Tennessee Chapbook Prize. She now lives, writes, and studies classical piano in Oxnard, California.

Eisha A. Mason is a Baltimore-born, Los Angeles-based writer. A poet, spiritual therapist and community facilitator, Eisha's work focuses on the intersections of social justice, spirituality and the "soul work of social change." She explores the relationships between the personal and communal, spiritual and political evolution. Her first book of poetry, *Red Door*, was published in February, 2023.

Maisie McAdoo published a science-fiction novella, *Myra's Flight*, in *The King's English*. She was long listed for the 2020 Fish Prize for her short story, "Michael L, Straight from Hell," and she is at work on a historical novel. She was a senior reporter at Reuters and an award-winning columnist for *New York Teacher.* She teaches journalism at Brooklyn College.

Ted Millar's poetry, essays, and flash fiction have appeared in *English Journal, Moss Piglet, October Hill, Isele Quarterly, Rabble Review, Sycopation, Grand Little Things, Words and Whispers, Fleas on the Dog, Straight Forward Poetry, Reflecting Pool: Poets and the Creative Process, Crossways, Caesura, Circle Show, Third Wednesday, Cactus Heart, Inkwell,* and others.

Jeanette Miller, a graduate of the Iowa Writers' Workshop, is retired after teaching writing at the University of Southern Indiana, then practicing as a psychotherapist in Iowa clinics. Her book of poems, *Unscheduled Flights*, was published in 2019 and poems have appeared in *Phoebe, Main Street Rag, Shenandoah, Prairie Schooner, The Blue Mountain Review,* among others including anthologies. Poems are forthcoming in *The North Dakota Review*.

Randy Minnich is a retired chemistry professor and researcher. He has published two books, *Wildness in a Small Place* and *Pavlov's Cats, Their Story*. His poetry has appeared in *Blueline, The Main Street Rag, U.S. 1 Worksheets, Uppagus*, and other publications.

Keshawna Mooney is an emerging writer born and raised in Brooklyn, New York. She holds a degree in English Literature and Creative Writing. "A Predictable Crisis" is her first publication.

Ellen Birkett Morris is the author of the poetry chapbooks *Lost Girls: Short Stories*, *Abide* and *Surrender*. Her poetry has appeared in eight anthologies and numerous journals. Morris won top prize in the 2008 Binnacle Ultra-Short Edition and was a finalist for the 2019 and 2020 Rita Dove Poetry Prize. Her poem "Abide" was featured on NPR's A Way with Words.

Sharon Lask Munson is a retired teacher, poet, old movie enthusiast, lover of road trips, with many published poems, two chapbooks, and two full-length books of poetry. She says many things motivate her to write: a mood, a memory, the smell of cooking, burning leaves, a windy day, rain, fog, something observed or overheard, and of course, imagination. She lives and writes in Surprise, Arizona.

Geetha Nair G. is the author of two volumes of poetry (*Shored Fragments* and *Drawing Flame*) and two collections of short stories (*Wine, Woman and Wrong* and *Love, Lies and Laundry*). She has compiled and co-edited two international anthologies of short fiction. She is a former associate professor of English from All Saints' College, Thiruvananthapuram, Kerala.

Jason A. Ney holds a PhD in English from the University of Denver. He works as an associate professor of English and the director of the Writing Center at Colorado Christian University. His creative nonfiction has appeared in *The Kindness of Strangers* (Wising Up Press) as well as *Fiction Attic Press, Little Did She Know*, and *How to Pack for Church Camp*.

Isabella Ojeda-Ahmed is a queer Muslim writer based in Southern California. She studied sociology and Spanish literature at Occidental College. After a brief stint in law school, she rediscovered her love of creative writing. You can read her musings about adoption, mental health, and identity on her Medium blog, *Working Toward Okay*. This is her first publication.

Nancy Werking Poling's most recent books are *While Earth Still Speaks*, a novel, and *Before It Was Legal: a black-white marriage (1945-1987)*, non-fiction. She lives and writes in the mountains of western North Carolina.

Linda Quinlan's work has appeared in such journals as *Sinister Wisdom, A Fine Madness, The New Orleans Review*, and *Conditions: The International*

Edition. She has also published a book of poems, *Chelsea Creek*. Linda currently lives in Montpelier, Vermont where she cohosts a cable access news/interview show called *All Things LGBTQ* and is one of the founders of Rainbow Umbrella of Vermont.

Ranjani Rao, PhD, is a scientist by training and a writer by avocation. Originally from Mumbai, India, she spent several years in the United States and now lives in Singapore. Ranjani is the author of *Rewriting My Happily Ever After—A Memoir of Divorce and Discovery*.

Sarah Rosenblatt is a poet and therapist specializing in intergenerational trauma. Sarah's poetry has been published in myriad journals including *Ploughshares, Poetry East, Heartland, The Portland Review, The Brooklyn Review*, and others. She is the author of three books of poetry published by Carnegie Mellon University Press. Sarah lives in Shorewood, Wisconsin.

Mary Kay Rummel's ninth poetry book, *Nocturnes: Between Flesh and Stone*, has recently been published by Blue Light Press. Her first book, *This Body She's Entered*, won a Minnesota Voices Award from New Rivers Press. *The Lifeline Trembles* won the Blue Light Award. She is Poet Laureate emerita of Ventura County, CA and divides her time between Minneapolis and Ventura.

Richard Schiffman is an environmental reporter, poet and author of two biographies based in New York City. His poems have appeared on the BBC and on NPR as well as in the *Alaska Quarterly, New Ohio Review, Christian Science Monitor, New York Times, Writer's Almanac, This American Life in Poetry, Verse Daily* and other publications. His first poetry collection *What the Dust Doesn't Know* was published in 2017 by Salmon Poetry.

Sherry Shahan lives in a laid-back beach town in California where she grows potatoes in the cardboard box that delivered a stereo. Her poetry has appeared in *Open Minds* (1st Place Poetry Contest), *Last Stanza Poetry Journal* (Editor's Choice Award), *Zoetic Press, F(r)iction, Critical Read*, and elsewhere. She holds an MFA from Vermont College of Fine Arts.

Laurence Snydal has published more than 150 poems in magazines such as *Cape Rock, McGuffin* and *Columbia* and in many anthologies, including *Visiting Frost* and *The Poets Grimm*. His work has been performed in New York City and Baltimore. He lives in San Jose, California.

C.P. Surendran is a poet, novelist, screenplay writer, and columnist. His five collections of poems are *Available Light* (Speaking Tiger, 2017), *Portraits Of The Space We Occupy* (HarperCollins, 2006), *Canaries On The Moon* (Yeti Press, 2003), *Posthumous Poems* (Penguin Viking, 1998), and *Gemini II* (Penguin Viking, 1993). His novels include *One Love And The Many Lives of Osip B*, *Hadal*, *Lost And Found*, and *An Iron Harvest*. He lives in Delhi.

Wilson R. M. Taylor writes fiction and poetry in New York City. His work appears in *Club Plum*, *duality*, *Superpresent*, and a number of other journals. He is currently at work on his first novel.

Johnny Townsend has published fifty books, including *Inferno in the French Quarter*, the first full-length account of the UpStairs Lounge arson at a gay bar that left thirty-two people dead. He was also an associate producer for the documentary *Upstairs Inferno*. His op-eds on social justice have been collected into several books, including *Racism by Proxy* and *Recommended Daily Humanity*.

Jen Webb is a distinguished professor of creative practice at University of Canberra. Author or editor of thirty scholarly volumes, she has also published eighteen poetry collections and artist books and is co-editor of the Mandarin/English anthology *Open Windows: Contemporary Australian Poetry*. Her recent poetry collections are *Moving Targets* (Recent Work Press, 2018); and, with Shé Hawke, *Flight Mode* (RWP, 2020).

Sarah Brown Weitzman was a National Endowment for the Arts Fellow in Poetry and twice nominated for the Pushcart Poetry Prize and for Best of the Net. Her poems have been published in hundreds of journals and anthologies including *North American Review*, *Rattle*, *New Ohio Review*, *Verse Daily*, *Alaska Quarterly Review*, *Mid-American Review*, *Poet Lore*, *The American Journal of Poetry*. Her fifth book, *Amorotica*, was recently published by Main Street Rag.

James Wyshynski is a former editor of the *Black Warrior Review*. His poems have appeared in *American Poetry Review*, *Connecticut River* Review, *Hayden's Ferry Review*, *Nimrod*, *River Styx*, *Stoneboat*, *Terminus*, *The Beloit Poetry Journal*, *The Cincinnati Review*, *The Cortland Review*, *Valum*, and others. His manuscript, *Emigrant from an Imagined Country*, is in search of publisher.

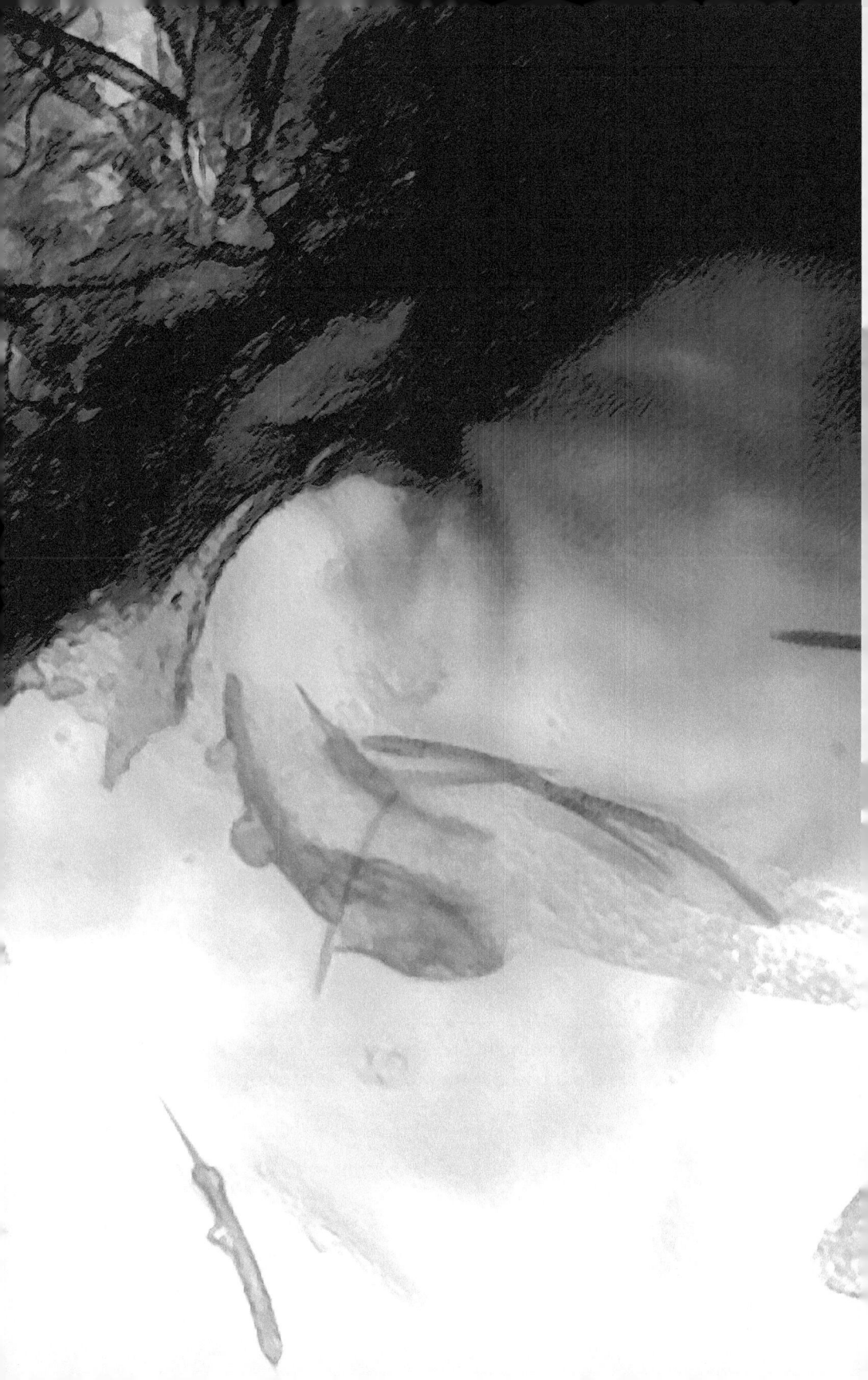

EDITORS/PUBLISHERS

HEATHER TOSTESON is the author of seven books of fiction, poetry and non-fiction, including the novel *The Philosophical Transactions of Maria van Leeuwenhoek, Antoni's Dochter* and the spiritual listening project *God Speaks My Language, Can You?* She has worked in health communications with a focus on communication across disciplines, racism, social trust, and how belief systems develop and change. She has an MFA (UNC-Greensboro) and PhD in English and Creative Writing (Ohio University).

CHARLES BROCKETT has a PhD from UNC-Chapel Hill and is a recipient of several Fulbright and National Endowment for the Humanities awards. A retired political science professor, he has written two well-received books on Central America and numerous social science journal articles and book chapters. With Heather Tosteson, he is co-founder of Universal Table and Wising Up Press, co-editor of the Wising Up Anthologies, and co-author of *Sharing the Burden of Repair: Reentry after Mass Incarceration*.

Visit our website and learn about our other publications,
our readers guides, and calls for submissions.

www.universaltable.org
wisingup@universaltable.org

P.O. Box 2122
Decatur, GA 30031-2122

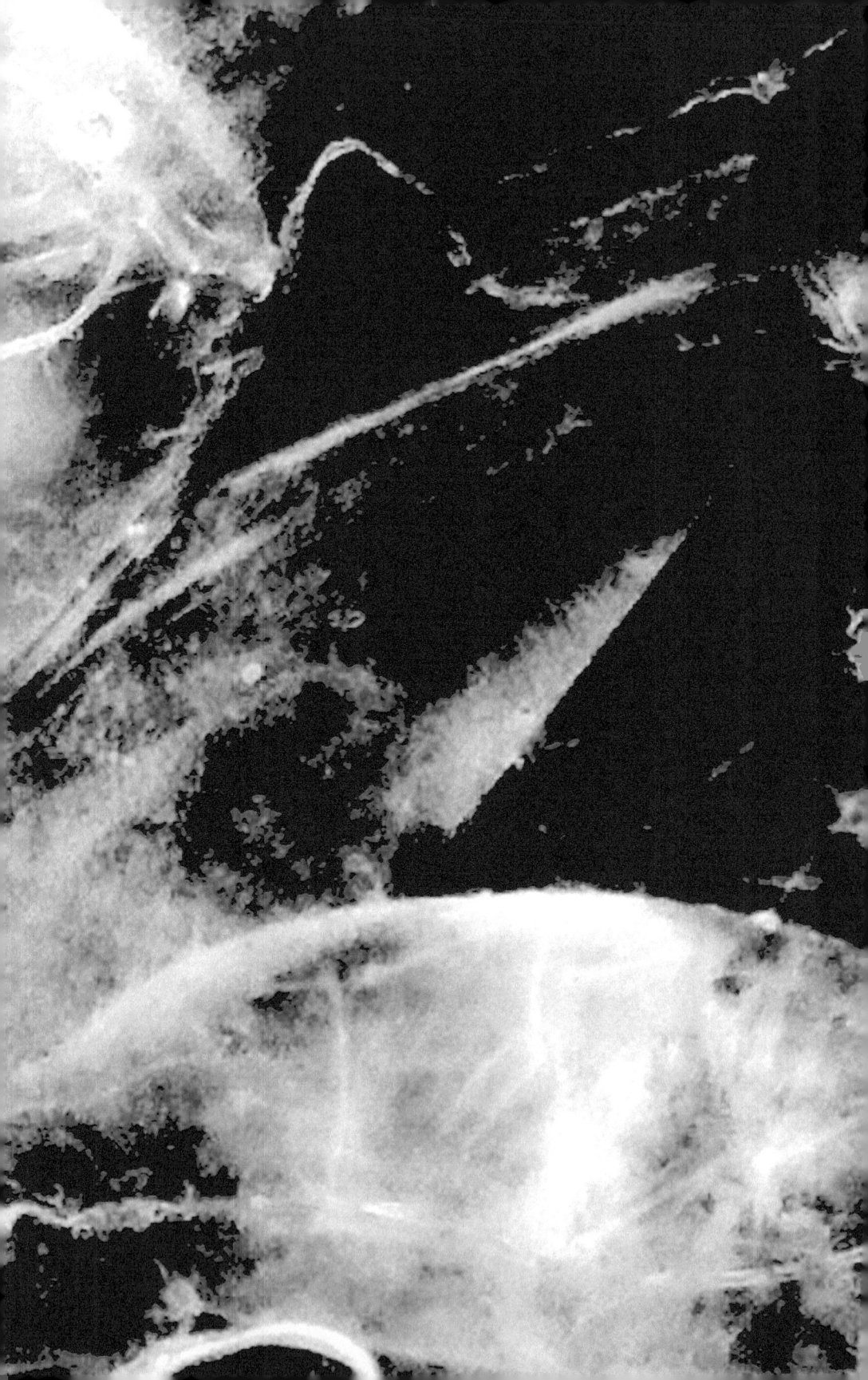

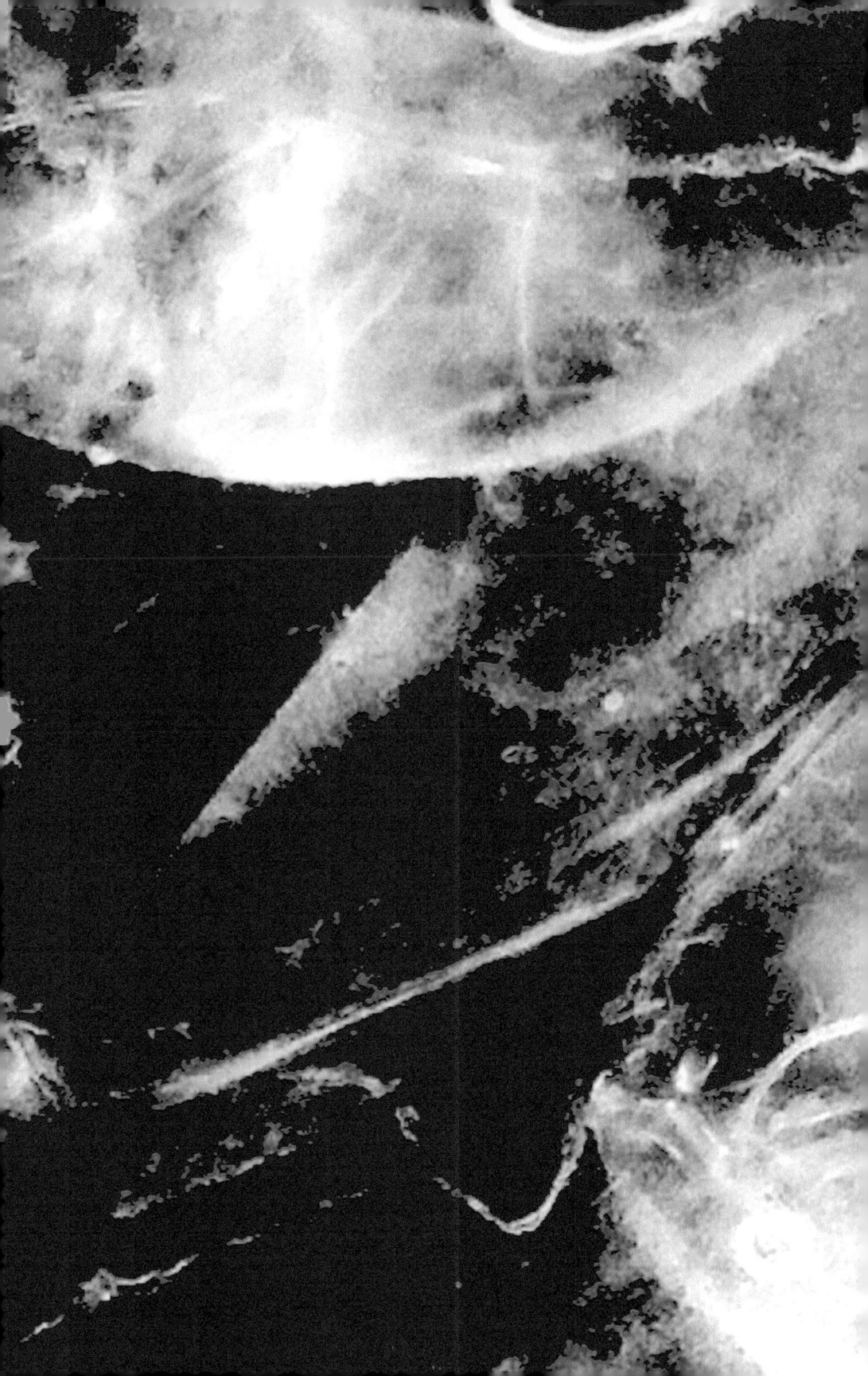

www.ingramcontent.com/pod-product-compliance
Lightning Source LLC
Chambersburg PA
CBHW022350020726
47500CB00002B/205